The
Finder

a Beatrix Patterson mystery

EVA SHAW

The
Finder

a Beatrix Patterson mystery

EVA SHAW

Torchflame Books
Durham, NC

Copyright © 2022 Eva Shaw

The Finder: a Beatrix Patterson mystery
Eva Shaw
www.evashaw.com
evashaw@att.net

Published 2022, by Torchflame Books
an Imprint of Light Messages Publishing
www.lightmessages.com
Durham, NC 27713 USA
SAN: 920-9298

Paperback ISBN: 978-1-61153-484-9
E-book ISBN: 978-1-61153-485-6
Library of Congress Control Number: 2022917659

To Days for Girls International

Thank you, all of you, who understand that
menstrual health management is a matter
of human rights and a critical component of
achieving gender equity.

ABOUT THE BOOK

As you hold this book, *The Finder*, welcome to my mind. Does that sound magical or plain creepy? Read the paragraph below and then consider this concept.

Cosmologist Carl Sagan once said, "A book is a proof that humans are capable of working magic. It's a flat object made from a tree with flexible parts imprinted with lots of funny dark squiggles. But one glance at it, and you're inside another person's mind, maybe somebody dead for a thousand years."

Those I meet for the first time before they discover I write about crooks, hoodlums, swindlers, murders, and assorted good-for-nothings, accept me as an ordinary woman. They probably see me as a gardener, maybe an artist, and "Fifi" to Gwen and Dane, two beautiful youngsters who crowned me with this grandmother's name. Many others know me and my little Welsh terrier, the intrepid Coco Rose, as neighbors as we ramble around my "village" of Carlsbad, California.

Possibly once we've moved from acquaintances to friends, they realize I'm often overwhelmed by a body count that's adding up. A serial killer on the loose? A kidnapping that isn't going to have a happy ending. They might be surprised that while they're thinking of what to have for dinner, I'm working wicked ways to off the bad guys/gals, plan intricate deceptions, range of blood splatter, and pull the entire manuscript together with a surprise or three before I have written a word.

I'm often asked, "How do you find these ideas? Where do the ideas come from?" They're everywhere, from the nightly news to a conversation I've eavesdropped on while waiting for a barista to hand me a coffee. Besides mysteries, in every shade and color, are my jam. I keep a file of peculiar stuff that may or may not find its way into the next mystery.

More so, life is excellent for primary research, especially for a mystery writer. Life is full of broken hearts, disenchantments, regrets, sorrow, grief, and guilt; if we let it, supreme joy and possibilities. Yet, even in the worst times, the yucky stuff that hits like a blizzard of spit wads can improve our writing and give it more depth.

My husband Joe died in November 2021 of Alzheimer's Disease. I've included a character wrestling with that cruel ailment in this book. Yes, primary research at work. Further, I've always wanted to write about my childhood hometown of Santa Barbara when it was not an enclave for the rich and famous but a small city. I wanted to shed light, also, on the autocracies committed against Indigenous people during the Spanish mission and colonial periods and racial discrimination just under the surface.

When I finished "The Seer," I thought that would be the end of my time with Beatrix and Thomas. One and done, that kind of thing. So wrong. They would not stop "talking" to me, and while I tried not to listen, they had other ideas. Without meaning to, I concocted a plot dangerous enough to stop these two in their tracks and threw them into the middle of it.

However, both characters matured in the years between the beginning of World War II and the now, which is 1946. War does that to people. While they floundered and were frightened, they managed to stay in character. At one point, they both stared at me to get them out of some frightful situations.

If you've thought of writing a book or have one in progress, carve out time and make it a priority. Make some magic, as Dr. Sagan advises. I've done that for you, and you can do it, too.

Here's *The Finder*. I hope you enjoy it.

ACKNOWLEDGMENTS

ARE YOU A READER OF ACKNOWLEDGMENTS? If so, you've noted how a writer gives thanks to the team who has supported her/him/them. That's because a book doesn't magically appear. It takes a writer to start and doesn't get into a reader's hands until it's been through a team of unsung literary heroes.

My heroes for *The Finder* started with the first readers, and the book you're holding wouldn't have been possible without them. Thank you: Ellen Hobart (bestie forever), Susan Meibaum (can't wait to read your novel), Andy Meibaum (for NOLA tips like Club My-Oh-My), Nico Garofolo (a wise and creative friend who always listens), Celeste Mergens (for always believing) and Danielle Light Corwin (always there, no matter what or when). I've come to depend on each of you for truthful feedback, gracious, unwavering support of my writing, and for giving me more than my legal limit of laughs as I craft novels. Thank you for believing in me.

Huge thanks go to the staff at TorchFlame Publishing: Betty, Wally, Meghan, and the talented designers and proofers; all of you made my writing shine.

Thank you to all my former and current online writing students, booksellers, librarians, book club members, podcast providers, and bloggers. The book world is better for all your unfailing support.

Finally, I'm blessed to be surrounded by amazing friends and loving family, both chosen and bio, who encourage my creative efforts, even nutty ones, and let me talk about plots, murders, twists, and the characters who reside in my brain. If they think I'm weird, they don't let it show.

It is an honor to support Days for Girls International; fifty percent of this book's profits have been pledged to the organization. Days for Girls advances menstrual equity, health, dignity, and opportunity for all girls and women worldwide in the most-dire situations. Without sanitary products, they cannot go to school or work and are left in poverty simply because they are female. Days for Girls transforms periods into pathways. Please join me in furthering their message and sharing it by reading more about their work at daysforgirls.org.

You're all the best. Thank you, big time.

CHAPTER 1

Santa Barbara, California, November 1945

"EXCUSE ME, YOU'RE BEATRIX PATTERSON." This was a statement, not a question. The speaker towered over the sidewalk café table and Beatrix. The accent was as smooth as honey on a warm biscuit.

Pure New Orleans, she thought.

Every morning since moving back to her hometown, Beatrix walked to downtown Santa Barbara for coffee and to buy the newspaper. She chose one of three cafés each day and relished the time alone to organize her thoughts and memories. If she didn't "process" them, as she called this period of reflection, it was hard to concentrate. She was afflicted or fortunate, depending on the situation, to have a gift of hypermnesia, a condition that allows one to retain details with great precision. Forever.

Right then, the person staring down at her stepped back and looked around, scrutinizing, evaluating, and surveying the area, as if expecting evil to jump from the mellow surroundings. They looked at Beatrix in the same way. Cloying, treacly Tabu perfume grabbed the sea breeze as the tall individual in a hip-length black and white tweed jacket, a crisp white shirt with a frilly lace collar, and shiny black gabardine pants stared down at Beatrix. *Waiting for an invitation to sit? Waiting to be recognized?*

"I believe we've met." Beatrix could not remember a time when she'd forgotten anything, a detail, or a person. Everything once seen, heard, smelled, or tasted was engraved in her mind. However, there was a niggling feeling that this glamorous and oversized female butterfly in front of her was someone she'd met, but she was even more dazzling when they'd first been introduced. Beatrix looked more closely at the chocolate brown eyes and prominent nose and knew the truth.

The *Santa Barbara News Press* was open on the little table before her, and her finger still lingered on a story about the despicable Manzanar Internment Camp that housed innocent Japanese Americans during the war. Beatrix knew the Owens Valley area of California and remembered the constant, piercing winds and desolation. So isolated, so other worldly. Brutal. It was as if these blameless people were responsible because their ancestors happened to have immigrated from Japan decades before. It was a shameful black mark for America, and she hoped now that the war was over, kindness to all people would be achieved.

Supposedly the final detainee would be released in a few days, said the article. *And how will they get their lives and livelihoods back now that the government has stripped them of their rights as citizens, their honor, and their pride? These scars will last this lifetime, and into the future of their children and grandchildren.* These thoughts were stuffed into a compartment of her brain to ponder later as she waited for the looming figure in front of her to reveal their identity and reason for finding her. It was obviously not by chance.

The stranger tapped the table with a long index finger. "Are you the psychic?" The voice was deep, throaty, and not at all matching the curvy figure in front of Beatrix.

"Definitely not." *Not anymore,* she thought. "Why are you asking?" She recognized the person, but she had no idea about the reason for the visit.

The visitor pulled out a wrought iron chair, its legs screeching on the cement, and maneuvered carefully to join

Beatrix at the tiny cafe table, one of a half-dozen outside the coffee house that would soon become a popular lunch spot and trendy Santa Barbara tourists' eatery. The morning fog, perpetually clinging to the central coastline in the fall, had just receded, and yet, Beatrix saw dots of sweat on her companion's overly made-up face.

"You were a psychic when you lived in New Orleans, right?"

"Yes, for a time. I tried to help people, but that's been years. Who are you and why are you asking? If you're looking for a fortune teller, you're mistaken to come to me." Beatrix's auburn hair, now in a long page boy style like fabulously successful actress Lauren Bacall, inched her chair back. Feeling the body heat from this stranger made her feel ill at ease, which was unusual since Beatrix thrived on meeting new people and diving into mysteries. She crossed her legs in the other direction and the seconds ticked by as she waited for the stranger's response.

Dressed in fashionable high-waisted gray slacks, a thin black belt, and a red gingham shirt, complete with trendy western stitching, Beatrix could have passed for an actress. Perhaps not the leading lady, but one with a memorable face. She would have been the strong-willed sister or a supporting player. Maybe even the murderer in a detective film. Resolve and strength were etched on her young face. Since the central coast city of Santa Barbara was just becoming an enclave for the rich and famous, as it was close to Hollywood and Bel Air, no one would have been surprised if she were in films. Even locals took a second look at the striking woman whenever she was out in public, proven as a couple slowed on the sidewalk when they spied Beatrix and the tall individual across from her.

The visitor said, "John Brockman sent me."

One mystery solved, thought Beatrix. *Now onto the next.* "Yes, John and I are old friends." She thought of the decent man she'd become close to during her time in New Orleans. He wasn't good to everyone, but then again, who really was?

"He told me how you helped him and provided information. He told me I could trust you. John said if I had trouble to look you up."

Beatrix watched as the stranger took a cigarette from a pale white snake-skin clutch purse and placed it into a theatrically long holder that telescoped out, then fumbled with a matchbook. The match cover read The Nightingale Club. It was a strip joint near the navy base at Port Hueneme, a gritty flipside of the more gentile Santa Barbara. Beatrix hadn't been there, but had read in the paper, perhaps a week before, of a scuffle between police and a rowdy crowd.

The visitor took a long drag, blowing smoke high above Beatrix's head, watching it disappear into the vapors. "What details do you need to know to help me? If, in fact, you help people? John said you were a finder, could find anything."

"Would you like some coffee? It's quite good here," Beatrix offered as she scrutinized her companion, picking up clues from the pricey purse, finely pressed outfit, the fire engine red painted fingernails, and the eye-catching diamond brooch, in the shape of a *fleur de lis*, that took up most of the jacket's broad lapel. Long raven locks cascaded over the jacket's shoulders. *A wig?* She wondered why, but there were numerous reasons.

The hands were large, but the movements were graceful. Beatrix realized she'd misjudged the visitor's age. *No more than thirty.* However, weariness pulled down the person's shoulders and felt as heavy as the thick layer of facial foundation that didn't quite conceal a pebbly surface. But the little black hat, complete with peek-a-boo veil, shielded more from inspection, and that seemed to be the reason for wearing it.

"Yes, thanks. John and I have known one another for a while, too. He's been a faithful friend. Yes, I'm good at discovering the truth and no, there are no guarantees."

John Brockman, fixer, loan shark, tycoon, opportunist, among other things, including being the owner of an antiquated bookshop, which was a façade for a gaming hall, had been Beatrix's neighbor in her tiny office on Royal Street in the

French Quarter in New Orleans. He had most of the politicians in Louisiana in his pocket and rumor had it that this was also true throughout the South. Yet, this slight man with immense power had single-handedly attempted to save Beatrix's life when two misguided women kidnapped her. Even more, he'd helped discover the original and misfiled adoption records, proving that the Patterson's had officially adopted her as a toddler, hence their fortune went to her. Finally, when the dust settled, he became a friend, one she could trust with her life.

"John is in Louisiana, or that's what I understand. Are you from New Orleans too, Miss...'"?

"Ramsey. Frankie Ramsey." The smile that started on the generous lips never made a full appearance. "Just to clear the air, you're not the first clairvoyant I've talked with about the issues. However, you are the first here in California. I'm at a loss of what to do. The police ignore me. The FBI refuses to let me make an appointment. John said to find you. That Asian guy working on your house said you'd be here, at this café, or sitting outside one of these others here on State Street. John told me you'd know what to do."

"One moment. To clarify your statement, I am not a clairvoyant, so I need to ask you questions. You live in New Orleans, then? That is quite a train ride, two or three days straight, to get here. Or did you fly? Did you come to Santa Barbara for other reasons than to talk with me? What do you want?" Beatrix knew this was a time to be blunt because she no longer wanted to pretend to read minds. In fact, she'd left that life behind, forever giving up faking to be a seer. She no longer pretended to get her knowledge from the ethers or the dearly departed. She had stopped after British scientist Dr. Thomas Ling turned her world and heart upside down. The earth continued to revolve on its axis, and without the weight of being a fake, Beatrix could now pass a mirror without cringing at her unscrupulous image.

"Yes. I need your help because of what happened in this backwater. I'd have friends in New Orleans, people who could find answers, but I'm lost in this hick town. I much prefer city life and feel like a fish out of water in this sleepy little berg. That's what makes it even more difficult."

A waiter came hovering with the coffee pot, but the visitor flicked a hand and sent the man away. "You are willing to talk with me? If you're not comfortable I'll understand, but honestly, I'm a person just like you. I need help."

Being blunt works both ways, Beatrix thought. "Sure, but why seek me out?"

"Like I said, if you were listening to me, Miss Patterson, I need answers." The tone was condescending and put Beatrix on guard. "Forgive me, I've been through an ordeal. Do you want me to spill the entire, sorted story right here? This is a confidential matter. My future depends on what happens. Shall we talk a walk along the beach where there's more privacy?"

Beatrix's eyes followed the legs of the shiny black slacks right down to large, open-toedshiny black snakeskin stilettos. Thinking of this person walking on the beach in those shoes, digging into the golden-colored sand was ludicrous. She placed a napkin to her lips, so the final sound was more like she was clearing her throat.

"Right here will do." Beatrix looked around. "It's quiet. The tables aren't close. You can talk freely." The years she spent pretending she had supernatural powers were over, but she was still curious about people, as everyone was fascinating with their own joys and heartbreaks, including the person in front of her.

Because of her incredible memory, she'd never forget anything at all about that moment or any other in time. For instance, there was a couple in Navy uniforms at the next table. The WAVE was older than the young sailor, but her face glowed with lust or love. They whispered and Beatrix caught the words "Biltmore Hotel." They were planning a few hours of intimacy for later, perhaps. A smiling young mom pushed a baby stroller, bouncing along as she sang "Don't Sit under the Apple Tree," a favorite war-time song. Across the street, two lanky boys shoved one another, probably brothers or best friends on their way to the high school on Anapamu Street, near the Victorian house that Beatrix and Thomas were renovating at the pace of a sleeping snail.

The war had been over for three months now, and there was a feeling of freedom, optimism, and untapped possibilities hanging in the air. America and her allies had vanquished the enemy, although it would take patience for life to return to normal, if it ever could. That included getting everyday things accomplished, from finding building supplies like lumber and nails, to water pipes and bath fixtures. The future didn't look bright for things to speed up anytime soon. Electricians, plumbers, wood finishers, and carpenters were impossible to hire, as most men had not yet returned from active duty, even though reports in the newspaper said the troop ships were leaving the ravished combat zones.

Beatrix was currently resigned to living in a moldy, dilapidated house for a good long time unless a miracle happened, and in life, miracles were silly to hope for. The once opulent dwelling deserved to be restored, and if she and Thomas did not do it, who would bring the "grand lady" back to life? This was not her childhood home, as that had been sold years back before a fire destroyed it. However, it was on the same street, with the same quiet memories whenever she walked the tree-lined lane.

Beatrix had dreams of the house being a place to raise a family. Thomas, her soon-to-be husband, had nuzzled her neck the evening before, after they'd spent the day hauling rotten banisters out to a pile in the yard. Thomas's lithe body belied his strength, from years of practicing martial arts and his hands became toughened from the hard work. He was no taller than Beatrix, yet his personality seemed to fill a room whenever they were together and they worked hard, and laughed hard, about the ruined old mansion, as neither had any carpentry experience.

Early that morning, he'd kissed her hand and then smoothed his now work-calloused fingers over her cheek. "I am learning a great deal in my attempts at carpentry, my darling Bea, but I don't think I will ever want to give up being a scientist. As for this house, I wish the work was coming along faster. Imagine what a good time we'll have filling up all these bedrooms."

"Thomas Ling, excuse me, but there are eleven bedrooms in this house," she pushed him back, chuckled, and then snuggled more deeply into his arms. As an only child, she'd longed for a large family, but it seemed that she and Thomas must have "the talk" about how large would be large enough.

"I see your point." He cocked his head and winked at her.

"Thank you." She sighed.

"We need to keep one at least for guests." Beatrix laughed, shaking her head.

"We're going to revisit this discussion, Dr. Ling, you can be certain of that."

They'd been engaged for four years, most of which they'd spent apart. During that time, Beatrix studied psychology and passed her state board exam to be a therapist, although she wasn't ready to set up a practice.

By the grace of God, Thomas returned to his home outside London and to his work in Britain. With each of his daily letters, he'd vowed to "button things up" so he could return to his future wife. Because of the ferocious bombing and battles in war-torn Europe, one year moved into the next, and it was only in the middle of 1945 when it was somewhat safe to cross the Atlantic that Thomas planned his trip. He'd made it without incident along with the first travelers who dared to cross the waters once patrolled by Nazi U-boats. While apart, Beatrix left New Orleans and came back to her childhood hometown. She rented a studio near the harbor. The home she'd purchased about three months prior, was just barely repaired enough to live in and the kitchen remained in pieces.

"Let's try to focus on the immediate, Thomas. We must get this house done, or at least get it off of the Health Department's watch list. Plus, we have a wedding to attend, that would be ours. After that, I'm all for getting started on those babies. You are aware, Thomas, that babies turn into toddlers and then suddenly they're surly teenagers, right?" She shoved him, more playful this time, only to pull him closer. The wedding was to be on New Year's Day, in London, in Thomas' family home, which had managed to escape the decimation of the city.

Their plans were simple. The wedding would be an intimate affair. None of her family would be attending. Beatrix's adoptive parents had passed years before, her biological mother preferred not to travel, and her birth father, General Charles de Gaulle, now head of the French government in exile, was organizing relief plans in Europe for France. Besides, de Gaulle had never publicly acknowledged to his wife or adult children that Beatrix was his offspring. Now, Beatrix forced thoughts of the wedding out of her mind. She focused on the person across from her.

"Morty, um, my father, Mortimer J. Ramsey, was always on the move and came from a family that fell apart right after he was born, when his own father killed his mother's boyfriend. Once a string of them, I've come to learn. Granddad escaped the law, moved to Mexico, and let my father, then about a year old, be raised by a series of strangers with good hearts, eventually reuniting with his mentally ill mother. 'I've survived by the skin of my teeth,' Morty always bragged about scrapping and fighting and loving every moment of life, he did. Or so he told people," Frankie said and looked into the distance, down State Street, toward the Stearns Wharf and the Channel Islands now glittering just a few miles from the shoreline. By late afternoon, the fog would circle around and creep into the city, shrouding the town with a damp blanket.

"I saw him just a month ago, some business with Mr. Brockman that's mostly real estate and finding backers for hotels and bars that are springing up everywhere now that the war is over. We spent the evening at Preservation Hall in the French Quarter, listening to music and talking about old times. He had plans for something really big here in Southern California, he told me. He seemed genuinely excited and easier going than I've ever seen him. This was a far cry from the way he'd work a scam, where he'd calculate every detail as if a profit and loss statement ran his heart. Yet, when I asked for details, he got secretive and vague about who or what he had in mind."

"Something happened?"

"He returned here, to Santa Barbara, and a week later, he was dead. Suicide. That's what these backwater cops said and their coroner, who is about 105 and is forever attempting to hide stinking whiskey breath, confirmed to me. Saw his young assistant and had the feeling the guy wanted to say something, but didn't. Yes, I'm frustrated."

Beatrix had read about the death, yet, while sad, she had been more interested in following a story about a possible Chumash shaman found near the beach in Gaviota, a tiny bump on the California map, just thirty miles north of Santa Barbara. A woman's body, with inked art on her breast, at least that's what the newspaper said of the concentric circles. They didn't show the corpse and only reported that the body had been discovered days before, crumpled below the sheer cliffs. No one, including the Chumash indigenous peoples' community, had claimed her or had any knowledge as to why she would be there. Did she fall? Beatrix read the report and it seemed that the local police were shaking their heads about the incident.

Beatrix was listening and yet, still thought of the woman, dying alone, no family. She'd once been that woman, alone, with no next of kin, no close friends, no one to care. *I care. I need to find the truth and tell her family that she's gone. Would anyone have done that for me before meeting Thomas? Beatrix wondered.* The answer was no. *I'm going to find out the truth,* she vowed.

The police seemed to think the dead woman chose to end it all. The tribe's people eventually did explain she was an infrequent visitor, although many visited the reservation. The elders knew her but refused to say more. She'd lived on the sovereign nation's land for the last five months or so, but not full time. That's all the report said. Beatrix wondered where else she'd been and why.

Beatrix thought of all this as she patiently waited for Frankie to say what she wanted. She slowly folded the newspaper that had been on the table in front of her and took one more look at the photo of a lifeless form covered by a sheet and the rising tide, taken from the sheer cliffs above. She smoothed the tablecloth and centered the vase with its single yellow rose and sat still. She knew it was the time to listen even if the quiet felt awkward to her companion.

"Morty wasn't ill, never a day in his life. He didn't tolerate weakness or illness. Okay, he was overweight, but not ailing. He had money in the bank, which in itself was a surprise as Morty didn't trust banks after what happened in 1929, when Wall Street crashed. A lot of money actually. He had friends I've learned, an apartment on upper State, and there might have been a girlfriend. Or three, he liked to do things big. They wouldn't have stuck around long once Mr. Sugar Daddy wasn't paying the bills. If I meet them, I'll make it clear that I'm not picking up their shopping tabs or footing any bar bills." The words came in a huff followed by obsessive picking at a flaw in the scarlet nail polish on the beefy thumb.

CHAPTER 2

"COULD THERE BE ANOTHER CAUSE OF DEATH?" Beatrix could see it all in her mind's eye and the more she heard, the clearer the picture became of this person's father. So there was Morty Ramsey, a flamboyant southern gentleman, romancing local ladies and living the high life in California, now in the morgue. She remembered the term "unfortunate accident." Suicide had not been mentioned.

"No. That's the simple answer: It was caused by a rope. Tied over the beams in the garage. Then around his neck. A chair knocked over. A parttime manager supposedly found him the next morning, as if my father wanted to be discovered. If not, wouldn't he have closed the garage door? I think it's more complex than it seems."

"Sorry. It sounds conclusive. There is a but here, right?"

Frankie slammed a fist to the table and the flatware, the dishes, and even the pretty, little rose quivered. "Damn right there's a but. A big one."

"What then? It's a tragedy your father took his own life. It's okay to be angry, Frankie. It's normal that you're distraught."

"I got a call from these hick cops in Santa Barbara. I could tell they were not interested, and I wanted details. No suicide note, by the way. Yet, that same afternoon, the mail brought a letter from Morty, written the day he supposedly killed himself. Yes, it was his handwriting. I checked. He had just purchased tickets for us to go to Squaw Valley, for Christmas and a skiing holiday, like we'd done once when I was a kid. He'd gotten the best accommodations, the works. Said he had a big surprise to tell me, something that could even change my life if I wanted to be part of it. Tell me, Miss Patterson, why would he do that, spend all that dough, and then bump himself off? Besides, Morty was high-strung and extravagant to those he liked, conniving and manipulative, always looking for an edge, and yet, the eternal optimist except with me. He always wanted to trick me or prove he was smarter, even when I was a kid. I grew up knowing I was never good enough for Mortimer Ramsey."

"Addictions?" Beatrix had to ask the hard questions, no longer faking being able to read minds.

"Yeah, pretty women, the occasional bottle of expensive bourbon, and Dixieland jazz, the louder the better."

"What is your role then? Why are you here? Why are you talking with me?" Beatrix had an intuitive feeling that this was far from the truth and all Frankie's reasons for finding her.

Frankie sighed, deeply. "I want to find out why he took out a one-million-dollar life insurance policy. I'm the beneficiary, but the executor won't tell me anything else about the Mortimer Ramsey estate until after he's buried or cremated. This was not at all like my father, and the only time he gave me anything, there was a hitch to it. He had to get something in return. If I amto get a million bucks, there's a catch. I need to know what that is. Wait, don't get this wrong. I don't want his stinking money but I'm not stupid either. My business has been doing well. Although I'm surprised you don't recognize me."

"I have known that you are Francesca Ramsey, the celebrated drag queen, since you walked up to me, Frankie." The last time they'd met, he'd been wearing bright red feathers and a gown loaded from top to bottom in sequins and a lot more makeup. "By the way, adorable hat." Beatrix flashed back to the show, remembering that voice that should have recorded gold records, except that Frankie was a man and most of middle-class America wasn't ready for flamboyant cross-dressers. "It was at the Sapphire, on Bourbon Street. Think it was June 10, 1941. No, it was June 13 of that year. You performed the songs from some of my favorite Broadway musicals. I was amazed. You had the audience jumping up and down."

"I'm flattered. That was an entertaining gig, and I remember meeting you, too. Heard there was a real psychic in town, but never pictured it to be anyone but some old crone. You surprised me. Good old days. It wasn't too long after that I got drafted. I refused. The Army insisted. When there was no possible way to procrastinate anymore, I traveled to Mississippi and walked into a recruitment office there. I signed up using Franklin, my given name. The Army isn't safe for people like me. We all know that. I kept my feminine side in the closet throughout my unspeakable experiences as a G.I."

"Frankie, as awkward as this is, should I use a male or female pronoun when thinking of you?"

"Male will do. I'm a drag queen. I'm a celebrity who likes to dress up like a woman. Right now, I'm in costume, in case there are any Hollywood producers around this middle of nowhere, boondock berg."

Beatrix smiled, nodded, and said, "Got it, and next time we meet will you be Frankie or Francesca?"

"Does it matter?"

"Not at all. Not to me. Let's return to what you were saying about your father. You mentioned there would always be a catch, payback of some kind, for any thoughtful gestures by your father. Are you suspecting there was a note that's disappeared or evidence that was removed before the police arrived at the scene? Or by the police?"

"May I call you Beatrix? Feels like I know you. Mr. Brockman said you'd help me and I could tell you anything. I didn't believe John, actually. Now I do. I have thought this through and even toyed with the idea that Morty was playing one last horrible practical joke on me. I can see him laughing, in hell, about how he'd made me the beneficiary and then took his own life. From the lawyer, just today, I got the news that there's a stipulation in the policy that if the police cannot find a suicide note giving his reasons for taking his life, I don't get a penny. I talked with my attorney about this and as wacky as it is, it is, evidently, legal. Regularly, there's a clause in a policy that says if a person dies by suicide, the contract is void, and the money is gone. But not old Morty. Always working a scheme."

Beatrix was starting to make sense of the situation, but she still wondered about her role in all of this. "Does that sound like something he'd do? Had he scammed you before?"

"Yes, the man took perverse pleasure in tormenting and conning me. Like I said about the money, Beatrix. I thought I was too smart to play into Morty's scams and now I think I'm caught again because that money could do some good." He thought of the money lenders, greedy, and threatening. *Yeah, I need that money for my own good, but she doesn't need to know that.*

Frankie dusted a crumb off the table and said, "If it's true, and he offed himself and didn't leave a note just to spite me, my life will go on, quite nicely, thank you very much. I'll kick myself and focus on my film career." He crushed out yet another cigarette. "However, if you investigate, and find out someone killed him, or if you find a note, that's easier. Been considering sharing this good fortune."

"That's noble."

"Not really. Morty kicked me out of the house once when I was about ten and I got picked up by the police and transported to Poydras House, that asylum for abused women and kids. Thought I'd died and gone to heaven with regular meals, That lasted until they learned Morty was my father. They sent me home. He did hire a housekeeper after that so there was food."

"Now? Thought of spreading the wealth, some to save kids and ladies at Poydras House. John said you'd know it, had some dealings there. Been thinking, too, about the Japanese Americas who lost their livelihoods, farms, businesses, and of course, homes, before being prisoned away in internment camps. Might give their organizations some. Feel like the USO needs to help those who are unsure of their gender, too. Then there's the shock of seeing war close up and personal, never leave me for one second. I'm not alone, I know, but I'll never be the same."

Bloody battles and horrendous losses were all that Beatrix could think about when Frankie muttered the words, "The Pacific."

"I ended up landing with the walking dead, us sailors trying to take back Iwo Jima. First attack. Bloody as hell. I was a medic and a conscientious objector, so they gave me a stethoscope, bandages, and a kick in the ass rather than a gun and sent me into battle. That's our government for you. I still can't get the scenes of my buddies being mowed down by machine gun fire. Still get nightmares. God, it was vile. That's war for you, senseless and cruel. The guys just followed orders, orders I didn't agree with, but orders nonetheless. Now, I see people as people and maybe that's because of this. War changed me, heck, made me care more than I want to care. I disappear in costumes and play roles," Frankie waved his hand down his body. "I'm me inside and the sum total of all my experiences. I have no doubt that this outside sometimes puts others off and truthfully, I like that."

Beatrix wondered if it were all true. "Including Morty?"

He didn't answer and that was telling. She felt his memories of the war were honest and how people around him seemed to die, but what about his opinion of his father? Sometimes our own truth isn't really true at all.

Was this suicide one final, terrible prank by his father? Would Frankie really give away such a vast amount of money? Who knew there were these types of clauses in insurance policies? She played with the coffee cup thinking that when one has money, anything can be arranged, especially in New Orleans. The questions burned more deeply as Beatrix asked, "What is it that you need me to find out? Want me to somehow prove it wasn't suicide, or find out who killed him? Or find a note?"

"Exactly. Yes, Miss Patterson. I've been grilled by the police for hours and yes, I was in the city. I did come to meet Morty, but I never got to because, well, I didn't have the b---," he swallowed, "the chutzpah to do it. but 1 did not kill him. They even gave me a lie detector test and it proved, 1 guess, that 1 was telling the truth because the cops have backed off for at least twenty-four hours.

"Frankly, this ending to my father doesn't scream Morty, doesn't even whisper his name. If Morty did it, what I'd like to find out is why. Maybe then I'll accept it. Or not. Hard to anticipate how grief affects us, right, Beatrix?"

"Enemies?"

"Here or in New Orleans? Or heck, how about all of North America? And maybe a few in Eastern Europe as well?" He snickered a joyless sound. "That list is rather long, and 1 don't believe 1 even know a tenth of the names. Morty told me once he kept a list of those who wanted him dead, kept it in his desk."

"Since your father was a colleague of our mutual friend, John Brockman, you have to know there may be secrets that could come out which could be disturbing? John's associates aren't always on the moral or ethical side of the law."

"No surprises there. Thought 1 told you. Morty's entrepreneurial game started out with him being a pimp and then morphed into a lot of other things. Mostly shady. Enemies come with that territory, although it would be far more likely if he'd crossed someone here on the West Coast since Morty pretty near had everyone east of the Mississippi scared of him. Well, except me. 1 was terrified."

"Nevertheless, you were going on a Christmas holiday?"

"1 leaned early on it was dangerous to say no to my father."

Beatrix had met people who were overbearing and Morty sounded like he belonged to that human subgroup. "Frankie, give me the phone number and address where you're staying. I'll be in touch. 1 promise." She passed him one of her contact cards, just her name, address, and telephone number.

"I'm not particularly patient, Beatrix."

"Me, either, Frankie."

CHAPTER 3

FRANKIE WALKED DELIBERATELY through the streets of Santa Barbara, tiny compared to New Orleans. He admired the Spanish-style colonial architecture, the old trees, and the crisp breeze from the Pacific. He purposely made eye contact with anyone he met, nodding to those who passed by, even if they stared at the six-foot-tall person dressed for Sunday church. Intimidating people made him feel powerful. Yet, when a woman dragging a screaming toddler stopped and stared and the kid wailed even louder, he thought, *Maybe the pillbox hat with the flirtatious little veil is too much. Nix the hat next time,* Frankie told himself. Still, he swayed his hips, and smiled. *Some guys couldn't pull it off,* he mused. *I can.*

Turning the corner, he reached the Hotel Santa Barbara in the heart of the city. The clerk at the high, mahogany desk didn't need to ask his name but handed him a key to 211. Forgoing the elevator because it was like being smashed in a sardine can, he climbed the tiled stairs, unlocked his room, and opened the window over State Street. He tossed the key, purse, and hat onto the desk in the corner, and stared at the foothills above the town. The day was clear all the way to the Santa Ynez mountains. Growing up in New Orleans, the highest peak was a place in City Park, built on a trash dump, and affectionately called Monkey Hill. He and other kids would madly ride their bikes down the slope of a good ten feet, feeling like daredevils all the while. "I could get used to that view," he said.

Frankie poured a glass of water and kicked off his high heels, sitting on the edge of the bed to rub his toes. He'd told Beatrix that it would have been typical of old Morty to scam him, to take his own life without leaving a note just for one final, dramatic trick, and go to hell laughing about how the con was his best. "Did he hate me that much?" Frankie asked the breeze coming from the Pacific, rubbing his large hands over his face, and again, thought of the bizarre stipulation in his father's will that without a note or conviction of his killer, Frankie would get zip.

He sighed. Beatrix seemed to understand, just like Brockman said she would and that made him briefly smile. "She's probably met people like old Morty before. She didn't seem perturbed by me, either. That's good."

Frankie removed the now-sweaty wig, and shook out of the tight-fitting slacks, blouse, and jacket. He peeled off the false eyelashes and fingernails and scrubbed away the thick foundation and eye shadow. He placed the raven wig, worn on stage and often in public, on a hat stand, took a handful of cold cream, and removed the blazing red lipstick, just as he'd done a million times before. Then, he put on denim jeans and a blue checkered shirt, sliding his feet into loafers. The hotel room felt as if the walls were inching in, a sensation he'd often experienced since he was a child. His heart beat faster, his palms were getting sweaty, which happened when he was in confined spaces and sometimes even as he wore the tight sequined gowns for the shows. However, he refused to think of that part of his life, a life of two people in one body, each trying to control his mind and actions.

Instead, he repeated his mantra: "I am not Morty. Nothing like Morty. I will never be like him." Then he thought of the younger Frankie Ramsey, just a good old boy from New Orleans, happy to have beans and rice for Monday supper, kick back some bourbon, and talk trash with the guys. "Can I ever be just that guy again? Would I want to?" he asked in a whisper.

Visions of his childhood raced through his mind as he looked at the masculine image in the mirror. He was never good enough or clever enough according to Morty. He'd learned to shoot a rifle and a pistol and then was punished for refusing to go deer hunting with his father. Punished for not being quick enough with an answer or punished for being too quick. He was called a dumb ass and a smart ass and plenty worse.

Mortimer didn't reserve his criticism for Frankie, but aimed it squarely at Frankie's mother Vivian, petite and painfully introverted, who after ten years of marriage and constant belittling retreated into her own world and refused to speak. She felt safe if she turned off all emotions. Frankie remembered he was eight when Vivian was dragged from the house by medics and a doctor, only to be shut away in an institution outside of Shreveport. Frankie could not visit; Morty wouldn't let him. He was too terrified to ask anyone else, even if there were people he could. After high school when he left the Ramsey house without a note or explanation, he moved closer to see Vivian.

Frankie jolted back to reality and stomped down the stairs, exiting the hotel as if the nightmares could catch him. Somehow, in his daze he'd managed to get to the wide promenade along the coastline, Stearns Wharf, that jut out into the sea. He looked around, startled, and then saw the telephone booth.

Popping a nickel into the machine, he dialed the number. Beatrix answered on the second ring. "Frankie, you sound tense. Are you okay?" she asked after he thanked her for taking the call.

"Yeah, yeah, fine. I've been walking and thinking. I don't know if you can find out, but he might have told John why he no longer wanted to live. I need a reason, or the suicide note."

"You're sure his death was a misguided punishment toward you?"

"No, well, well. Yes. It just came to me." Frankie continued to explain, "One of the last times Morty saw me in a show in New Orleans at the Club My-Oh-My, the group he was with, and he always had an entourage, went crazy for my act. I remember their faces and the applause and Morty scowling. He growled at one of his flunkies and stormed out. He'd never took interest in my career and was shocked out of his mind to see me on stage. At least that's how it looked to me."

"He was angry about your success?"

Frankie sighed. "I thought that at first, but maybe he was embarrassed about me. Then the next week, he summoned me into his office on Decatur Street, not to the house mind you, and then all business told me about the life insurance policy. Beatrix, he was like this, mercurial and dangerous, loving and gentle. The problem was I never knew from one moment to the next, which one he'd be. Always trying to scam people but there was something different in him after his upper-class friends enjoyed my show. They even came back stage to meet me and we all went to dinner at Antoine's afterward. Without Morty. I'm sure that news got back to him. Had to."

"Wait, Frankie. You don't think your father's dead?"

"Okay, it was a wild thought. Of course, he's gone." He gulped, knowing that he was talking too much, but he couldn't stop. "The police confirmed it. Chalk it up to irrational me, Beatrix; I've been fighting the demons of bad memories since I got to town. I just can't get it through my head why Morty did this, why he was so generous to me when he could barely speak to me."

They ended the phone call. Frankie stared out at the Pacific; his breathing was shallow. Not for the first time in his thirty years did Frankie wonder what life would have been like had his father not been a bully and his mother had been a mom like other kids had, worrying about soiling their Sunday clothes and patching their skinned knees instead of retreating to her bedroom with the blinds always drawn. He started walking away from the sea, toward the hills, and finally a long trek to the Santa Barbara Mission. Eventually, he sat on the steps, looked out at the Channel Islands, and ground his right fist into his left palm. Walking had always helped him figure out problems. Or had before. Not now. This time, the biggest problem was in the morgue. *Not the biggest,* he corrected himself. *Those are the loan sharks. They're circling, snapping at my ankles, out for blood.*

My blood if I don't pay them off soon. Damn. Should have asked Brockman for money for my theater scheme. No need for him to know about the gambling or debts. Not now, not ever. He'd only tell Beatrix. He looked back at the grand mission, supposedly the jewel of all that were built when California belonged to Spain. He'd never been religious, scoffing at those who were now filing in for Mass. *If I prayed, would their God help get all this sorted out?* He shrugged and retraced his route to the hotel, all the while making plans to drive to Hollywood the next day, in a Francesca outfit, to try to catch the eye of producers.

CHAPTER 4

THE WHITE VICTORIAN THREE-STORY BUILDING with the peeling trim that was once cobalt blue seemed to hold court over the cottages and craftsmen homes it shouldered in this former enclave for the elite of the city. Even in the house's current state of deterioration, her grace and architecture could be seen. While State Street was a main thoroughfare in the city, Anapamu was a regal branch, and because of the stately mansions and a few architecturally striking homes, cars moved along at a dignified twenty miles an hour in their honor. It would have been unheard of to rush through these blocks, disgraceful even to the few estates left.

Beatrix walked the six blocks from State Street toward her residence, smiling and briefly talking with neighbors. One woman was trimming back a ginormous rose bush. She picked a stem and handed it to Beatrix. "It's called Cecile Brunner."

"Thank you, and now I know what to call the gargantuan one that's trying to take over my patio."

The woman, tiny compared to Beatrix, pulled off her cotton gloves and stuck out her hand. "I'm Josephine."

"Beatrix," she replied.

"Are you new in the city?"

"I spent part of my childhood here. I know this is a big ask, but there are some rose bushes in the garden of the house I'm renovating, and if I have questions, can I come to you?"

"Certainly. That'd be fun. Mind you, I'm not formally trained. I just garden with advice from Mama," she replied, yet her garden was a kaleidoscope of late-blooming flowers. She tucked a strand of black curly hair back into a bun. "Come anytime."

They waved goodbye and Beatrix stopped. She'd used a single pronoun, calling it her house. Why? She'd studied so long a time to become a psychologist, and realized she needed to dive into this issue. Was it telling? Was she afraid to share the home and future? No, the house belonged to Thomas as much as to her. Did she not trust him? She was afraid to think too deeply into that notion. She turned to wave again to the kind neighbor, and watched a small boy with gorgeous chocolate-colored skin dash at her from behind a hedge and hug the woman. The two laughed at what seemed to be a game. Beatrix's heart did a worried flip. "No, again. Just pre-wedding jitters. Who would have thought I'd get them?"

Seeing the mom and the child, questions swirled in her head about Frankie and his father. She needed time to think, and imagined sitting in the garden with a cup of English Breakfast tea would help.

She stopped on the sidewalk directly across from Santa Barbara High School and looked up at their house, once a grand lady. It would be known as the Ling home. She imagined children running in and out, and roller staking on the front sidewalk. She could nearly see a manicured front lawn, where weeds thrived, yet, it would be perfect for soccer or football and picnics on a lazy Sunday afternoon.

The years before she'd met Thomas, and fell in love with him at once, were like a bad dream. Now joy replaced all of that. Now she was going to be a bride, a married woman to the most handsome, kind, and gentle man she could ever imagine. Not ever did she, in the past, think that love would be part of her future.

She stood on the sidewalk looking at the house, but she was picturing herself in the trim white wool suit she'd picked out for the wedding. No frills or lace, but sapphire pipping around the collar and cuffs. England was still struggling with food shortages and rebuilding of the city was painstakingly slow after the terrible years and constant shelling by the Nazis. A grandiose wedding seemed absurd.

In her mind, she imagined Thomas's parents and his grandmother, all of whom she knew she'd adore, standing near the fire, his sisters and their families grouped around. The local vicar had agreed to come to the house for the ceremony and that pleased Thomas's family. The honeymoon was going to wait until March or April on the cruise ship Queen Elizabeth, once the grand vessel was finished its war job as a troop ship ferrying our soldiers home from war-torn Europe. Thomas had booked the best suite on the ship. Then they'd take the train across the country, making stops so Thomas could get to know America. They planned to be gone for six months, but there was so much to do on the house, and no work would be done while they were away. Should they cut their trip short to get the house habitable?

Beatrix was jolted from her thoughts by the echo of hammering. *It can't be from here,* she thought and looked around. The street was quiet. She opened a side gate to enter the garden and it squealed, screaming for oil. The broad front steps with the wrap-around porch were too termite ridden to use and that repair would have to wait. They really needed a functional kitchen now, and she was just grateful that at least one of the baths was nearly done. But the full renovation at this speed could take a decade.

She tried to peek at the homes on each side. Certainly, elderly Mrs. Turney would not be creating all this commotion. She lived in a well-maintained shingled craftsmen home, with manicured gardens and white bush roses clustering near the sidewalk, roses that now waited to be trimmed for winter. They'd often seen her with binoculars hanging from her neck waiting for a warbler or a goldfinch to roost in the trees. On the other side, Beatrix knew the couple just from saying hello. They both left carrying briefcases each morning, and returned about four going straight into their cottage and pulling down the blinds. "Maybe they're spies," Beatrix said one afternoon as she saw the couple walk from the bus stop, not look up, and retreat into their house.

Thomas and she were hauling rubbish bins at the curb. "Teachers at Jefferson Elementary School, up there, overlooking the city, Bea. I asked, since I have had a bit of experience being a covert courier, myself," he chuckled.

All was still for a few moments and then the clattering resumed. It was definitely coming from inside the house. The sound of construction was a glorious symphony of hammering and sawing.

Beatrix was stunned. Then he saw her approach. Thomas rushed to her side and closed the squeaking metal gate, again making a noise like cats fighting at midnight. "I have a wedding present for you, my dear." He waved his hands like a showman at a circus. "Surprised?" He kissed her soundly and then pulled a hammer from his toolbelt and motioned for her to enter the mudroom that connected to the kitchen in the back of the house.

She tried to take his hand, but he put the tool into her fingers, instead.

"How? Where did you find anyone willing to help us?" She heard voices but couldn't understand the words. They were most certainly in the kitchen.

"Never underestimate me, my darling. Middle of last month, I happened to meet someone we both knew in New Orleans. Major Davies. Sorry, I just forgot to mention it with all that has been happening."

"Here in Santa Barbara?" Her nose wrinkled as if there was a foul smell, then she quickly recovered. Frankly, she'd secretly hoped Major Davies and that part of her life would be over.

"We happened to meet here at the store called Woolworths on State Street. They sell everything you can imagine, and they call it a five and dime, whatever that means. Was it here when you were a child? I must take you there. I'd just ordered at the soda counter when Davies walked right up to me and started talking. He was out of uniform. Shook my hand as if I was his longtime best mate and even bought me that root beer. He is still waving that unlit cigar around and told me he had retired."

"Sounds fascinating, but how does that explain carpenters in our kitchen?"

"Davies said he was trying to find you, heard you returned here after the 'incident' in New Orleans, and how it was a mighty lucky break that he found me. He wondered if there was anything you needed, anything his connections might help in these times of shortages. Mentioned we were in a bit of a spot with the house."

"You trusted him?"

"Okay, not totally, as you've often said. However, America is the land of second chances, and I gave him that. We sat at the counter and had a fizzy pop. I prattled on about restoring this wreck of a house. He actually smiled, well tried to, and offered some assistance."

"I'm sure he's still working some scheme, Thomas. Have you seen him again? Did he stop here at the house?" They were in the kitchen by then and it was a beehive of carpentry. Five workers stared at her for a short time, nodded hello, and then returned to the jobs at hand.

"Yes, the next day. He arranged to have these fine gentlemen, who previously had been incarcerated at the Tuna Canyon Detention Station, near a neighborhood called the Tujunga in Los Angeles, come help us out. These fellows were prisoners of war, and are still stuck in the maze of red tape."

She turned away so she could whisper, pulling on Thomas's shirt front, "That's a POW camp? Major Davies helped?"

"Yes, well. Surprised me too, but since I thought it was an empty offer, I didn't mention it to you. Then a government bus pulled up in front of the house at about nine today, and off came the answer to our renovation prayers. Real workers. To answer your questions, we will house prisoners of war along with perhaps some Japanese Americas who were sent out from Manzanar, that despicable internment camp in the high desert."

"We have POWs working on our house?"

"Now you understand. Bravo, my lady. Major Davies has quite possibly retired after the sorted details of the debacle in New Orleans finally came to light. Seems he still has enough clout to mention to the warden at Tuna Canyon how he alone saved New Orleans from being invaded by the Nazis and the end of the threat to all of North America. I'm sure he didn't volunteer the truth. However, he had to fess up, I imagine, after the article came out in the *Times Picayune* that Mr. Brockman had leaked to the press. I doubt he mentioned those facts locally. Well, the warden checked with a contact in Washington, and found it was you who owned the home. The rest is history. We've got a crew working on this house and since across town another Victorian home is being demolished, we'll have lumber, too. Say the name of Beatrix Patterson and cell doors open."

"Again, Thomas, we have prisoners working on our home?"

"No, of course not, you silly girl. These fine men are in your custody and are being paid $1.00 an hour. That is well above minimum wage, as I've just learned. Wait? Should we be paying more? Is that why your forehead is wrinkled? Yes, you're right, we need to pay them a dollar and a half an hour. We're going to house them and offer them meals. Brilliant or what?" Thomas rubbed his hands together, smiling like he'd just discovered new deposits of gold in the California Sierra foothills.

"They know what they're doing?"

"These are upright and good men, my darling. I talked with each although my Italian is rusty and they're all from Sicily. Well, most of it was pantomime. Yes, until the government can send most of them back to Italy, they'll be lodging here. All were in the building trades before that egomaniac Mussolini took power. Giuseppe worked in the Vatican." Thomas gave Giuseppe the American sign for "okay," and continued with an innocent smile. "I apparently had a premonition when I said we'd be filling the bedrooms, however, accommodating a bunch of grown men was not what I intended." He chuckled. "The Japanese American workers will stay here for the most part, but a few will return to their homes when any family that's still at the camps are released."

Beatrix put the hammer on the counter and circled the large kitchen. Two men were securing the frames around the windows, another was replacing a sagging pantry door, and a robust carpenter was replacing floorboards that had rotted away. More noise came from deeper inside the mansion. "Buongiorno," each shouted, tipping their hats as Thomas introduced them.

Then in Italian, he said, "Lads, this is your boss, Miss Patterson. Soon to become Mrs. Ling. I told you at one time she saved all of North America from a Nazi invasion, so don't underestimate her small stature. The woman can be downright evil." Thomas translated into English what he said. The workers nodded and returned to their tasks and Beatrix wondered if they'd understood her fiancé at all. Yet, everyone was smiling.

In just three hours since they'd started, the workers had done miracles in the kitchen. Cabinet doors were attached, the window didn't tremble in the ocean breeze, and from what Beatrix could see, the rotting floorboards, twelve inches wide and made from California pine, that had once frightened her if she wanted to go into the garden, were strong and safe.

"They'll stay as long as we need them, Thomas?"

"Davies figures the Italian government and your Army won't get around to processing their paperwork until mid-June, and it could even be August. These men, of course, have families and loved ones in Sicily. I thought, and tell me if you think I'm out of line, that you might ask your best friend, former First Lady Eleanor Roosevelt, if the families might be able to immigrate, if they want to, of course. I know it is wishful thinking, yet these gentlemen are hard workers and would be a credit to America. I can tell."

"It never hurts to ask, and I'm thrilled to get the kitchen done. Having a working sink is going to be the best wedding present you could ever imagine. Thomas, you are aware that we're leaving for England in two weeks? Who'll make sure they have everything they need while we're gone? Or will we have to stop the work?"

At that moment, there was a thudding on the back door. A booming voice called out, "Miss Patterson? Doc? Are you home?"

"Henry? My goodness, it is you." John Brockman's driver and their friend bent his head to enter the kitchen, his sizeable body eclipsing the door frame.

"Yes, ma'am. Doc, how the heck are you?" Henry shook Thomas's hand and soundly patted his back, then reached out to hug him as if he couldn't help himself. The first time they'd met, Henry was suspicious of any Asian since his brother had perished in the attack at Pearl Harbor that had started the war, but after their "escapade" as the two joked, all animosity evaporated.

"My friend, Mr. Henry Berto, it is just brilliant to see you again," Thomas said, although the words were muddled as he was being smashed into the visitor's muscular chest.

Thomas, still stiffly British at times, seemed to be making an effort and returned a one-armed hug. A few days prior he'd asked Beatrix, "Must I actually hug men, other than family?"

Beatrix put her arms around Henry's massive middle. "What a lovely surprise. I don't understand. Is Mr. Brockman with you? Are you on vacation? Stay with us?"

Henry nodded to the workers now all staring at the mammoth African American who seemed to fill the kitchen. "Howdy, gents," he said. They continued to stare.

Beatrix motioned to the men. "These are our new workers, originally from Italy. Currently, they're guests of the US government. This is our friend," she explained, hoping that her smile and wave would explain.

One or two said something she couldn't understand, however, at that second, Henry broke into Sicilian, speaking without hesitation and the men left their posts and shook his beefy hand. He must have heard them talking as he didn't even try speaking Italian. He continued to chat and listen as Beatrix and Thomas blinked in surprise.

"Good men you've got here," Henry said as the crew returned to work. "Been hard for them, away from their families. The Italian government forced them to fight, treated them as second-class citizens, and deserted them. Their country is in ruins."

"You're fluent?" Thomas asked.

"Guess that fact doesn't come up in conversations for us, Doc. Yes, Mama is from right in the Ninth Ward in New Orleans, a long line of city folks, but Dad? He came from a town of forty in the Palermo region. Lots of Berto's there, I hear. He immigrated and landed in New Orleans, but never got any further because he married my mom, started the family, and then realized the First World War was going to devastate the country. He returned to Palermo, packed up my grandmother, Nonna, who had just lost Nonno, and brought her back. She refused to speak English, so Mama and the rest of us learned Sicilian."

"No wonder they weren't clear when I spoke my best Italian," Thomas thought about want a wanker he could be and laughed at himself.

"Unlike Italian, which is almost entirely Latin based, Sicilian has elements of Greek, Arabic, French, Norman, Byzantine, Hebrew, Catalan, and Spanish. Grammatically, Sicilian is also very different from Italian," Henry explained. "Probably more than you need to know, but the Sicilian language isn't commonly used today except for in the more remote villages of Sicily. Like I said, that's where my dad's family came from. Most Italians find full-blown Sicilian incredibly hard to understand and to be a total departure from traditional Italian. There are also minor differences in sentence structure, as well as a unique accent. More than you ever needed to know?"

"You are wicked smart, my friend, although I've known that for years," Thomas again patted Henry on the back.

The three got out of the workers' way, now retreating to a weedy jungle supposedly to be transformed into a private garden. The dew was dotting the wildflowers like sequins on a ball gown. The patio was brick and spacious and had the potential to be the favorite gathering place.

"Tell us everything and how long you'll be here," Beatrix said as she spied Mrs. Turney's face peeking over the hedge that divided the properties. She quickly bent down, but Beatrix was certain that the woman was listening and using her birding binoculars to get a better look.

"Never thought I'd get to California, Miss, but then Mr. Brockman bought a house, in Montecito, right near the ocean and I've come out to be his major doe doe, at least for a while. Said he might not even need me back in New Orleans at Christmas, but I've got to be there for Mardi Gras to drive him around for the parties and parades as I always do. Said he may come west and stay the whole summer, getting away from the humidity and hurricanes. Never had a vacation so I've got to enjoy this while I can."

"Major doe doe? Do you mean major domo?" Beatrix smiled, so pleased to have another friend in the city.

"Yeah, that, too." Henry laughed and looked at some of the windows and the disrepair of the house's façade. "His place is posh, sorry, ma'am, not like yours, here. Got to hire staff and asked me to see if I could find a cook, gardener, and folks like that. Thought you might have an idea where to locate potential employees. I don't know what I'm going to do here. Don't know anyone but you. Hope you don't mind I've called just barging in like this. Mr. Brockman said to look you up."

"We are delighted to see you. But you do know someone else, and it might be a surprise then," Thomas said. "That the military man we came in contact with in New Orleans, a Major Davies, is here in the city, too."

"Up to his usual shenanigans?" Henry winced. He had the ability to see through any pretension, as perceptive as Beatrix.

Beatrix replied, "Hard to tell. Thomas met him downtown, out of uniform, and he asked to see me."

"Not my business, ma'am, but that man seems to bring trouble with him no matter where he goes. Mr. Brockman ranted for a week about how the officer tried to cheat him and his buddy Andy Higgins. Mr. Brockman sends his regards and wanted you to know if you need anything, that I'm here to help."

"Even with the tensions and drama, it turned out okay. Just curious why Davies wants to see me. My days as a psychic are over." Beatrix smiled and gave Henry another hug. "I have an idea, and say no, please, if it doesn't work. With Mr. Brockman's permission, might you consider looking in on and overseeing the workers while Thomas and I go to England for our wedding trip?"

Before a reply could come, a baritone voice echoed from the front of the house, "Miss Patterson? Are you here? It's Major Dav--." There was a crashing thud, shattering of lumber, a string of swear words, and then intense moaning. "I'll sue you. How dare you booby trap the entrance," came painful screams possibly heard throughout the neighborhood.

"That's my cue. Miss Patterson, Doc," Henry started to leave. "Count me in to be your domo here, too."

"Henry, wait, please," Beatrix reached out to stop him. "From the sounds of that racket, Thomas and I might need you to help extricate whoever fell through the porch, especially if it was that beefy military man."

CHAPTER 5

IT TOOK THE THREE OF THEM, plus two workers, and Mrs. Turney, cheering and waving as she stood in the middle of her tidy herb garden, to extract Major Davies from the twisted and termite eaten wreckage that once had been the front porch. As soon as they determined that the officer, battered, but safe, was in one piece, Henry backed up and said goodbye. "I'll call you tomorrow, Miss, and you can tell me the dates. Mighty sure it'll all be fine with Mr. B, but if you can talk with him, that's better as well."

Five minutes later, Beatrix put a tumbler of whiskey into Davies's trembling hand, and two swallows later, he was calm enough to begin breathing regularly, which only allowed him to scream more obscenities. Then, like watching a tire slowly deflate until it was flat, he explained why he was there but not before grumbling, "You need a sign shouting that there's danger, Ling. Could've killed me, died right there. Damn it, the war didn't get me, but your front step would have. Miss Patterson, whatever are you doing here in this wrench of a house? You've got plenty of money, yeah, I checked and no, I am not going to sue you for negligence. But you owe me, now. Big time. Don't forget that."

"You didn't come here for a social call or to destroy my front porch, did you?" Beatrix asked.

His face was rounder than she remembered and the lines more engraved into his forehead and cheeks. The bravo he threw at everyone four years ago when he'd hired Beatrix to flush out Nazi terrorists in New Orleans seemed to have withered. She saw his fingers quiver as he ran them through the sparse hair valiantly trying to cover his bald spot. "Social call, with you? Madam, the truth is, when I learned from Dr. Ling you were in the city, I was shocked. What are the chances of that?"

"Quite good since this is where I spent my childhood, sir. And you probably just asked around in New Orleans to learn of my whereabouts." She waved her hand toward the house. "No, this was not my family's house, but I lived in another Victorian-style home a few blocks away. Unfortunately, that home burned, was left in disrepair, and consequently demolished. Or I would have tried to save it, as well."

"I'd forgotten you were a native." He rubbed his elbow, then his shin, and onto his shoulder. "Yeah, so's my wife, Mary."

"Mary? Might she be my age? Could we have known each other from school or the social events in the city?"

"Mary Hernandez, that was her family's name, and she's a little younger than me, and she'll be 45 in July. Parents owned an ice cream parlor on upper State Street and that's where I met her. Maybe you remember it? She was working behind the counter. Prettiest girl I'd ever seen. She smiled and I would have bought every gallon of ice cream they'd had. Played hard to get, let me chase her until she caught me," he said, as he smiled slightly and looked toward the eucalyptus trees swaying in the breeze, clustered on the hill above the home. "Know it's crazy, yet I stopped at the shop yesterday. It's now called McConnell's. Didn't make it inside. Just stood in the doorway. Drank it in, the smell of sugar and cream and suddenly I was twenty-five again. Somehow in my mind, I pictured Mary behind the counter, offering samples. I thought she'd be there to wink at me." His voice dwindled to a whisper, quiet at the end. Desolate. Drained. Lost.

Beatrix tilted her head, giving him time to form his words, to remember, She looked east, as well, from the garden, a riot of weeds, to the knoll in back of the house, then to the hillside where she planned to build a gazebo in the future. Eucalyptus, tall and unruly, clustered on the slope. The Eucalyptus trees were what she'd missed most when she'd moved to New Orleans and while traveling the world. The trees had originally been brought in from Australia to be used as railroad ties, until it was discovered how brittle and cracked the wood became when it dried out. Now, the forests dotted Southern California, and especially the low foothills east of Santa Barbara. They could be dangerous too, as huge limbs shot off in gravity-defying directions. When the annual hot, dry, and powerful winds came, called Santa Anas, hefty branches just snapped. They were called "widow makers" in their native Australia for good reason. *It's right to be home again and oh, how I've missed the pungent smell of the trees,* she thought.

She watched the facial expression on the ex-officer. When he turned back toward her, she said, "She's not here with you." It didn't take a once fake psychic to see the sadness clouding his eyes.

"Yes, I think she's here in town, but well, not with me, not living with me. Don't exactly know where she is. Mary and I hit a rough spot, a big fat pothole, actually."

"Oh?" Beatrix looked at Thomas and sensed he knew what she was thinking. "You mean she got tired of your string of illicit affairs? Or perhaps the years of philandering finally become public?"

"How dare you?" he snapped, his body rigid. He tried to struggle up, but Thomas put a hand on his shoulder and the major flopped back into the chair.

"Dare me? Major, this is pointless. Remember, I've seen how you use people, how you manipulate women, to get what you want and so there's no need to be untruthful with me."

"Oh, yeah, because you're psychic and all," he glared.

"No, because your lies are as transparent as the unlit cigar in your jacket pocket."

He pulled it out of the pocket, twisted it in his fingers, and shoved it back in. "The fact is, Mary and I separated right after some humiliating events came to light, and that coupled with the things you were involved in, Miss Patterson, was the straw that broke our marriage, how I broke the marriage. The Army transferred me, the highest-ranking officer in the American South if you remember that, to a tiny, far-flung camp in the Sierras, at least five hours from any town of any importance. They then assignment me to be in charge of...nothing. Absolutely nothing. How the bloomin' chiefs of staff in Washington found out that I didn't realize the Nazis were controlling Camp Algiers is beyond me, but they did. They didn't demote me and there was no court-marshal. Nothing formal. My little Mary, so used to the finer things in life, gentle and innocent that she is, up and left. Out the door. Gone."

"You've found her here in the city?"

"She tracked me down, not that hard, actually. Got a letter from an LA attorney. She's suing for alimony and my pension. I am paying, of course. No options. I send the check to a box at the main branch of the Santa Barbara post office. She won't even give me her address. Don't that frost the cake? When I finished my tour, I retired, and now I'm here. In North Hollywood. A studio apartment. Here in Santa Barbara to find answers."

"And to get revenge?" Both Thomas and Beatrix watched his face harden and he pulled the cigar out of his pocket and this time ground his teeth into the soft black tobacco.

"Payback? No. No. Not at all. I want her. I need her. I'll do whatever it takes. I'll get down on my knees or put my face on the floor to ask for forgiveness. I just pray to God that she'll have me."

Beatrix wanted to believe him, yet intuitively, she knew there was more to his tale of woe, which lacked all the emotions that had been there two second before. "Why the change of heart, Major? Or should I call you Mr. Davies?"

"My first name is Herbert. Friends call me Herb."

"Alright, Mr. Davies, why are you so eager to get your wife back? The money? Costing too much in alimony? You've got a good pension, I assume."

"You get right to the juggler, don't you, missy?"

"You may call me Miss Patterson. Not missy." She stood up and Thomas followed.

"Wait, sorry. I've barked orders for my entire adult life and it's a rotten habit that won't die."

Beatrix didn't sit. "I'm quite busy today. Why not get to your point? There's no use wasting our time and I really don't know why you are here, except that now we don't have to have hire anyone to demolish the front porch. You took it down, at least a goodly part. Thanks for that." She smiled only to see Mr. Davies eyes darken.

He looked at the distance, then muttered, his face more pinched than before as if he were sharing a terrible confession, "I don't want to admit it, because I never have. However, I truly need Mary, like I've never needed her before. There's no one else, Miss Patterson. I don't have anyone else. My siblings are all gone, and our adult kids and their families have no use for me. She told all four of them everything. I've been to the doctor." He squeezed his hands into fists, let go and shook his fingers, but his face turned to stone. "Damn if I'll be one of those pitiable men who deteriorate in some gosh awful, grimy Army hospital bed reeking of chloroform, urine and rotting flesh until the Grim Reaper decides he's ready for me. I'd jump off Stearns Wharf with a boulder tied to my chest before I'd do that."

Beatrix sat down and said, "You're dying." At one time, Beatrix would have played this clairvoyant card, coaxed a client into giving more information. In return for lies, she would have been paid handsomely, and the client would have purchased a smattering of hope, but not truth. If in fact, the major was telling the truth.

Davies closed his eyes, and Beatrix could read on his face that he was debating if she was worthy of honesty.

"It'll be easier if you are open with me, sir. If you want to locate your wife and sway her to return to you, then you'll need to give me as much information as you can. Remember, if you choose not to tell me everything, then I may miss a connection that could bring you results."

"Yes, well. It started with my fingers shaking a bit and then things happened as I tried to read reports and directives. The words started jumping around. Then I lost things. The doctors told me to knock of the alcohol, tobacco, and coffee. Like that was going to happen when I was waging a war against homegrown terrorists infiltrating New Orleans and trying to invade the Good Old USA.

"Before the reassignment to that hick army camp and after Mary left, I was driving back to the barracks and got lost. My heart was racing. I felt nauseous and I was sweating like a pig. After that, the wine, women, and song went out the proverbial window and as you've noted, I chomp on a stogie but there's no way I'm going to light it. Wasn't too long ago, I started to lose even more things and blamed the folks at the apartment I rented in North Hollywood. Then I'd forget where I was going or what I did with stuff, bank books, my wallet, or the car keys. One day, I went out of the house without my pants. Forgot to put them on. Cops were called as I was trotting down Hollywood Boulevard and were going to charge me with indecent exposure. Had my doctor's card in the pocket of my shirt. They sent me back to the doctors. There's no cure. Bad news all the way as it's going to get worse."

"Are you saying you have Alzheimer's Disease? This is the doctor's diagnosis? Yes, I have heard of it." If it hadn't been so sad, Beatrix might have smiled at the idea of pristine former Major Davies walking around Hollywood in his boxer shorts and being stopped by the police. "Let me understand this. You want to find your wife and lure her back so she can become your fulltime caregiver when things become are more problematic."

"Damn straight." He growled. "She signed for in sickness and in health. She got the health and now look at this." Davies raised his right hand and it quivered. He made a fist and the shaking got worse.

"What are you willing to give her to encourage forgiveness, if I should be able to locate her, in exchange for a life as your personal nurse, Mr. Davies? What's your plan?"

"I'm her husband and she owes that to me," he snapped, and his face turned the color of an overripe tomato. His volatile personality hadn't yet been affected by the disease.

"On the contrary, your infidelity throughout the years, wait, don't deny that your infidelity cancelled your marriage contract long ago."

Thomas stood, "I think we're done here, sir. Let me show you out. Do I need to telephone for a taxi?"

"Wait, no, please. I've come off as a tyrant, Miss Patterson. Can we back this truck up and give me the grace to hear me out? This disease makes me short tempered. Angry. I am told it's a symptom, and damn near impossible for me to manage. Forgive me." He swallowed a few times.

"You have ten minutes. The workers are going to expect lunch. Thomas is the cook and I'm the sous chef. By the way, thank you for that arrangement."

The former military man shrugged as if he didn't know what she was talking about and then said, "My children, our children, have ganged up on me. They know me and what I've done to their mother. They have sworn that if I don't try to find her and heal our relationship, they'll never speak to me again and they'll keep our grandkids from me." His voice softened at the end, something that surprised Beatrix.

As a man who shouted to get people to jump, perhaps this was the first time he'd told his emotional truth.

"I need Mary. I want Mary back. I want us to have a family, with the little grands running around, making noise, and running to see me when I visit, at least until the stupid disease takes over and I won't know them anymore."

"Do you think Mary knows the bargain you're offering? Have your kids been in touch with her?"

"That's a damn good question, Miss Patterson. I hadn't thought of it. They all live in the Los Angeles area. Would it be out of line to hire you to represent my best interests? To go to them and find out if they know Mary's whereabouts? The next step would be for you to talk with her and see if she's willing to help her own husband or if she's as pig-headed as ever."

"First off, if Mary agrees, you've got to change your attitude. Being a care giver, Mr. Davies, is a grueling and fulltime position. How much longer do the doctors think you have?"

"This is just the beginning. Could be a year or could be ten. It's all a crap shoot. Next, I'll start forgetting people and even the things I've done hours before."

"Before that happens, sir, write down any addresses and telephone numbers that I might need, especially those of your adult children, and I will contact them. I need to know the post office box number and when you send the check so I can make sure to be there when Mary picks it up. If I find you have not been fully truthful with me, Mr. Davies, then our relationship is over, and I will not share any information I might discover. Do we have a deal?" She extended her hand, and he took it.

"I'm not rich, however I want to offer you $500 now," he withdrew an envelope from his jacket pocket. "And another $500 when you find my Mary. If you find her and she refuses to take me back, I'll believe you and still pay you. I really don't deserve your forgiveness, but I had to come and ask for help."

"Then we have a deal. I'll try to find her and see if she's willing to talk with you. No promises, Mr. Davies. Sometimes, the truth hurts more than the lies that we prefer to tell ourselves."

CHAPTER 6

"In all honesty, my darling Beatrix, I do not like that chap. He's rude and we both know he's a bully. Hoped we'd never see him again, and then there is the issue that I do not trust him, either, never did. I know my opinion matters to you, and yours to me. I am also acutely aware that you will not be swayed by anything I say. I respect that." Thomas paced back and forth with the floorboards of the front parlor creaking with each step. "I love you. I want to protect you. I think he's crazy and dangerous."

"If he is sick, and it could well be a rouse, then he's truly unable to control his anger, and he's afraid. Rightly so, Thomas. Lots of old people get this disease, if they live long enough, but the major is young-ish from what I understand. I have sympathy for him."

"He was instrumental in trying to cheat a friend, and bamboozle the government, and nearly got you killed."

"Yes, I know. Yet, if I can find Mary, his wife, and at least let her know he's not well, then she can make the call. It's not up to me. I'm just the finder."

"I do not like this, and I am also having mixed feelings about you getting mixed up with Mr. Ramsey, well both of the Ramsey's, the cross-dressing one, and the recently deceased one in the city's morgue."

"Thomas Ling," she took his hand to stop him from pacing. "You may as well get used to my life. I am a do-gooder. Did you really think I'd stay here, in this big house, raising kids and planting herbs, flowers that attract butterflies, and those weird-looking succulents in the garden, like Mrs. Turney, next door?"

They moved to the sofa. He smiled, but his forehead was lined with worry. "A man can hope."

"Darling, I do want that, a family, and the garden, but I want, no, I need more and that's why I want to counsel. I can't just be a stay-at-home wife and mama, and I always plan to do something. I know I do not need to work for a living now that the trust has been settled and for that matter, you do not need to work either. That said, I would never stop you from the career that you love, the sciences that you've devoted your adult life to. I do not want to become a hard-boiled detective or a Miss Marple, but if there's a mystery that needs to be unraveled, then I can't help myself. I want to better understand human nature, why people do what they do and perhaps even focus on how to change thoughts. I don't know yet, Thomas. I was going to wait until we returned from our honeymoon to talk this over with you as I might need to study abroad to enhance my education."

"I have known forever that you need all this, and I would never stand in your way," he replied, pulling her close, but not holding tight. He chuckled, "Why we'd then be doctored squared, or Dr. and Dr. Ling when introduced formally."

She laced her arms around his back and said, "Are you going to fret each time I walk out the door?"

His eyes closed. "It is unfair. I am an old-fashioned man, Bea. Hopelessly prehistoric. If I choose to agonize, then that's my prerogative, my dearest." Then Thomas attempted to work out a clandestine plan to keep an eye on Beatrix. "May I go with you when you meet with the people you are trying to help, like when you find Mary Davies? Because you will find her, of that I'm certain."

"Thomas, I don't need protection. My goodness, this is 1945. I'm not strolling down back alleys trying to capture hoodlums hanging on street corners. It's Santa Barbara. It's California. There are no murders or kidnappers hiding in the bushes."

"You think that Mortimore Ramsey was murdered? Or do you actually believe the guy took his own life? Why, for goodness' sake?"

"I wish I knew. Could he be so selfish that he killed himself and did not leave a note or some explanation in order to have the final nasty act to totally torture Frankie for the rest of his life? Can people be that ugly to each other?"

"We have just finished two of the worst wars on the planet, Beatrix, and ugly does not even come close to describing the atrocities that happened in those times." Thomas sighed, knowing he'd never forget the broken souls of shell-shocked people milling hopelessly around after each of the German bombings pelted London. He was often one of those horrified by the brutality. He'd always remember his mother's sobs when she heard of the massacres taking place by the hands of the Japanese in her homeland of China. Images of friends who had enlisted flashed in front of his eyes, half of whom he never saw again, and the other half changed forever broke through his memories. No, there was no end to the horrors that people could inflict on one another.

He held Beatrix's hands, knowing he was reliving memories that would forever contaminate his thoughts, if he bottled them up and did not talk them through.

Knowing this, Beatrix would continue to seek even more experience and education in psychology, and then practice with those suffering after a traumatic experience, whether it was war or abuse.

Thomas cleared his throat and tried to smile. "After the honeymoon, and if we ever get the house to the point when it's not crumbling at our feet, let's drive up the coast."

"I'd love that. You must see Morro Bay. Thomas, there's a lovely long and incredibly wide stretch of beach with this huge rock mountain in the middle of it. It's unbelievable. Why, we should drive all the way to San Francisco, and you, with your superb language skills, can take me on an adventure of a lifetime through Chinatown. Let's put off the wedding until summer and take that trip now, a pre-honeymoon?"

"Put it off? My mother would have a fit if without warning the wedding was postponed, Beatrix. You do not know what she can do when she's disappointed. You might think she is sweet and gracious from the letters, but that lady has the determination of your General Eisenhower. Besides, I want you to be my wife. You want that, right? Have you changed your mind? I am not easy to be with, set in my ways, not adventurous like you."

"Silly, handsome Brit. The wedding is still on, but you must take me to San Francisco."

Thomas looked at Beatrix and tried to read her face. *Does she not want to marry me? Is she worried about the mixed race of our future children?* His heart tumbled to his knees. His dreams of their future crumbled like dry all leaves under foot.

"Thomas? What is it? I know that look."

"You do understand that I want a family, want us to have children."

She smiled. "As do I. Let's not start to work at that until we at least make the bedrooms in this drafty house inhabitable."

Thomas's smile was quick and then faded. He took her hand, "Have you considered that our children will be neither one race nor another?"

"I understand how this stuff works and since we're already living in sin, by some standards, I don't quite know what you're getting at. Are you worried about how our kids will manage and their roles in society?"

There was a long pause. "Yes." He looked down at his hands, clasping his fingers and then releasing them.

"We are entering a new time, Thomas. There will, unfortunately, be events when mixed-race children and adults won't feel comfortable. Our goal as parents will be to instill confidence and strength into our kids. Don't tell me that with your Chinese heritage and even in academia, you've never been discriminated against? I cannot even imagine how difficult that would have been."

"Yes, there were times when I was passed over in university or thought stupid by professors who were not used to seeing an Asian in their classrooms. Passed over for a few grants, as well."

"What did you do?" She took his hands and made sure he knew she was listening. Beatrix knew if they were to make their future work, this was a topic that had to be discussed.

"I strived to like everyone. I also learned that some people just take longer to like."

"Did that work?"

He laughed and relaxed. "Of course not. I depended on my own moral compass. Yet, truthfully, there were periods when I did want to fit in and wasn't allowed to."

"You know, it's going to be up to us to raise our children as citizens of the world, people who make their own lives, and have strong opinions. We can help them to have hearts for those who do not look the same, act the same, or live cookie-cutter lives."

"Truly, Beatrix. I have never thought about how hard it will be as a parent. Mum and Dad made it look uncomplicated. Even my sweetly obnoxious sisters are all great mothers, and their husbands instinctively knew how to take off and put on fresh nappies and burp the babies. I never even knew I wanted to be a parent until I met you, Bea."

"You're going to be a wonderful, loving, and funny dad, Thomas. Now if I can just get you to stop worrying so much."

Thomas looked at Beatrix, a smile hinting at his lips. "You know what we need right now?"

"A good night's sleep after some serious cuddling?" She longed to feel his body, his warmth, close to her ear all night long and forever.

"Well, that, too, and a bit more. I was thinking ice cream. Let's go to that little shop that Davies said was once owned by his wife's family, have a treat, and you can ask a few questions."

"This is why I'm going to marry you. You know exactly what I want and need." She kissed his forehead.

Now, however, the niggling concept of her diving into other people's lives, dangerous lives, still caught in his throat each time he thought of it. *Is this a forecast of our life, with me fighting fear each time she walks out the door? What about when we have children? Won't that be worse?*

Thomas made the decision. *I will just follow her. I will be her bodyguard.* The thoughts made his racing heart rate nearly return to normal. *How can people love each other this much? How do they handle the anxiety?* He would not tell her she was being guarded, as she'd fuss and turn down his offer. Instead, he'd stealthily follow her and then, just maybe, once he could see she was in no danger, he would be able to find peace.

A few minutes later, she was ready, and she backed the bulky '35 Ford Station Wagon, with its classic wooden doors, out of the carport. She honked the horn and Thomas got into the passenger seat as she began chatting about the weather and plans for the house and what they could do during their time in Britain. "We should take the train to Scotland and even hike in the Highlands. Oh, to see the countryside again."

"Do you know, Beatrix, that part of the Ling clan is now living on the Isle of Skye? I haven't seen these cousins since I was ten or eleven."

Thomas had secretly hoped that once Beatrix and he moved to the West

Coast, with the madness of war over and reconstruction painfully underway, that his future wife might choose to become more domestic, perhaps he even mused, take up a hobby along with her career plans. Maybe learn some tips from their elderly neighbor? That, of course, wasn't the Beatrix he had fallen in love with and realistically, he knew that it was her gift to champion for the underdog, the righter of wrongs, that drew him to her. Her persona would never mesh with that of a homemaker, and the sooner he forgot that tiny fantasy, the happier he'd be. He knew when he met Beatrix, that fateful day in New Orleans as police swarmed the city looking for a terrorist who vaguely resembled him, that his life would never be dull or predictable. He'd once thought the world of science would satisfy his soul, then he met Beatrix, whom he initially believed was an evil spirit, and every plan for his future was turned upside down.

Sitting in the pleasantly warm evening on a tiny bench outside McConnell's Ice Cream Shop, licking ice cream, vanilla for Thomas and Rocky Road for Beatrix, she leaned in and licked his cone. "Thomas, darling, if you don't finish that soon, I'll have to do it for you. Why are you staring at me like that? Like I'm going to disappear? I told you that you're cursed with me, remember?" she grabbed the cone from his fingers and cleaned up all the drips before handing it back. "Now isn't that better? Really, Thomas, vanilla? You need to live on the wild side."

Walking back to the car, she said, "While I was paying for the ice cream and you walked out to the street, I got to talk with the current owners. I thought the current owners might know something about Mary Hernandez Davies, or maybe her family. They remembered the husband-and-wife team, possibly a daughter or two, however the sale of the shop was some fifteen years in the past. They didn't have any insight. Oh, this is the best ice cream ever and just some future marital advice, if you ever can't find me, Thomas, I'll be here at McConnell's. Wait, what is it?"

"I was walking along the beach last week, and I strolled out on Stearns Wharf to get some fish for dinner. There was an ice cream street vendor, and I got a cone."

"You're telling me this, why?"

"Don't be cheeky. I have a reason. The cart said Manny Hernandez on the side. You think perhaps that Hernandez is related to Major Davies' wife?"

"We need to find that cart. Tomorrow, though, as this is enough dessert for one evening."

"Not quite," Thomas said and winked at her.

"Oh, now that's exactly what I have in mind."

CHAPTER 7

THE HOUSE WAS A BEEHIVE OF CARPENTERS, and a few more arrived in the following days. It was all Thomas could do to keep up with making meals and doing odd jobs, if they let him.

The first floor's floorboards in a downstairs bedroom no longer sagged, and the iffy boards in the walk-in pantry were secure. The brown water-stained spots, possibly in the past caused by an overflowing tub on the second floor, were replastered. November in California is not a traditionally rainy month, but Beatrix and Thomas stood outside their house as a light sprinkle dampened the grounds which were weed infested and desperate for attention. They looked over at Mrs. Turney's immaculate garden, and she waved to them from the front window.

"Do you suppose we'll have to get the roof repaired?" Beatrix looked up. She shook her head.

"Add that to the cost of everything else. I thought we might call this the Ling Home, but maybe the Poor House would be a more appropriate name," he replied. "I am not keen on heights to see if the shingles are secure. Is the roof fifty feet off the ground? I will beseech one of our workers to go up there and see the extent of damage before winter sets in- if there is winter in California. However, I will brave the attic."

"You're terrified of spiders, Thomas, among other phobias. I must psychoanalyze you someday. Now no arguments. I'll go

49

into the attic and see if there are obvious leaks or if I can see the sky."

"How did you know I cannot tolerate those creepy things? Psychic messages? Of course, I'm also afraid of mimes, air travel, the thought of meteors hurdling themselves toward earth, public speaking, oh, the list continues."

"I'm just good at observations. I watched you scream like a five-year-old girl the other morning when you walked through a cobweb. I'll check the attic and then I need to go to the city's newspaper archives, called the morgue. I have a hunch."

"About where to find Davies' wife?"

"No, not that. About the woman found below the ocean cliffs on Gaviota Beach. From what I've read that is not a place one goes without a reason and the article alluded to a previous incident in that same area. It even said, quite grisly, that the cliffs there were the suicide location of choice for the entire county. I need to find out what happened to this one poor girl. Somewhere she has a mother, a dad, maybe even a family. There's no follow-up in today's paper about her death. I wonder if the coroner would talk with me, just as a concerned citizen."

"It is curious. Yes, I read she was nude? True? What happened to her clothes? Pretty breezy to be running around naked. Did the police ever find them? It mentions that she was wearing bright red lipstick. That's odd."

"My thoughts, exactly. Why take the time to put on makeup? Come on, my sweet prince. You can hold the ladder while I explore the attic. It's better to know if the roof will cave in than to wake up in the middle of the night with shingles all over our bed."

Thomas and Beatrix struggled to get a tall ladder up the staircase, making Beatrix giggle as if they were watching a silly Laurel and Hardy slapstick movie at the Granada Theater. When they had it balanced enough so she could climb to the attic, she did so without hesitation. She might tease him about being afraid of spiders, but she had her share of phobias, from circus clowns to potluck dinners, so additional jesting about his anxieties wasn't going to happen.

"Can't see any daylight, Thomas, and that's a good thing because we will eventually get rain," she hollered down, holding a flashlight to illuminate the corners of the spacious attic. "Oh, shoot and ouch. Oh, no."

"Beatrix? What is it? Speak to me." He dashed up the ladder and peered across the ceiling beams. "No spiders, please. Oh, tell me you didn't get bit by a black widow."

She balanced on a trunk and rubbed her foot. "Stubbed my toe, should have been more careful. Wow, look at you. My knight in shining armor coming to my recuse. Wait, Thomas, stay there, some of these beams don't look that solid. Oh, what's that? Look over there," she pointed the stream of her flashlight toward a wooden chest. It was a style she remembered as a child, even then it was too old fashioned for her mother, as it had been popular for long-ago sea voyages. There were also wooden crates. "There's a mystery here. You know I love a good mystery."

"I think I will, with the most care, slowly descend the ladder and wait for you to tell me all about it, if you're sure you're alright?"

Later that morning, and with the help of their carpenters, the sea chest and crates were muscled down the ladder. Now their contents were scattered on the second story's floor.

"This is absorbing and a treasure trove," Beatrix said between wiping dust and cobwebs off her back. "Look at these like old newspapers wrapping up keepsakes from the turn of the century. What a lovely vase, Thomas. We must use it. Oh, a baby's Christening dress. Shall we save this?" She smiled and cocked her head. "Actually, these things aren't really that old, Thomas." She read a short piece about contributions from the Women's Christian Temperance Union and a possible partner organization called Onus Organista. "I've heard of the WCTU but this other group. Odd name. Wonder what it was all about."

She sighed, "Geeze, Thomas, 1 hoped just maybe we'd find photos or money."

"You are dreaming, my dearest. 1 don't believe the house is cursed, yet it has a way of sucking money out of us."

They sat on the floor, close together scanning the newspapers as the treasures in the chest were a complete tea set, some fancy China plates, two cast iron frying pans, and what seemed to be a silver coffee service, but bumped and bruised. "Look, Thomas. Here's an article excitedly reporting the 1906 earthquake in San Francisco and days of uncontrolled fires. Why save all these neatly clipped articles telling details on the history and end of stagecoach service that connected other coastal cities?"

"Maybe the owner at that time was involved in the enterprise?"

"Oh, here's a keeper. A detailed piece on getting rid of bedbugs with turpentine, no less."

"That is unscientific and unquestionably dangerous." Thomas cringed at the notion.

Beatrix slowly examined the next neatly trimmed article. "Wait. Listen to this. There was a 'cult' called the Guardians of the Light, all hush hush apparently, and this reporter is scandalized. The cult was raided by police for their covetousness and carnal activities. The cult was considered armed and dangerous. Unlawful and lewd. It was disbanded after the Women's Christian Temperance Union marched on city hall. Wait, here's a follow-up from the next day. Oh, it just gets more indecent."

"Then please continue"

"It says that, and 1 quote, 'the lustful, lascivious, libidinous group fled to the hills as mounted possies roamed the mountains for the perverted congregation'. No one was apprehended or spotted, which makes it seem like the police didn't try very hard. This is wild, Thomas. All this happening in our little sleepy hometown. 1 wonder if Mother and Dad knew anything about it?"

Thomas took the yellowed slip of newspaper and walked toward the window. The day's sprinkles disappeared as the two were immersed in what a former inhabitant had treasured enough to save. "Why would people keep this, unless they were involved or knew someone who was? Wait, what's this? Some type of club or ceremonial staff in their hands? Torches? Looks like they have a carved head and circles around the edges. Are they indigenous American symbols? The people are not dressed in indigenous clothing? Do indigenous people still wear buckskin like in the movies?"

Beatrix moved even closer to his side. "Do you have a magnifying glass?"

"I found one, yesterday, in the elephant-sized armoire in the first-floor bedroom. Why?"

"I know exactly where I saw something like this, yesterday, in the newspaper. They showed a magnification of the image in a photo. Thomas, it's the same type of circle motif I saw on the grizzly closeup photo of the body of that woman who supposedly took her own life, jumping from the sea cliffs in Gaviota. The photo showed just the woman's head and upper chest exposed."

"No, that cannot be. What is the date on the article?"

"It's 1905."

"Forty years ago?" They climbed down the stairs and rummaged through the cabinet. "Here, let's take this stuff and go outside where the light's better," Beatrix said.

Near the collapsed front porch, they stopped to examine the clipping. "As Americans say, 'I'll be a monkey's uncle'. Whatever that means. The tiny. linked circles look the same to me. Do we still have yesterday's paper?" Thomas asked.

"I used most of it to start the woodstove in the kitchen. However, I kept the article about the woman's death. I must find out who she is and why she died, especially why she's holding a ceremonial staff from a long-dead cult. Now I really need to talk with the authorities and locals who might know more. There's a particle of truth in all gossip."

"Do we know anyone who likes to talk? A lot? Like Mrs. Turney?" Thomas nodded toward the lady, sitting on her front porch, always watching, always knitting, always waving. Heavy binoculars strung around the neck of her lacy blouse, in a fashion that was popular before the Roaring Twenties.

"Good day, madam," he waved and at first, she pretended she was too busy with the wooly garment she was knitting. He called again, and she smiled timidly, wigging her fingers in a coquettish wave. He waved back, and then said to Beatrix, "What an enchanting lady, so proper, and definitely out of another generation, don't you think? Her parents immigrated to Toronto when she was a teen and then they moved to California a few years later. You can still hear her British accent, and sometimes, while you're studying those psychology books after lunch, she and I visit over the hedge. Once or twice, she's invited me for a chinwag, a visit, with tea and biscuits, cookies to you, dear. We always chat about London and Shakespeare and Cambridge, how it was before the war. She grew up near my college, Beatrix. Is that a coincidence, or what?"

"Never underestimate a woman of a certain age, Thomas." She waved at the neighbor. "I've talked with Mrs. Turney about what she remembers of the previous owners, that couple who were going to turn the place into a hotel and backed down when they saw the price tag for the work. I haven't chatted about who first lived here," Beatrix said, sweeping dust from her shoulders and something sticky from her face. "Okay, heaven help me swallow another cup of her herbal tea, because it's time to talk with our neighbor."

He looked at his hands and dusted them on the front of his trousers. "Beatrix, please don't think I'm one of those lewd men who looks down ladies' blouses, but when having tea with Bunny Turney, she bent over to get a biscuit and I swear there was some kind of blue tattoo." He patted his upper chest.

"You haven't let it slip that you're a man who admires cleavage, did you?"

Thomas swallowed and then saw she was teasing. "You are so cheeky. Should I answer that, it would be certain that I'd make a pig's ear out of it. I'm not that barmy. I have to get down to Ott's Hardware store for some plumbing supplies. Giuseppe said we must replace the pipes under the sink, at least I believe that's what he said. You know, I had better take him to the store with me. Truthfully, until we got here, I had never been under a kitchen sink."

"Then, Thomas, do not attempt to do any plumbing, every, by yourself. Ever." She hugged him, then with clippings in hand, she walked toward their neighbor.

Chrysanthemums in shades of rust to egg yolk yellow lined the brick path to the front porch of the Craftsman bungalow. A liquid amber tree was just starting to turn autumn colors and in another few weeks, leaves of red, orange, and gold would be sprinkling down on her pristine garden.

Mrs. Turney smiled and put her knitting back in a basket. It could have been a pink baby sweater or a potholder, but Beatrix wasn't sure and didn't want to ask. "You two are just the cutest couple working together on the house. Now that you've got helpers, it'll go so much faster. I remember when my Clarence was alive, well, he liked nothing better than to rip out walls and install the latest gadgets. We moved here when there was an outhouse, can you imagine? No, I couldn't either, being raised in conservative Ottawa. Clarence was the love of a lifetime, and I would have agreed to live in a shoebox if it made my beloved happy. That man you've got, Dr. Ling, he's a first-rate gentleman. Oh, and his accent, reminds me of England. If I were forty years younger, I'd give you a run for your money. Haha, just kidding, my dear.

"You know he brings my newspaper right up to the door every single morning. The nasty boy who delivers it just throws the paper willy-nilly anywhere the winds take it, often in my herb garden and sometimes right into the roses. But your handsome husband is so kind to this old lady."

Beatrix hoped Mrs. Turney would take a breath. She didn't want to bother correcting her that Thomas wasn't quite her husband, yet. That would be news that didn't need to be shared.

After a thorough discussion on the weather and "what a lovely sunset that was last night" and "I think our milkman and that neighbor lady are cozy, don't you, dear?" and related gossip on the street, she slowed as Beatrix didn't remark. The commentary fizzled at last. "I couldn't ask for better neighbors than you two, especially after the others I've had, especially years back."

"How very kind of you. I do hope we'll be good neighbors to all the charming people on the block. Actually, that's what I was wondering about, Mrs. Turney, who were the people who lived in our house, perhaps even the first neighbors? I found a box of old newspaper clippings in the attic this morning and it seems someone collected articles on the oddest topics."

The lady reached down and fiddled with the knitting needles. "Now I'm not one to spread rumors, mind you, but when Clarence and I married in 1901, well, he built the house the year before and I remember him saying, 'You don't go and make friends with 'those kind' next door'. My Clarence was so outgoing and he was always polite, passing the time of day, but unlike other neighbors, he didn't spend time with the folks, think their name was McIntosh, in your house. I just admired how he could talk with anyone about anything, and I was just a shy little farm girl, mind you, and I still have trouble talking with people, don't you know. The folks who lived in your home, just a couple, seemed to be happy. Oh, their parties, where everyone would dress up. I was, well I guess I still am, a member of the Women's Christian Temperance Union, so I didn't really mingle with that sort. Clarence agreed that we were too homespun for the rich neighbors."

"That sort? What sort?"

"Drinking," she made a face as if she was sucking a bitter lemon. "Then when Prohibition passed in 1920, well, I tell you,

I assumed it would all change. Nonetheless, the parties just got wilder."

Mrs. Turney's dark eyes brightened, and she cupped her hand near her mouth as if the house would tattle on her. "I often think about those rum-running days and the speakeasies. I heard that sneaky sips could be obtained at places like Casa de Sevilla on lower Chapala Street. Why, there was a bar beneath the Balboa Building, for members at the Santa Barbara Club, and, during the last years of Prohibition, El Club Chico opened as a private club atop the Arlington Theater."

Beatrix saw the lady's eyes twinkle at the memories which were in direct contrast to how she was talking about the shocking past. "I'm confused. If drinking was against the law, didn't anyone raid the parties?"

Mrs. Turney's eyes sparkled recounting the history of the house and then abruptly stopped. "Oh, Mrs. Ling, how silly I've been. Let me make some tea. Here I've been talking old times and forgot my manners. You know I grow all the herbs and spices for tea right here in the garden, as I told you when we first met, and you and that handsome husband had my chamomile tea." Her hand swept out to indicate the patches of plants, neatly trimmed in beach rock. "Or would you prefer lemonade with a sprig of lavender? The lemons this year, as you see from my tree, are just full. You must come over with that fine-looking husband of yours and pick some, or perhaps you're too busy and your fetching husband could come by himself?"

Did she change the subject on purpose or is she a tad forgetful? Beatrix had a gut feeling, from her days of reading people, that this woman was not the proper lady she hoped everyone believed. It didn't matter a bit, but it was amusing food for thought.

Later, when Beatrix extracted herself from the nonstop chatter of Mrs. Turney, and drinking enough herbal tea for a lifetime, she relayed it all to Thomas. "It's your turn next time. She's got a major crush on you, you precious naïve man, so just a warning, do not let her lure you into her house or your virtue could very well be compromised."

Thomas chuckled. "Americans. When will I ever understand any of you? As for my virtue, you've compromised me already, and it was most satisfying. So, no need to worry about our neighbor."

Beatrix just shook her head. *My Brit is warming up.* She shared the details about the wild parties, even after alcohol was against the law, and how the owners seemed to be in the upper echelon of the community. "Their name was McIntosh, a variation on the famous Scottish architect. When I get to the newspaper's archives, I'll try to find something on the family as well as that beach and the Guardians of the Light."

"Did Mrs. Turney say they may have been part of this sect or perhaps an alternative religion or maybe it was a club?"

"I think cult is probably a better word for it. She recounted in detail the years between 1901 and 1917, and when Mr. Turney was drafted and left for fighting in France, she talked about how young girls, dressed to the nines, traipsed through the house and gardens at all hours of the day and night. She was quite clear on what was happening inside as they left the windows open, and she saw it all."

"Orgies in our family home?" Thomas pretended to be mortified. "Beatrix, if I am an exceptionally good fiancé and husband, will you join me in orgies?"

"Only if we pull down the blinds, because otherwise, I swear our neighbor will be snooping on us. There's something needy about her, don't you think?"

"Bea, she's an isolated, lonesome old lady. Apparently, she and her late husband had no children and she told me that there is no close family left."

"Still, she seems curious about us. By the way, I did ask about any special emblem or mascot or insignia, the interconnecting circles that had to do with the group. She nearly hyperventilated getting overly excited but didn't choose to comment. Suddenly managing to spot a goldfinch or jay, but I asked again, and she seemed to regain her sense of the delight in some most risqué memories. I showed her the clipping and I swear her cheeks got rosy, if ladies in their eighties can actually blush."

"Do you think that when good old Clarence was off fighting the Great War, the little Mrs. was right here, actually in our house, keeping her home fires burning?"

"Frankly, yes, I was thinking the same thing, especially after her enthusiastic reaction to relaying those stories. I'm heading to the newspaper, and I might just try to find out something on Mrs. Bunny Turney at the same time."

CHAPTER 8

IT WAS JUST A SHORT TWENTY-MINUTE WALK from the house to the offices of the *Santa Barbara New Press* on Anacapa Street, and Beatrix enjoyed every step. The air was brisk, but not cold. The constant breeze from the Pacific was briny, with a hint of dried seaweed, a testament to a healthy ocean she was told. It was comforting to be in her hometown, and she hadn't realized how much she missed it when living abroad and in New Orleans. The sun warmed the back of her navy woolen jacket as she walked along Anapamu Street and finally, she turned left, toward the Pacific and to her appointment with the paper's archivist in their morgue, where copies of each edition of the newspaper were stored since it began in 1868.

"Miss Patterson?" A slip of a woman behind the desk asked when Beatrix arrived in the basement. "Thanks for calling ahead of time as I'm only here half a day. You're researching information on quasi-religious groups from the 1900's? Are you also interested in the Women's Christian Temperance Union? You've read, I'm sure, that the city was voted to be a dry town even before Prohibition? There were at one time over twenty-six saloons and bars here with a population of just 3,000. Quite an intense topic and one wouldn't think Santa Barbara would have groups like these, especially the cults."

"One would be wrong, is that correct? Yes, thanks. and any help you can give me on the cults, would be appreciated."

Beatrix had changed out of the wide-legged denim jeans and western-inspired cotton shirt into a smart navy and white suit, feeling like an actress ready to plan another role. She'd found a stenographer's tablet and a pen at Woolworth's on State Street hoping to look the part of someone researching the history of the city. She steadied the tablet and wished she'd had a pair of eyeglasses to make her look more studious.

"I see you're a writer. There is quite a lot of history to go through, some of it quite shocking at the time. People often think of California as the land of fruits and nuts and I must say that's what attracted me to Santa Barbara when I moved from North Dakota. It was pretty wild here even during the Depression," she giggled and it came out at the pitch of a first-time violist, squeaky and long.

Beatrix smiled. "This is the exciting part for me as I start to research, and I never quite know what I need until I assemble the facts and tidbits of information. I'm specifically looking for two things: The Guardians of the Light organization and a bit of history on a person who I've heard might still have a connection. It's just a rumor, so please don't repeat this."

"Guardians of the Light were quite prominent for a time, bringing the rich and famous from San Francisco down here, and even movie stars from Los Angeles trekked to Santa Barbara. Why, there were frequent visitors from Hearst Castle. All about having a good time, at least I think that was their quest. Chitchat had it that there was a dark side, and you may find it in your research. I hope you're not easily embarrassed." The lady flipped through a heavy book. "Yes, you'll be able to read the information in our 1933 files. Right after Prohibition ended, the group, as I remember, fell apart when the unofficial leader, a Mr. McIntosh, had an accident, although I can't recall what happened to him. I'm sure you'll discover what occurred. I was employed here, however, that was nearly eighteen years ago. You can find the archives down the second aisle. As for the person?"

"I'd rather not say at the moment. Are there any listings of people who might have been involved in the Guardians of Light or their organization?"

"Not here. Other than reading the newspapers at the time, I don't know of an easy way to get that info, however, have you checked with the public library? It's just around the corner, well nearly. It might have some kind of reference book on that." The clerk went back to sorting papers, or was she just pushing them around on her desk, knowing that whatever Beatrix was looking for was far more interesting than shelving newspaper stories?

"No, I didn't. Not yet." Beatrix didn't move. There was something that the woman wanted to say, something holding her back. Beatrix had learned to be a patient listener.

The clerk said, "You know, ma'am, that some folks think the organization still exists? I don't believe that, however."

That was it. The clerk turned her eyes away from Beatrix, then looked down, a sure sign that she knew, that something had been left unsaid.

"Where might I locate any info on the Guardians?"

"The paper had covered it a lot over the years. It'll take a lot of digging. There's no list or catalog or directory. Sorry. But you do know, of course, that some folks say they were always a part of the Chumash, the tribe with a compound north of town, but I think that's hooey, since when anything odd happens, well, the tribe gets blamed."

It's always been that way to those of color, she shook her head and withdrew a card from her pocket. "If you think of anything, for my book mind you, could you call or contact me? I would really appreciate that."

Beatrix scrubbed her hands before leaving the newspaper morgue, but she still felt gritty as if the dust penetrated the fabric of her clothing while digging through the dusty archives. She'd learned that the Guardians of the Light, with a double connected circle emblem, was an unacknowledged branch of Holy Grail Family of Friends, another unrecognized off-shoot of the Light and Love Universal Family Church, and a vague chance of being connected with some established religious congregations, as well.

The most enlightening moment was when Beatrix read that they had a large gathering of sorts on the cliffs and sand at Gaviota. They had called it The Awakening. Beatrix inhaled as she read: "Shocking to locals, the Santa Barbara sheriff's department counted thirteen bodies. Witnesses who came forward said that the gathering turned into a frenzy with cult members dancing and singing along the sand and around massive bonfires before wading into deadly rip currents. Witnesses say that the leader, unnamed at press time, perished too, as he attempted to cleanse every one of their sinful natures. Some members, on the cliff above, threw themselves into the rising tides."

The grainy, unsettling photos showed nude bodies lined up on the beach, much like sea lions enjoying a break. A crowd was held back by police, seemingly circling the bodies. She tucked that away in her brain and knew she would need to put more of these "puzzle" pieces together. She waved thanks to the clerk as she left that morgue. She walked into the sunlight, unable to shake the tragedy of members choosing to blindly follow a misguided leader only to perish in ravishing waves.

I wonder if there were survivors? Not every member might have died, she thought. *How can I find those who were part or may even now be part of the cult? Do I need to? More so, do I want to?* Then her thoughts returned to the young woman who had died, and she knew the answer.

CHAPTER 9

THERE WAS NO DOUBT that Bunny Turney, sweet and frail now as she might look, most definitely would have followed the sensational scandals, especially since she knew her neighbors rubbed elbows and nude bodies with those found on the beach. Beatrix would visit with her new best friend to share whatever scoop she could to incite Mrs. Turney to say or even wrinkle an eyebrow about the incident on the beach that had made headlines and the Guardians of Light. *Could little Mrs. Turney have been part of the cult?* It didn't take much for Mrs. Turney to talk, but would she tell the truth? Would it only be her own conception of the truth or gospel?

As for finding any further insight on her neighbor, Beatrix cringed when realizing she'd have to read every single copy of the city's newspaper to find anything. Maybe the public library would be able to help.

"But first, to the next morgue," she said out loud and headed to the police station just blocks south. Inside the Spanish and Moorish-influenced style building with the red-tiled roof, a style she'd missed dearly during her time in New Orleans, she dashed to the restroom, took water, and smudged her mascara. She looked up and yes, it did appear as if she'd been crying. She took a hanky from her shoulder bag, and crumbled it in her hand as she put away the steno pad. She pinched her cheeks to make them look spotty. The reflection in the mirror showed a woman in distress.

"Excuse me, sir," Beatrix looked down and fluttered her eyelashes, to indicate she was fighting back tears. "I saw this." She shoved the day-old newspaper photo of the dead woman lying on the beach across the counter to the desk sergeant. Right then, another brief article in the paper caught her eye as she waited for a response. It was about the Women's Christian Temperance Union and a local dignitary had made a large, charitable contribution to one of their subcommittees called Onus Organista.

"You knew the deceased?" he asked. He straightened a bit and when he looked at Beatrix, he attempted to suck in a protruding belly.

"I fear it might be my," gulp, "sister." She blinked, hoping tears might form in her eyes. "Is there any way of checking? She hasn't been home for five days."

"Could you kindly sit over there, miss? I'll get somebody to take you, um, well, to see if it could be your sister. Now, don't you worry. Santa Barbara's police are always helping people." He dashed to another office and Beatrix marveled. *That easy?* she wondered.

A sturdy officer in an ill-fitting uniform, two sizes too large, and with the cuffs folded up as they, too, had been made for someone much larger, waddled toward her. She had the bearing of military personnel, and now with the war over, many returning veterans hoped to find a niche in law enforcement. *Good for you,* thought Beatrix as the woman said, "My condolences, Miss..."

"Thank you," Beatrix replied, keeping her lips in a straight line as she got to her feet. She let the question of her last name hang. If she didn't have to lie any more than was necessary, although she was very good at it, it would be easier. However, she was prepared to do it, if it let her take a look at the body.

"Sarge, here, thinks our Jane Doe might be your sister?"

"Jane Doe?" She tried to look grief-stricken. "Yes, that could be true," Beatrix replied, again pretending she was blinking back tears.

"Be prepared for a shock, miss. She fell or decided to end it all. Then was dashed against the rocks, the detectives think. It was the fall, not the ocean, that got her. No water in her lungs that would concur she'd drowned."

"Could she have been pushed? Those cliffs are high out at Gaviota Beach."

"Suppose so, but the coroner told me he thought she'd just wanted to end her misery."

"What misery? Was it that, um, cult? What are you saying?"

"You didn't know?"

"Know what?"

"You would have been an auntie. Our Jane Doe was two months pregnant."

"Oh, no," Beatrix blinked back genuine tears, real ones, and sat down, then abruptly stood. *Darn it all, a baby. Such a waste of life,* she thought as she steadied herself and followed the officer down a long, cold corridor to double doors with glass windows and a sign above saying City Morgue.

The officer pulled open the door and stood out of the way for Beatrix to enter. "I'll leave you alone, but I'll be right outside the door. I asked the coroner's clerk to pull her body out for you. I hope that's okay and again, miss, my condolences."

The coroner's assistant was just wheeling out the drawer that held Jane Doe from a chilled locker as Beatrix entered the lab. He looked barely old enough to drive and had the tack of a grocery clerk flipping food into sacks. He looked at Beatrix. "Ready?" Then turned back the white sheet from the young woman's face, made a tut-tut sound, and withdrew a pack of Camel cigarettes from his ill-fitting white medical jacket. "Want to be alone?"

The young man didn't wait for a reply but headed out a side door for a smoke break. It all surprised Beatrix because in this small community, it never crossed their minds, apparently, that people really weren't who they said they were. In any big city, she would have been asked to prove she knew the deceased or present some type of identification. Their naiveite was good for Beatrix's investigation.

Beatrix shook her head as she looked down at the woman, "You're not even twenty, you were going to be a mama, and now you are dead. Both of you are dead. What do you want me to do? Why end your life? What can you tell me?" She pulled back a corner of the sheet covering the body and held the woman's hand. It was icy and stiff, of course. Her palm was rough, and her skin was tanned, but only half way up her arms, as if she'd been a laborer, or worked in the strawberry or lima bean fields around the outskirts of town. Beatrix looked at her nails, broken. Her black hair twisted and tucked under her head and Beatrix imagined that at one time it was luxurious and shiny.

She gingerly pulled the sheet back further to expose her upper torso and there was the answer. There was a small tattoo on her chest, just above her heart. It was two intertwining circles, and the flesh looked irritated around the marks. *Fresh, it's new, or there wouldn't be inflammation. Did she get this tat before dying or is it post-mortem, and if after death, why?*

It was plain. The circles were that of the Guardians of the Light.

"You were a member. What else? Were you a sacrifice? Did you jump off the cliff during a wild party that got out of hand? Did you struggle as someone tried to push you? I'll try to figure it out, my friend. You will not be forgotten. I promise." She searched the woman's deathly still face and brushed off a tear that fell right in the middle of the tiny tattoo.

There were no sounds inside the morgue. The police officer was sitting with her back toward the window reading the newspaper, and the coroner's clerk was apparently still out smoking. She pushed the unidentified woman back into the vault and looked at the names on the other drawers. Mortimer Ramsey was two drawers over and one down. Beatrix took a chance, not knowing how much time she'd have, but the opportunity could not be passed up. She pulled open the drawer, and if the officer glanced up, she would assume Beatrix was still mourning her sister's body, but instead, it was Frankie Ramsey's father lying there. Puffy, fat, and the color of wet cement.

With rope burns around his throat.

CHAPTER 10

BEATRIX LOOKED AT THE ROPE BURNS and couldn't understand why the police hadn't released his body for burial. *Perhaps they, too, realize it was possibly foul play, although Frankie said that wasn't the case. Then why keep the body?* From the sutures in a huge Y pattern on the man's chest, the autopsy was complete. Maybe there was paperwork or something like that still to be done, but it seemed fishy. Beatrix pulled the sheet back even more. There was bruising on his right forearm and a long slim laceration. He could have been bruised right after kicking out the chair and hanging himself, but there wouldn't have been a cut that size. It seemed to her that someone had reached out and sliced the man. She gingerly touched his scalp. At the back of his head, right where she'd expected it, there was a lump.

That too could have happened from a previous fall or was it from where someone slugged him? Hit him hard enough to die or cause him to black out. It would have had to be someone of strength to lift this sizeable man up, slip a rope around his neck, and then knock him so that the chair fell. Someone big and strong like the famous drag queen Frankie Ramsey.

There was the sound of the door handle twisting and Beatrix slid Mr. Ramsey back into his chamber of death. She turned and swayed, and made a little whimpering sound as if she might faint. The act did the trick and the police officer's eyes were diverted from the fact that Beatrix had been inspecting another corpse. "That was horrible," she said and grasp the counter. "Would you mind sitting outside with me for a moment?" hoping she sounded like a delicate flower.

The policewoman patted her shoulder. "Come on, honey. 1 was at Pearl Harbor the day of the attack and 1 have been in battle, saw much worse, but my legs sometimes feel like wet noodles, too. Death isn't pretty. That came out wrong, sorry. 1 am not recommending war to beef up a woman, mind you. You sit right here, and I'll get you some water."

Beatrix knew the moment the officer returned, she would ask her for details of that unnamed woman, supposedly her sister, and then be expected to make plans for the release of the body and which funeral home to contact. She looked both ways and quickly headed straight to the exit, outside the back of the police station and city morgue.

The coroner's clerk, now outdoors standing in a patch in the sunlight, seemed even younger looking than inside. He glanced at Beatrix and smiled. "Want a smoke?" he asked, offering the packet.

"No, thanks. 1 do have a question. Has anyone else come to see the woman you're calling Jane Doe?"

He leered and then looked embarrassed by it as he took in every inch of Beatrix's figure. "Your sister?"

"No, she wasn't, the poor dear."

"Visitors? Yeah. An old lady came from some church or something, 1 think. She had me pull out the body, held her hands, and prayed. Then she got out a bottle of water, I'm guessing water, and sprinkled it over her. 1 thought maybe she was going to claim the body, but then she turned and just walked out. It was weird. That happened one other time, the first week 1 was working here, too, about two years ago. Seems like Gaviota cliffs are a popular place to off yourself. Another lady, 'bout the same age, and naked as a jaybird, too."

"In 1943, when you started here? Was it the same older woman who came to 'visit'?"

"Yeah, it was June, I remember. As for the woman, all old people look alike, don't they? I can't be sure, but I am of the year. Yeah, '43. I'd gotten a deferment because of my job, thank God, and the fact that I lost this foot in a farming accident when I was a kid," he pulled up a pant leg to show an artificial limb. "You saying you might have been related to the other one?" He cocked his head, not making sense of the stranger's curiosity. "You writing a book on the Guardians of Light? Yeah, that circle thing. Heard about them my whole life. My mama thinks they were all doing the work of the devil, by the way. Or are you scouting out gossip or scuttlebutt on other wacky religions that have branched up here in town?"

Now it was Beatrix's turn to be surprised. "Why do you ask?"

"The first person I'd ever seen dead also had this, um, well she had those two little circles on her breast. I notice those things, um, not just the breasts, well, those too," the babbling excuses didn't matter, and his cheeks were blotched with youthful humiliation. The connection was there. "I remember my parents, strict Pentecostals, being horrified about some of the goings on with that group. My mama loved a good gossip with her lady friends, mind you, and I guess that wasn't against their religious rules, which always seemed flexible to me. I spent too much time in the house after the accident, and I liked nothing more than to listen to Mama and her friends dish the dirt."

"What happened to the last woman back in 1943?" Now Beatrix took out the steno pad and a pen, letting it hover over the tablet, just for show, and it worked.

"For the newspaper or a book, huh? Okay, we'll, let's see. Like I said, it was my first week on the job and everything was bizzarro. I graduated from Santa Barbara High one week and the next, was looking face to face with a corpse. After nobody claimed the stiff, the lady got buried in a pauper's graveyard at the mission. They've got a special area for the John Does and Jane's we bring in. My mama doesn't think folks who kill themselves should be buried near God's house, but I believe they're still God's kids, whether they do something stupid or not. I've done my share of stupid."

"Haven't we all," Beatrix said and scribbled notes, as if she were going to write a book or article as the assistant lit another Camel cigarette, seeming to enjoy his celebrity status with a writer. "Any others in your two years here?"

"Once. Another girl showed up. I'd gone to high school with her. Shocked the crap out of me. Excuse me, sorry."

"Because you knew her or how she died?"

"Both. Had the same connected circles on her chest. I had to get out of here after her parents claimed her. I didn't know her well, mind you. She was prom queen. Being with her, even her smile was magic. I was this crippled kid from a bean farm, but I do remember how everyone loved her. Me, too, I suppose, but from such a distance, I was, if I'm honest, not even a speck on her radar. She seemed to light up a room just walking in. It was Christmas Eve this past year, and since I'm the low Joe on the totem pole, of course, I was working. The parents fell apart and the mom tumbled to the tile floor. The mother crashed down after one ear-splitting scream, then fainted dead away.

"Later that day, on my way back to the farm, I got my mom a box of See's candy for Christmas. Nobody should go through what they did. Yet, right there on the slab is another luckless girl." The boy's face was long and serious. In barely above a whisper, he said, "I often think I'm not cut out for this job, but with the GI's coming home, Mama says there's going to be a lot of guys who would take it, so I'd better just shut up and keep it. My desk sergeant says you can't have a heart to be a coroner."

"If you think of her name, could you call me?" Beatrix jotted her phone number on the edge of the tablet and ripped out the page.

"Oh? Why didn't you ask if you wanted her name? You could have asked. It was Suzette McIntosh. She was called Suzi by the cool kids, of which I was not one."

"You're sure it was Suzette and the last name McIntosh?" Beatrix blinked. *Could it be a girl from the same family that once lived in our house?*

"Miserable business." He nodded and frowned. He opened his mouth and then stopped, looking at the door that would lead him back to keeping an eye on dead people.

"Something else you remember?"

"Just a rumor, mind you, but I heard after high school, that she got mixed up with the iffy bunch. 'The wrong crowd' were the words Mom would have said and then gone on, at length, to define just what she meant. Mind you, it could be nothing. I remember seeing Suzi down on the wharf and one time at McConnell's ice cream. She looked right through me, but it made me glad to see her laughing and looking like she was on top of the world. That's why this troubled me when not too long after that she was wheeled in here, taken her own life." He squished out the smoke, his knuckles white with pressure. He grimaced and returned to work. He stopped and turned and walked back toward Beatrix. "It's probably nothing."

She waited.

"When she was brought in, I swear she was wearing a necklace with a shamrock charm, a little green stone was in the middle. Then later, after the visitors left, including another couple of Bible-packing church ladies, I had to check on something and the chain was there, but the charm was gone. Probably fell on the floor and got swept up by the cleaner. Like I said, it's probably nothing."

"I do not trust coincidences, like this one," Beatrix said out loud. "Thanks, you've been helpful." She was glad to get out of the morgue, where the air was intense from chemicals. She breathed deeply when she got outside and headed toward the public library to see what she could find about neighborly Bunny Turney and the McIntosh clan, and just maybe a book about the Guardians of the Light, whatever that truly proved to be. "Maybe it's a social club that lights Christmas decorations," she chuckled, knowing that the truth had to be dark.

She crossed Anapamu Street, turned her face to the sun, and tried to slip the puzzling pieces together. Before she'd visited the morgue, she'd felt as if someone was following her. A few times, she'd slowed and pretended to examine the contents of a store window. She had turned abruptly, but nothing seemed amiss. Then, she spied Thomas sitting on a bus stop bench, hiding behind a newspaper, and peeking around the corner of a page. Even if she hadn't seen his spiky black hair, she'd have known him at once from his choice of footwear, those snappy British shoes he preferred. She was tempted to wave or even sneak up and yank the newspaper from his fingers. Yet, if his surveillance made him feel better, she'd pretend he wasn't there, following her, for now. She smiled and tried to shake off the unsettling emotion of possibly being stalked that had first crawled up her spine. *So sweet, in a creepy way. My bodyguard is back.* While the idea made her quietly chuckle, a bubble of concern surfaced and she wondered, *Can I marry and live with a man who doesn't fully trust me?*

CHAPTER 11

SANTA BARBARA'S CITY LIBRARY was just slightly more inviting than the city morgue, she thought. *No, the morgue felt more human.*

In unison, bespeckled librarians frowned as Beatrix's heels clicked across the marble floor. She squared her chin, looked at each one of their reactions, and in practiced unison, they turned away. *I've faced down crazy kidnappers and lunatics with guns. Certainly a librarian isn't about to intimidate me.* She almost let loose the laugh threatening to escape, but that certainly would have caused her to be expelled from these hallowed halls at once.

She might be five-foot-six inches, but their looks were attempting to make her feel as if she were five again, and blowing Bazooka bubble gum among the collection, which she actually did on a visit with her mother decades earlier. It was one of her most cherished memories, because after they left the library, Jennie Patterson, shoved three wads of gum in her mouth and proceeded to blow a bubble the size of a watermelon. Beatrix screamed with delight. Best yet, her mother let her pop it, and the film coated her normally sedate face. They both laughed, tumbling over, and each time one stopped, the other's laughter started again. One of the best library visits of her entire life.

Now, Beatrix placed her palms on the counter near the sign that read "information." Here stood what seemed to be the youngest in a half dozen librarians. This one hadn't perfected that literary frown of the others. She tried to contain the smile lines crinkled at her eyes. "Good day, ma'am."

"Good day, Miss Smith," she read the lady's name tag, secured on the lapel of her suit jacket. She looked at the long-painted nails again, and the slim gold band on her right hand, third finger. There was a slight indentation on the third finger of the left hand. *Newly divorced? Hiding her marriage from the other librarians? Husband a casualty of the war and just now taking off her ring?* Beatrix knew there was a story there.

"Thank you for coming into the library," she said and truly did smile. "How may the library assist you today?" She grabbed a piece of unruly yellow hair, a color never seen in nature, most definitely not in the realm of hair colors. She tucked it into a loose bun snuggly scrunched against the collar of her crisp white blouse with the lace trim. Her mannerism was welcoming and fresh, while the other staff put fingers to their mouths and shushed.

"I need some help," Beatrix tilted her head and smiled the words, hoping this could melt the frosty persona of another librarian who joined Miss Smith. The second librarian's frown was etched deeply by her mouth, a mouth that seemed ready, at least to Beatrix, to shoo her out of the library for even speaking.

Miss Smith's smile showed perfectly aligned, bright white teeth. "That is why we are here," said the pretty librarian, possibly younger than Beatrix, but it was hard to tell with her thick glasses. The only hint that the librarian might be wilder than her appearance tried to report was the thick coating of hot pink lipstick and matching nail polish. Her clothing was far from glamorous, but neat, and from the tweed fabric of her jacket, it was pricey.

"Is there a who's who directory of the city? I'm trying to find information on a family I knew when I lived here in the thirties with my parents, Jennie and William Randolph Patterson."

The librarian's entire posture changed. She blinked and only then looked like a well-composed woman who had a curious streak. "Your family? The benefactors that financed all of our nationally known genealogical collection and restored the building after the earthquakes? You are the child of Mr. and Mrs. Patterson?" The whispered question could have been a shout, as all the staff turned and stared at the woman in front of the waist-high counter.

"Yes, I'm Beatrix Patterson." Who knew that the Patterson name, and their generous donations, had the ability to turn Beatrix into a minor celebrity?

"An honor to meet you, Miss Patterson. Darla Smith." Efficiency poured from her, and she quickly added, "Yes. We do have a social register and I can direct you to a book with the clubs and their officers, but not a who's who directory of the city. Is there a specific group or family you want to reconnect with?" The librarian was already making notes and moving toward a bookshelf of red-leather-bound reference books, apparently too priceless to be out in the open where the grubby town's people might come into the hallowed hall and touch them.

Beatrix didn't want to give out the names of the McIntosh clan or that she was seeking information on the club for fear that gossip, always a delight within small organizations, would spread. This was the time to be quietly searching, not scattering rumors. Besides, she wanted to see if Bunny Turney possibly had any history in the city, as well. The activities of the late Mortimer Ramsey, Frankie's father, would best be found by asking around, in the shadier parts of the community and perhaps by gathering tidbits from her loyal contacts in New Orleans.

"Would you mind terribly if I looked at the books on your reference shelves myself?" She was pulling the "Patterson name card" and didn't care. She remembered how her parents had been major benefactors for the various buildings, the art museum, and the renovation of the grand city hall buildings. They loved the city of Santa Barbara and were financially lavish with that adoration.

The librarian squeezed her lips together and glanced behind her. A forgettable man, in a gray suit, with not more than ten strands of melancholy hair covering his bald spot, had been monitoring the conversation. From his posture, he seemed to be in charge and displeased with Beatrix's intrusion into the deadly quiet of the library. He frowned, sighed and grudgingly gave a quick nod. All archives opened to Beatrix.

Not only was the library noiseless, but the air inside was absolutely still, as if a breeze would disrupt the librarians. After two hours of reading, Beatrix stood, stretched, slipped off her bolero jacket and placed it over the back of the chair, found the restroom, dabbed a bit of water on her face, and returned to her quest. Time slipped away, and only because her stomach was insisting that she forgot to feed it, did Beatrix look at her watch. She had far more to dive into. It was a rabbit hole, and one topic bled into the next. *It's enough for now,* she thought, closing the tablet that didn't require any notes as she would remember everything she'd read in detail.

She strolled the five or so blocks back to the house that they'd begun calling a 'work-in-progress' or WIP. Sometimes it was a work in pieces, yet, in the last few days, the construction crew had made incredible strides.

The shady sidewalk and the sea breezes seemed to help at least compartmentalize all the confusing facts she'd uncovered. She stopped, as if to adjust the cross-over purse strap, and turned slightly knowing she was being followed. She recognized Thomas, even hiding behind a palm tree.

Approaching the house, Beatrix spied Mrs. Turney, so devoted to her garden, trimming and deadheading flowers with gusto. The lady was talking, apparently, to some lavender, holding it by the faded flower stalk before giving the stem a quick snip. Beatrix scooted by the chatty neighbor, trying to make her footsteps as inaudible as possible. She made it to her own garden's squeaky gate before the neighbor looked up, calling hello, and giving a jaunty wave with a dirt-covered cotton-gloved hand. Beatrix returned the greeting and headed to the back of the home. She bent to pull a few weeds, tilted her head, trying to plan for a vegetable patch in the back corner where it got sun most of the day, and stopped to smell the few old roses. One of her favorites, the delicate and perfumy Damask rose, was a bright pink one with scores of petals in each flower, like ballerina dresses. The breeze picked up the spent flowers and tossed them in the air like floral confetti. She smiled as they danced in the breeze as she waited for Thomas to dash around the other side of the house. If he wanted to pretend that he'd been home all the time, she'd do it too. She waited, shoved a hand into her jacket pocket, and felt the crisp edges of paper.

Whatever is this? She wondered. Standing on the pathway, she withdrew the paper, white and folded into four. "Stop sniffing around where you do not belong. A pretty thing like you could end up like the others."

Beatrix blinked. "Like the others...? Dead?" She'd been alone throughout that morning, had only talked with the youngish librarian with the glowing pink lipstick, yet here was a threatening note. She scrutinized the writing, it was tight and precise, but why and when? Then she remembered she'd visited the restroom, leaving her research on the Guardians of Light open on the massive library table. But again, "Why?"

She'd tell Thomas, of course, because a lie in a relationship made the relationship a lie, but not at that second. Not even that day. Clearly, someone wanted her to stop as she inquired after the truth. Plainly that meant something vile had happened to the young women with the concentric circles tattooed on their breasts. Once more, Beatrix stood straighter and thought of the promise she'd given to the young Jane Doe at the morgue. "I will find out why you died," she repeated.

Thomas's breathing was a bit ragged as she bent to kiss his cheek as he nonchalantly sat with the workers. They'd established a picnic area, under a sycamore tree, and were finishing off the sandwiches and fruit that had been prepared for them, once Thomas finished making their breakfast earlier that day. "*Bonjourno, Caramia*," Thomas greeted her, and the men laughed with him. It was obvious they were not threatened by their bosses and each day looked healthier and happier and even amused by the homeowners.

"Come sit with us, Beatrix." He patted the empty place on the bench next to him. "There's an egg salad sandwich left and apples. I'm afraid the Lemon-Ricotta cookies I got from the bakery yesterday have disappeared," he said.

"What a morning. Good afternoon, gentlemen." The men nodded and relaxed as they chatted in a language Beatrix had no hope of learning right then. "Are you practicing your Italian, my darling?"

"Apparently, I'm hopeless to their specific dialect. I know six languages and Italian is one, but not Sicilian. I'm thoroughly struggling with it. These courageous workers are quick to point that out, and I have a suspicion they're using 'baby talk' to converse with me, however, these blokes are lifesavers. Wait until you see how the bedrooms are shaping up."

"Thank you, all," she motioned to the men, "for helping us to get our house into habitable condition." Beatrix assumed that the smile and hand gestures would convey her gratitude if they could not understand the words she used.

Giuseppe, who seemed to be the foreman of the group, nodded, and spoke in halting English. "You know, Doctor and Madam, we maybe can maybe understand most what you are saying," he said. "*Madrone.* English is not my friend."

Thomas was stunned. Beatrix laughed. He hadn't asked if the workers spoke English.

He continued and the men happily nodded in agreement. "We battled in North Africa. That pig Mussolini retreated. He left us Sicilian troops to perish in the desert and dragged the Italian soldiers with him. The Italians never trusted us; no talk to us. Finally, they shout that Americans will kill us, and we wave white handkerchiefs. There was no place to hide. It is desert. We believed what the Black Shirts said. We knelt and prayed for God to protect us. The GIs, your good guys, dragged and carried us to tents, to their camp. Most of us so weak we no could barely walk. Death was a day away. GIs gave us water. They gave food. They even had doctors and nurses give us medicine and bind our wounds. We would have died otherwise so when they sent us here to California, again not our choice but we understood, many of us started to pick up English."

The other men talked too, a rich mix of Sicilian and English. One said, "American is not that hard to pick up."

Another said, "You have weather here, just like on our island homeland."

"Well, that is a relief," Thomas chuckled, pretending to wipe sweat off his forehead. "Thank you for your kindness to me and my future wife. And to our house."

"Gentlemen, if you need anything," Beatrix looked closely at the workers, meeting their eyes, returning their smiles, "you must ask me or Thomas. If you need help sending money home to your families, please let us help you, too."

Much back patting ensued and finally, Thomas finished the untouched second half of Beatrix's sandwich and the workers happily returned to the massive rebuilding job. "Speaking of life saving and relief, you know if that house across town hadn't been sold and was to be demolished, and we bought it lock, stock and clawfoot tub, we would never be able to have this much lumber. Every building supply out there is being snapped right up. I have arranged for the light fixtures and even any furnishings that were left in the house to be transported here."

"What a smart man you are," she said. Once alone, she began telling him about her morning from the newspaper's archives to the city morgue and then onto the library, but she stopped short of the odd note found in her pocket. *It'll just drive him silly with worry. It's weird, but weird is often normal these days,* she thought.

"The young woman lying there, cold as an icebox, was pretty, or would have been if she wasn't dead." She looked out the window, the sky and the Eucalyptus trees dancing in the breeze. "She was pregnant, Thomas. Whoever murdered her killed two."

He circled her with his grasp. "I am so sorry, for her, the baby, and you. Are you sure you want to get involved in this, well, more than you already are?"

"No, yes. Yes, I do, but just until I can find out her name. Her family deserves to know the truth, just like I sought out my truth." She fiddled with a loose string on the hem of her jacket and then said, "I need to know more about Frankie Ramsey's father as he looked, unfortunately, as pathetic as a beached whale. All bloated. I need to talk with Frankie again."

"You got sidetracked?" Thomas asked.

"Yes, and it was Mrs. Turney's fault. The lady loves to talk. A lot."

"I've given up avoiding the little woman, Bea. We've been having afternoon tea and biscuits and she tells me more about the unseeming history of our house. Oh, it was wild at times, and you should see how much joy it gives our neighbor to tell the sordid stories. I swear her eyes light up. I stop in for a visit, just a half hour after you and I finish lunch, while you're in the music room studying. Are you aware that she makes a different, most intriguing herbal tea each day? I always return energized. You'll have to join us."

Beatrix took off the fitted jacket as November was proving to be warm, and smiled at the idea of her fiancé been pursued. "You realize the sexagenarian now will depend on your company."

"You didn't just make up the sexagenarian word to frighten me about her, did you, darling? For your information, I find her not in the least appealing." Thomas tilted his head and smiled knowingly, of course, aware that a sexagenarian was someone over sixty.

"It's not too late," she looked at her wristwatch, "I want to telephone John in New Orleans. He'll tell me why Mortimer Ramsey was here on the west coast, or least will be able to find out the truth, if he doesn't already know. I find it curious that Frankie was unaware as to why her father moved here to Santa Barbara. Or maybe I don't understand fathers and sons."

"You are right. Sometimes there are questions we want to ask our fathers about issues, opinions and preferences and do not have the courage or the words to do so."

She took his hand, smoothing her fingers over the palm now calloused by hard manual labor. "What would you ask your father, Thomas, if you could? If you wouldn't upset him and you knew he would tell you his reality?" Her eyes looked deeply into Thomas's soul and she knew this would not be the last time they'd talk about whatever had happened and why the truth was always concealed.

"I would like to know why in the early 1900s he left our ancestral homeland. He was the oldest son of five siblings, and in Chinese culture, as you know, there would be extraordinary disgrace for the oldest son to desert his family like that, Bea. It's just not done. Even now. I have tried to ask, but he evades the topic or flat-out says something like, 'It's complicated, my son, and to be discussed some other time'. Mum says, 'That's your father's story to tell, not mine. He'll tell you or not'.

"Candidly, I fear the worst. I believe it was because he had done something horrendous or unlawful at that time. Perhaps murdered someone or caused an accident. Or, these were traitorous periods and it could have been his politics were wildly unpopular or downright dangerous. Then there was the revolution. Before the war, and during a short period of somewhat calm in China, Mum took six months and visited her family although by then, my paternal grandparents had died. There's just never been any discussion about Dad's family."

"Perhaps when we're in London for the wedding, you could approach the question," she said. "Take a walk together and bring it up when you are outside of the house. Do something he enjoys. You said he especially liked the Albert and Victoria Museum. Go there, stop for afternoon tea and when you're both relaxed, ask him. He might still put you off, but you must try. Secrets have a way of becoming far more powerful than they really are. Remember how my parents wouldn't tell me anything about my birth parents? I could feel the weight of that secret on their hearts even when I didn't know I'd been adopted."

"What if he did commit an unspeakable crime, what if he had to flee?"

"Oh, Thomas, you are sweet. Your father, from all you've told me, is a kind, honorable man. Times dictate the definition of what crimes are. Perhaps, now in 1945, whatever happened back then to cause him to escape China is no longer against the law, if it ever was." She gave him a peck on the cheek, knowing they'd return to this conversation again before the wedding. "Now, if you'll excuse me, I need to call New Orleans before John leaves for the evening to see if I can find out why Morty came here to Santa Barbara and perhaps even if he had business associates in town."

John Brockman, a key player in gambling and money lending throughout Louisiana, and rumored to be head of wagering in all of the American South, who was also Beatrix Patterson's friend, answered the phone on the first ring. After the typical pleasantries from health to weather, Beatrix came to the point.

"Mortimer Ramsey has died." They knew each well enough not to sugarcoat the truth.

"So, I was told," John said. It came with a sigh, as it often does when a contemporary passes.

"Frankie, his son, is here in the city and as you recommended, he looked me up, asking for help, to find the truth. Frankie believes that his father would never have taken his own life. He has hired me to find the truth. Was Mortimer the type to end it all by his own hand?" As she asked that, she wondered if she'd be able to discover what happened to the woman on the beach and felt compelled to do so.

"I have wondered about that, too, Beatrix. Morty lived as large as his body, and he was a big man. Haven't heard anything about foul play, but then again, I'm 2,000 miles east of you. It's curious. I'm curious."

"How come, John, other than you had a history together?"

"This is speculation, mind you, but Mortimer didn't do anything halfway. We butted heads plenty of times on more logistical issues than moral ones. He stayed out of my business, and I stayed away from him. Although when Morty was in a good mood, there was no one better to be around. He was generous to those he admired and honestly? Fair with those who were his enemies. Like a lot of us, he had his own code of what was right and wrong. I thought his calls were on the money most times. That's an admirable quality, especially in the world in which Morty and I make a living. Are you interested in rumors, Beatrix?"

"Emphatically." She sat in the brown leather overstuffed chair, that had seen better days and was far too large for the small foyer where the big black telephone was balanced on a wooden packing crate. At least they were able to get the telephone company to install one, or she would have been having this conversation in a telephone booth near Woolworth's dime store.

"There's an organized sex trafficking ring of young girls, barely teenagers, in Southern California and run by, I believe, a Mexican cartel out of Tijuana, across the border from San Diego. That's nasty business, but we're not here to discuss my moral compass or you'd get an earful. I base this intelligence on the result of some inquiries and the whispers I've heard. Okay, I didn't see Morty when I was in Montecito to buy the villa there, which my man Henry says is in spick and span condition now.

"Excuse me for a moment, my dear, I need to handle a small concern." Muffled voices came through the line as if John had put his hand over the receiver.

Then she heard, "Well, tell him that unless he pays his past gambling debts, which is pushing a million, he's persona non grata. Yeah, that means he's not welcome here or any of the other joints in town. No, I will not accept the family's estate as collateral."

John's voice held quiet authority. There was no doubt he'd meant whatever he said to whomever it was and since Beatrix had been in John's office during other interruptions, she was sure that the messenger was obviously one of the bouncers at the door of the gambling hall.

"Sorry, Beatrix, a bit of business. You wouldn't be shocked if it was our state's attorney general trying to use his position to forgo repayment for poker losses, would you? I doubt it. Now, let's see. Oh, yes, keep in mind, old Morty may have looked like a loveable teddy bear, but only a fool would have believed that. He was too smart to mess with that gang south of the border, and I heard this from a source when I came to Santa Barbara, to your hometown, to buy the home. However, Morty knew the Central Coast, all the way to San Francisco, was pretty much open for his style of business and perhaps wanted to replicate the ungodly success of the Mexican cartel's business 'model'. If he wanted to get into that line. Rumor was he'd been a pimp in his early years, but keep in mind that would have been right after World War I, or the Great War as we'd called it, and when some of us did things we'd rather forget."

There were things in Beatrix's past she was not comfortable sharing or wanting to be made public. She understood and waited for John to continue, as she knew he would.

"This is just word on the street, Beatrix, and frankly I don't know why my source even had an interest in Morty. I have no facts on which to base the claim. The Morty from the old days probably would have been a pirate if he'd been born a hundred years before."

"He wasn't just a common street-corner pimp, right? How was he going to take over shoe-string operations from Ventura to Santa Cruz? If he was there to organize the trade."

"Was he? I don't know that. Best guess, if that is true, would be through intimidation. Perhaps protection. Fraud. Payoffs to local law enforcement. The same way it's always been done throughout the country. Again, Morty never told me what he was up to, and I never asked."

"How far along was he, do you know, if he was going to establish authority over the local pimps?"

"Mind you, Beatrix, this is not gospel. I did hear that Morty was content. I wished him the best as he'd rarely been happy. To your questions, the central coast, I've learned, is the Wild West when it comes to criminal organizations. Every town has a group, but they don't want to know what's happening in other areas and no one gang pushes the other. Must be the sunshine and warm weather."

"Could Morty's new business be all rumor?"

"Want me to dig deeper? Last I heard anything about Morty, other than he'd died three weeks ago, was when Frankie came to my office weeks ago as he wanted to turn a dilapidated venue built before 1920 called Le Petit Théâtre Du Vieux Carre, on St. Peter and not that far from Club My-Oh-My, and transform it into a legit theater. He came to me seeking financial backing. I gave it to him. Quite a bit of money, actually, and figured it could help him. He's got potential, he's driven, and he's got plenty of the opportunist, like his dad, in him, too."

"We talked about family and friends and told me his dad had been working Santa Barbara since summer."

Beatrix thought of how Frankie said he didn't need money. Why lie? Instead, she asked John, "Did he have an office, do you know?"

"Set up in a place called the El Paso, or is it Patio district? You say that Frankie is okay? I like the kid, a bit weird, but aren't we all." He laughed.

"El Paseo, and it's right downtown. An office? Yes, Frankie seems to be coping, and confused and angry. Death of a parent, especially an estranged one, will do that. Finding out if Mortimer took his own life won't solve personal issues, but maybe it'll give Frankie some closure. Did you know Vivian, Frankie's mother?"

"Met her a few times at some Mardi Gras affair or debutant ball. Yes, Morty was well connected and accepted with society here in town. His lady was the polar opposite of Morty. Odd couple. Then there was an incident. It caused a breakdown. She didn't recover."

"John, what accident?"

"Frankie didn't tell you? Don't see how it's germane to the issues at hand and while gossip can be enlightening, don't know if this is. Seems, as I remember, Vivian was into some type of voodoo blessing crap, had a dozen or more candles blazing in the living room, curtain caught fire, Frankie nearly died. Apparently, she was punishing him for some infraction and locked the kid in a closet. Morty, as you've found out, wasn't the guy to cross, although he respected me, and after the accident, neither were the same. Frankie stopped talking for a few years, dropped out of school, went to Europe before the war and came home a drag queen. Morty? I never heard him laugh after Vivian's death at that institution in Shreveport. She was there for at least ten years, as I remember. Know he visited her a lot. Out of guilt, perhaps, but we never really do know about relationships, do we? Sad business."

"As for Morty, suppose it could have been some weird accident?"

"Well, there's that, but hardly unlikely. Just a shame about that poor kid. Here's the rest of what I remember, Beatrix, since you need the details. Think Frankie was about ten or so. Fire department got the blaze out before it engulfed the house, and they found the kid huddled in a corner of the linen closet. He'd breathed in a lot of smoke and could have died. Vivian survived by needing mental care. She was most likely under some street drug. If not for the firefighters, she'd have died."

"Oh, my goodness. Is there more to this, John? No need to sugar coat things with me."

"As I said, he wasn't the type to stand on a street corner to rustle up business for his girls. He'd threatened the pimps who owned the girls, and always seemed to know dirt on all of them. Then when the low-level pimps agreed to Morty's terms. He brought them on board to his business or let them franchise as long as Morty got a sizeable kickback. I thought he'd gotten out of that business by the end of the thirties. However, we both know the war could have changed things."

"One last question and I know it's getting late. Thank you for being so generous, as always, John. Do you think Mortimer would have taken his own life?"

There was a chuckle, but it could have been a cough. "I was shocked when I heard that. Not the Mortimer Ramsey I knew. I'd heard him threaten to off a handful of people who got in his way, maybe even throw his son under a bus, but his ego was as massive as he was."

"You think he had plans to become the crime king of California?"

"Wish I could answer that, Beatrix. Morty kept his true thoughts to himself and yeah, he blustered and bit and badgered, so anything could be correct. Let me know when you find the answers to this mystery, because it certainly is one. I can ask around about Morty if you like, see if there are any other rumors that are worth passing on. Give Frankie my best and let Thomas know if he ever wants to give up a career in science, he can be one of my drivers. Henry still talks about how your fiancé drove like a bat out of hell through the crowded streets of New Orleans when he believed you were in danger. And stole a taxi to do it."

Moments later, Beatrix sat in an alcove near the front room's expansive bay window. The afternoon sun warmed the spot, and she imagined having it filled with laughter and love. She decided right then that the window seat needed a plump cushion so it could become her favorite reading spot or for storybook time. For a brief second, she could see red-haired kids with almond-shaped eyes yelling and screaming and thriving in the Ling House. *How many? At least three and maybe four,* she fantasized and then returned to the puzzle she couldn't seem to get a grasp on.

With the clarity of writing a list, Beatrix reviewed what John said, thought about Mortimer's possible scheme, and wondered if Frankie had keys to the office that his father had recently established in town. She dug into her purse for the scrap of paper with the Hotel Santa Barbara's phone number and called it.

Luck was on her side. Frankie had returned moments before and was in the lobby when the clerk answered, quickly handing him the only telephone at the hotel. Beatrix got right to it.

Frankie knew of the office, but hadn't been there. "When do you want to see it?" he asked, his voice just above a whisper. "Is it important? I feel like Morty's following me. His ghost mind you. Like he's peering over my shoulder. Do you actually need me to go with you?"

Beatrix looked at her watch. It was only three and even November, it should stay light until six. "I'll meet you there at three-thirty. Just walk across State Street and turn right. El Paseo is about three blocks north of your hotel. You have keys?" She looked across Anapamu Street at the neat little cottages and the high school, watching students and teachers leave the campus for the day.

"Um, no. Do you know how to pick locks?" he asked.

"Yes, Frankie, but let's see what's there when we arrive." Not for the first time, she wondered why Frankie was unsettled to look too deeply into his father's business, even though the man was dead in the city's morgue.

CHAPTER 12

BEATRIX CHANGED INTO high-waisted brown linen slacks and a snug-fitting long-sleeved white shirt, and slipped on an aqua-colored cotton sweater that just touched her hips. She found Thomas in the downstairs "library." They laughingly called it that as there were floor-to-ceiling bookshelves lining one wall and their vast collection consisted of a single volume of Homer's "Odyssey" long ignored and shrouded with an inch of dust, two volumes of an encyclopedia, a cookbook from 1886, and a tattered "Shakespeare's Sonnets."

"Going out?" Thomas was covered with white plaster. "It might be smart, my lady, if you'd take your bodyguard with you," he offered, adding a final swipe of plaster. She told him about the phone call with John and how she was going to meet Frankie shortly. He crunched his forehead.

"Stop that. as those wrinkles will be permanently engraved in your face, or at least that is what my mother would tell me when I frowned. It's daytime, Frankie is a big guy, I'll be perfectly safe. This isn't New Orleans or London."

"As you Americans say, 'Famous last words'. Did you make sure that Frankie changed out of the stiletto high heels? If someone tries to attack you, he'd be useless in those things," Thomas dipped the trowel back into the plaster and smoothed the gooey white substance over the pock-marked wall. "Be careful, my darling," he added with a wave of the trowel, flinging paster over his shoes.

He's tried to make his voice light and carefree as he wrestled with the intent to follow her. *I'm being foolish, as always,* he told himself. *If I cannot trust Beatrix to be safe, how will I ever trust our children in the world they will have to inhabit?*

"Careful is my middle name," she replied and bent to tickle his chin.

"I thought it was Louisa? Wait, that was one my previous birds." He laughed, but Beatrix saw concern in his eyes. "Well, now Bob's your uncle. You've found me out."

"Cad. This bird will be back before you know it. I'd wanted to get a good start on removing that gawdy mustard-colored yellow paint off the banister today, but this is urgent. I need to solve it."

"Beatrix? Wait." Thomas wiped his hands on the front of his trousers and took her hand. "Is it terrible of me to worry?"

She stopped at once. His face was deadly serious.

"Remember when we made a promise that I would always tell you the truth? I expect the same in return, right? If I am worried, I'll tell you. If I'm afraid, I'll tell you. You do not have to follow me as you did earlier today."

"Bullocks. You saw me?"

She kissed his cheek. "You were not good at blending into crowds when we were in New Orleans and you're still not. I'll be back by dinner."

He smiled. "Be patient with me, please. I've never been in a relationship like this, where I truly cared for another human. I don't know what to do most of the time and that's exhilarating and terrifying."

"It's new territory for me, too. Buck up, Mister. I'll tell you all about how it feels to enter a life of crime by breaking, entering, and trespassing. I promise I'll be fine."

"What?" He pulled her back to him. "That is supposed to me make feel relieved?"

"Not at all. Thomas Ling, if you go through with what you've promised and do marry me, you're going to have to put up with whatever I'm dishing out."

He clutched at his heart, swayed a bit, and then pulled her close. "I always keep my promises."

CHAPTER 13

BEATRIX COULDN'T REMEMBER when she'd been to the El Paseo last, although it was a popular tourist destination before the war. The locals liked it, too, and strolled through the pedestrian street savoring the quaintness that typified the little city.

Now with the chaos of restoring the house, it hadn't been a field trip that was high on her priority list. She'd forgotten the picturesque shops, the tiny cafes, and the delicious art galleries tucked into the old market place. *I'm taking Thomas to lunch here tomorrow,* she vowed, as she spied Frankie pacing the sidewalk on State Street. He stopped as she approached, looking like he wanted to bolt.

"Is there a sign or anything?" she asked.

"How would I know? Do pimps hang such things?" he huffed and they walked through the arches, finding Morty's office just by chance. The office's entrance was behind a shop Beatrix remembered selling exotic seashells. Now it was transformed into one displaying kitschy knickknacks and a few antiques with nautical themes. Bright purple clusters of Bougainvillea draped low over the windows. At least that was the same.

If Beatrix hadn't stopped to marvel at an oil painting of Stearns Wharf in a shop window she knew she must have, they would have missed the tiny sign above the door: Ramsey Inc.

Frankie looked at the placard and shivered, stepping back into the courtyard.

What causes so much fear about entering his father's domain? What memories are haunting this man? Beatrix wondered if he'd been there before without his father, as his feet had slowed slightly when they got to the nook of an office. Or maybe he was mulling over unpleasant recollections. Either way, he wouldn't be much help.

She could see him forcing his face into an expressionless mask and the only "tell" that showed nerves was a tiny muscle twitching in his cheek. The big man backed away, standing behind Beatrix.

In a whisper, as if the thick adobe walls would give their visit away, he said, "Do you want to wait here, and I'll see if there's another door or window in the back? Morty would never have given me a key so we should just break in." Yet, he still didn't move. "You're small. I should shove you through a window and then you could come around and open the door," he offered.

"Whatever are you thinking? It's daytime, Frankie, and there are lots of people shopping, some looking at us right now, like the food server across the way at that restaurant. Do you want the police to dash over here so we'd be faced with a dozen awkward questions at the very least and possibly be arrested? You know, we could try the obvious," Beatrix twisted the doorknob and the door swung open. *That makes me even more uncomfortable,* she thought.

It was just one room, organized with a desk, cabinets, and two freshly reupholstered chairs in a nubby, masculine green fabric. There was a window behind the desk, closed, with the lock down. Papers were in neat stacks; the place hadn't been ransacked. *Who left the door unlocked and why?* she wondered.

There was a lingering stench of cigars, although the ashtray on the desk sparkled.

Frankie held back, not crossing the threshold, plunging hands deep in his pockets of his jeans. "What are we looking for?"

Beatrix thought of Thomas's worry about being a good father and compared her beloved to the dad that Frankie had.

Thomas has no need to fret about his qualifications to be a parent, she thought. *Now me, as a mom.* She turned away from Frankie as she was smiling, thinking of future children. Again. *Oh, those kids are going to have to be born with a sense of adventure.* Then she responded to her client's question. "I don't know what we are looking for, Frankie. I'll know when I find it. Did he have an accountant in New Orleans or here?"

Frankie inched closer but still didn't join her. His body filled the door, making the inside even dimmer.

Beatrix wondered, *What is it that is stopping him from coming inside? It's like a child afraid of the Big Bad Wolf or the Boogie Man. Was that Morty?* She waited, learning from her days as a fake psychic, and as someone who was excellent at reading people, that Frankie was about to divulge something. His shallow breathing told her so.

He exhaled and the twitch stopped. "Morty was greedy. I swear he had the first dime he exhorted from a kid he was in first grade with. Loved to tell that story. He was a control freak, kept his own records. Always bragged about that and how he paid taxes, like a solid citizen."

"That's actually good. Then he must have ledgers right here in the office unless he left them in Louisiana. Flip through the material on those shelves, Frankie. It's okay. Come in. Morty is dead. I saw him. He's not going to storm in here. He won't accuse you of anything. You are safe." But maybe the demons he was wrestling with were torturing him in places only he knew.

Finally, he walked inside, looking at the corners, possibly seeing Morty's apparition or fearing he would. Beatrix did not want to ask and said, "Pull out the books and see if there's anything hidden behind each stack. If you find something, let me see it. Take the lid off that heavy glass vase thing, whatever it is. Good place to hide something. Would he have installed a safe? Check behind those ghastly framed prints of dogs playing poker. I'll see what's in the desk." The top of the desk held a big black telephone, the ashtray, a notepad, a pencil. and that was it, except a calendar. Each day in the past had a checkmark and then a dollar sign with an amount next to it. Dare she take the calendar with her to figure out this puzzle? Why not? As she had told Frankie, Morty was gone. He wouldn't be needing it.

Beatrix sat in the oversized leather swivel chair. It squealed as she turned to open the middle drawer, which was thankfully not locked, and saw Frankie jump at the noise.

"Frankie? Did your father normally keep a gun?" Squarely on top of white typing paper was a shiny black revolver. Either brand new or well kept.

Frankie stopped rummaging through a wooden filing cabinet and turned. "Not that I know of, but nothing that man did would surprise me. Why? I know at least in New Orleans, he'd have hired someone to do the dirty work, or so I heard, and bragged about."

Beatrix reached in her purse for a handkerchief and gingerly lifted the pistol. It was cold and heavy, menacing even to touch. "Because he seemed to think he needed protection or decided to keep this handy."

"Oh. No." If possible, he looked more nervous. "What do we do? I hate guns. Turn it over to the police?"

"The police don't seem to think anything is suspicious about his death. They're going with a verdict of suicide. There's no reason they'd care that Mortimer had a gun if he had committed no crimes in the state. That's what we assume, anyhow, but we aren't aware of his real business dealing. There's no law that says a citizen can't own one. Shooting someone, well, that's a different story." She put it back, closed that drawer, and then gave her attention to the files inside the drawers on each side.

Files, lots of them, were neatly placed in folders in alphabetical order. The handwritten labeling each was done with care, all uppercase letters. There was letterhead paper marked Ramsey Incorporated with matching envelopes. Beatrix surmised that there would be a typewriter somewhere in the office if, in fact, Morty did any business.

She fingered the files. Surprisingly, each contained tasteful photos of appealing women. These were glamour shots in evening gowns, full make-up on the ladies, and even in black and white, Beatrix could tell the lipstick had to be fire engine red. There was nothing scandalous and it was almost as if he were running a talent agency as these looked like photos to send to the studios, or she imagined so. Beatrix flipped through the listing and stopped suddenly when her fingers came to the letter D. Right after a file marked "Dane, JoAnne" was one marked Mary Hernandez. Out of order, that perturbed Beatrix for a heartbeat, before she grabbed the file.

Mary Hernandez. "Oh, my. What have we here?" she whispered, spreading the folder's contents out on the desk.

CHAPTER 14

BEATRIX OPENED THE FILE and held up the photo, considering the consequences of what she'd just found. Beatrix withheld comments; this was not Frankie's business. The woman was exotic with dark flashing eyes, thick eye lashes, and luxurious black hair cascading over bare white shoulders. The tasteful evening dress sparkled in the photo. Not old, but far from a teenager, as many of the women seemed to be. The image was slightly blurred as if the photographer had smoothed out the woman's smile lines and crinkles around her eyes. *No, this couldn't be. But it has to be,* she argued with herself.

Beatrix picked up a sheet and read it to herself. "Mary grew up in Santa Barbara, just a hometown girl. She sings and dances, won awards for tango and salsa, and acted in little theaters in Washington DC and Louisiana. She recently returned to Santa Barbara after living in New Orleans and is glad to be back. She likes to make new friends, go dancing, and enjoy all the fun that California has to offer. She's fluent in Spanish." *Mary Hernandez,* Beatrix breathed in and out. *What are the odds? Could Major Davies's wife be a paid companion? Is this a genuine talent agency or a veiled front for an escort service?* Beatrix mentally catalogued everything she'd read, so there was no need to jot down Mary's home address and telephone number. She'd read the folder and then returned the material filed under the letter D.

Beatrix dug deeper and found more folders containing photos of handsome men, all movie-star material and wondered if Morty had branched out to gigolos as well, if that was his aim.

The rest of the desk seemed to be organized, and held no additional firearms or explosive or incriminating photos. She sat back and stretched, kicking a trash can with her toe.

She pulled the receptacle out. It held dozens of crumpled pieces of typing paper. She picked up the top three, smoothing them out with her hand. Morty seemed to be designing a marketing campaign. Written in the same neat script as the names on the file folders, the first said:

"Ramsey Inc. – Get Paid for Your Talents."

The second had the phrases switched.

The third one announced: Ramsey Inc. Sign with Me and Head to Hollywood and Stardom."

Beatrix read more, all variations, and none seemingly pleased Morty. Or maybe one had. Was he tricking people into signing up with a suppose talent agency only to pimp them?

She unexpectedly felt a pang of regret encircle her heart for the former Major Davies, the blustery ex-military officer who was now dazed and befuddled by the beginning of a terminal illness. What would he say to this? Could she tell him? No. Not yet. If there was one thing she learned as a fake psychic, it was that not everything that appeared to be true was really true. The whole story, as truths unravel, was most likely far more complicated than Davies's wife being an escort, or one of Mortimore Ramsey's call girls. The search produced more questions than answers and the fat dead man in the city morgue wouldn't give up the solutions.

She exhaled deeply and finally started ruffling through the files in the credenza behind her. Pulling out a drawer, Beatrix stopped. It was stacked with letterhead that read, "Ramsey Theatrical Agency." There were business cards listing Morty as president.

Beatrix stared at the open door organizing her thoughts. Frankie looked at her. "The place gives me the willies. I can't breathe in here. Aren't you done yet?"

"It's nearly five o'clock," she replied. She wasn't ready to tell Frankie about the possible escort service slash talent agency until she understood how or if the businesses worked together.

Visiting Mary was her top priority. Beatrix had memorized the address the moment she read it, yet that trip would have to wait until tomorrow, as it was in Montecito, at least a 10-mile drive to the south of the city. After the walk home and the drive to Mary's house, it would be dark. Learning the whole story of why Mary Hernandez Davies was working with a possible pimp needed to be discovered in daylight. *First thing in the morning,* she thought. She left the office unlocked, as they had found it, and bid Frankie good evening.

CHAPTER 15

BEATRIX DRIED THE LAST COFFEE CUP from breakfast and placed it in the cupboard to the side of the sink. Thomas was inside the pantry nailing down some wayward shelves. "Do you want to go to Montecito with me? I'm planning on dropping in on Major Davies' wife."

"Whom you believe is part of Mortimer Ramsey's prostitution ring?"

"Let's wait to see if any of that's true, Thomas. For all we know now, he could have been launching a legit talent agency as well."

"Sure. Wink. Wink. Right? From what you told me last evening, after you avoided being arrested for breaking and entering and discovered the pistol in a known criminal's office, I cannot see where there could be doubt why her file was found there. Will you tell Davies where his wife is living and what's she's been up to?"

Beatrix smoothed her hand over the cool marble countertop. It was original to the house, distressed, and she liked it. There were stories and secrets in this house, like the clippings in the attic, which was, along with other period details, worth saving. The moment she'd walked through the ramshackle mansion, it felt like an old friend. She patted the countertop as one might a faithful dog. She stood at the kitchen window, seeing Bunny Turney with two muscular men, directing them to trim a massive Eugenia bush at the rear of her property. By her erratic hand movements, Beatrix knew that the neighbor wasn't keen on their work and wondered if she should go out and help the gardeners. Then she saw Bunny turn away, turn back, yell again, and return to the house. The gardeners continue as if nothing had happened, and Beatrix wondered if this was her usual behavior for laborers.

What surprises would the ex-military man's spouse be willing to share? "Again, this may have nothing to do with what we think is obvious and she might not even be Davies' wife."

"You're right. Jumping to conclusions is one of my finer forms of exercise. Seriously, I'm torn, Beatrix. I thought it would be wise to stay here and keep working with our crew. This house might not tumble down around us anymore, although that front porch is a disaster. It's a massive project. On the other hand, I was originally hired to be your bodyguard and I fear I will always be. Just give me ten minutes to change and I'll accompany you. Showing up with splatters of paint all over me might scare the woman."

"It's okay. You look fine, and please realize if Mary Hernandez Davies is involved in prostitution, you showing up dressed in a swimsuit like shapely movie star Betty Grable wouldn't shock her."

He pulled up the cuff of his paint-splattered jeans. "Betty and I have the same gorgeous legs, don't you think?"

"Yours are much better looking in my book. Go and change and I'll grab a sweater. Then we're off to find out who lives at 103 Butterfly Lane in Montecito."

Beatrix maneuvered the Woody Station Wagon through mid-morning traffic and headed south on Highway 101. The coastline sparkled in the clear sunlight, the sapphire ocean reflected the morning sunlight like a million sequins on a ball gown and the breezes were playfully tugging at the palm trees.

"If I were in London, I'd need an overcoat right now and an umbrella," Thomas said as they stopped for the traffic signal change to green.

"Do you miss England? Did you ever think you'd be marrying a Californian and ending up in Santa Barbara, a world away?"

"Certainly not. There were years when I didn't think I would ever leave my lab. I was often alone in the lab. I'm embarrassed to admit that was my entire life, and a few mates I'd meet at the local pub for quiz nights."

"I bet you guys won all the time,"

Thomas rolled down the window, lifted his arm out, and felt the softness of the air. "The breeze is as soft as cream." He was certain that there was no other place he'd rather live. "I long to see my family, Beatrix, you know that. They are loud and funny and I swear, Dad is always rolling his eyes at the things Mum gets into. Did I ever tell you my mother is an abysmal cook and yet, she keeps trying new recipes and nearly burns down the house once a year, or so it seemed. At least Mum is always volunteering to help fundraisers for the local fire brigade and taking them shortbreads and cakes, from the local bakery." He laughed quietly, privately relishing the memory. Then he patted her knee. "Once the house is finished, would you mind if we have Mum and Dad and maybe my sisters and their husbands and families come for an extended time? Summer is going to be lovely here and I can tell that already. Yet, I bet they would be thrilled to get away from dreary London in the winter."

"Since you clearly want to fill up those bedrooms however you can, I won't argue. You are a man of science, so you know doing that the old-fashion way of bringing babies into the world takes time. Seriously, do you think that your family would come? I hope we can convince them to be here for next winter."

"After we're with them for the wedding, they'll love you as much as I do. My sisters will not rest until they come to California. They're expecting movie stars on every street corner and mouths of fresh oranges, or at least that's what Mum wrote in her last letter, remember?"

The traffic signal changed, and Beatrix steered the bulky car down the highway, enjoying the drive, the ocean, and the pristine Channel Islands flickering in the distance. There was no rush to get to Mary Hernandez Davies's home, so she let traffic pass her and tried to devise how she'd approach Davies's wife on the topic of the evidence found in Morty Ramsey's office.

"The map said to take the next right and then a quick left on Butterfly Lane," she said. She checked the house number against what she remembered and pulled the car to the curb a few houses down the block from that address. The cottage, just three homes from the beach, was whitewashed and trimmed with black. It was tidy and smart. The lawn was recently cut and showed the diagonal lines of the mower. Pots of red Germaniums shouted a welcome from their containers on the porch and the scarlet perfectly matched the color of the front door. Looking from a distance, Beatrix could see the lacy curtains, pulled to each side. Everything seemed serene and homey. She started to slip the strap of her purse over her shoulder and stopped. "The door is open. Stay here, Thomas. I'm going to peer through the window. I have a bad feeling about this."

"Not a psychic one?"

"Just creepy. It's too quiet. Mary may have been carrying in groceries and couldn't shut the door. Or it could be something else."

He started to get out and to protest.

"Shh. You're better than me with a lot of things, but stealth isn't one of them." Beatrix didn't let the car door even click to close. She crouched slightly and made a mad dash from the sidewalk to a box hedge standing along the perimeter of the garden. Then, still seeing no movement inside, she crouched down to hide behind a massive periwinkle-colored Hydrangea and finally to the window where Mary Hernandez Davies supposedly lived.

Thomas clenched his fists, craning his neck to keep an eye on his future wife as she snuck closer. He saw her peering into a side window and then scramble around and into the house, screaming his name as she rushed inside.

When he reached the door, Thomas wanted to run. Quickly. Away. Yet his body would not move.

A woman was crumpled on the carpet and Beatrix touched her neck, trying to locate a pulse, just as he had seen in the movies. "It's faint, but there. See if you can find a phone in the house and if not, please, Thomas, drive as fast as you can back to that filling station on the corner near the highway. I saw a phone booth there. Call for a doctor, an ambulance, and the police. Take the car. I left the keys in the ignition."

He sprinted to the kitchen, to the bedrooms, and then returned. "I don't see a telephone anywhere. I'll be back as soon as I make the calls for help." He darted down the front steps, to the awkward Station Wagon, and with tires squealing, he rocketed toward the gas station to call for help.

Beatrix cradled the woman's head and her blue eyes flicked open. The bruising on her arms showing fat fingerprints pressed into her flesh were already turning purple and blood dotted her nostrils. Beatrix slipped out of her sweater, and held it fast to the woman's head in a futile attempt to stop the bleeding.

"You're safe now. I'm here and a doctor is coming. Please don't move. My name is Beatrix Patterson. You are safe. I won't leave you alone. Just try to stay calm and know that help is on the way."

The woman's eyes flickered and closed, but she did not look as if she was in pain. Shock, definitely. Beatrix gingerly rubbed her hands up and down the woman's bruised arms.

Beatrix spoke softly, "I don't know if you can hear me. Can you tell me your name?"

Sounds came from the woman's mouth and her eyes fluttered, but Beatrix could not make sense of the words. "Did Mary do this to you? Do you know Mary Davies?" It didn't take clairvoyance to see that the blue-eyed woman was not the ex-officer's wayward wife, especially since she'd seen the photo in Morty's office.

The woman gasped and once more Beatrix noticed a tiny cross at her neck. Both the chain and cross looked like gold.

Beatrix felt seconds turn into hours, waiting, listening, for the sound of sirens and medical help.

Just then the woman's eyes opened, wide and terrified. "Told me this was just a warning," came the rasping whisper, "Said there wouldn't be a next time. And pushed me."

Beatrix looked toward the coffee table, lying on its side just feet away. That would explain the head wound, but not the purple bruise marks on her arms. Whoever did this had shoved her. Hard. To make a point. The woman's head probably collided with the sharp corners of the table. "Tell me who did this to you."

Her eyelids slid closed as she breathed the words: "The pimp."

CHAPTER 16

THOMAS SQUARED HIS JAW and knelt next to Beatrix, as she continued to rock the slender body of the bloodied woman. "Is she...?" He swallowed hard and it hurt his throat as the truth was evident.

With a fist, Beatrix shoved tears off her cheeks and shook her head. "I'm so sorry, so sorry. I could not help her." She sat stunned as tears dripped down her face.

Thomas pulled a handkerchief from his pocket and dabbed at his beloved's tears, yet they continued to spill onto the frilly pale pink flowered dress of the dead woman.

First, in the distance, and then blaring down the lane came the police sirens. Yet, for Thomas and Beatrix, the world was still. The only thought was the woman lying in Beatrix's arms.

Seconds later, three uniformed officers elbowed into the cottage's tiny living room, each scanning the room, taking in the couple sitting on the floor and horrified at the sight. Thomas moved against the wall. Quickly, in the cops' footsteps, trotted a stout woman in a baggy gray cloth coat. Her hair was cropped, straight as her posture, and her lips a thin mark on her face.

The officers stepped aside.

"Who are you?" demanded the woman. There was no doubt that she was in charge.

"Beatrix Patterson, and this is my fiancé, Dr. Thomas Ling, who called you. And you are?" She still held the limp body, but straightened her spine. She would not be intimidated. Ever.

"Detective Stella Rodriguez. You know the lady?" She produced her badge and ID card, waiting for the couple to nod or acknowledge it. Then she stooped down and seemed to take in all of the details of the woman's still body. "Is she a friend of yours? Why are you here? Did you see who did this?"

Beatrix looked at the now-peaceful face. So young, under twenty, and completely void of any lifeforce. She nudged a lock of bleached blond hair from her cheek, slowly and gently, as if caressing a terrified child. "No. We came here at the request of a friend who is trying to locate his wife. This was an address I found and assumed the wife lived here." She didn't say that she broke into someone's office and stumbled on the address. It was not necessary to give out facts that weren't needed.

Beatrix wiped her nose and said, "However, this is not the woman we are looking for. I'm searching for Mary Davies. Do you know her?"

"No clue, don't know anybody named Davies. As for this girl, I haven't seen her in the drunk tank or on any lineups at the station. You can't identify her?" She looked from one place to another in the compact home, then to the white-painted coffee table with a spatter of blood clinging to a corner, and finally stood up. "'Gents, sniff around here. See if there are any bills or paperwork to say who lives here while I talk with these witnesses. We need to figure out a name for the deceased or there'll be another Jane Doe at the morgue. The coroner is getting tired of me bringing in unidentified bodies." She grimaced and while she looked gruff, Beatrix could tell that this officer cared.

The men branched out in opposite directions, three steps to the kitchen and two to the bedroom. Beatrix remained on the floor, holding the dead woman, knowing that her final words could possibly lead the police to the killer. Yet, withholding them for the moment was Beatrix's only plan, although it was not yet fully formed. Perhaps it was wrong, yet it was a matter of habit from her time in New Orleans. Beatrix silently promised the woman she'd find out who did this to her and not let it happen to anyone else.

The detective flopped into a small wingback chair covered in a pink and green cabbage flower slipcover and the chair quivered under her weight. Thomas was motionless. He'd seen the dead during the shelling of London, but never had he seen his future wife holding a body. The scene kicked him in the gut and for the hundredth time, he doubted if he was strong enough for such a formidable and remarkable woman.

"It's daytime. The neighborhood is quiet, houses close together. Potential witnesses everywhere. This was not a premeditated act," Beatrix said, more to herself than the detective, yet the other woman nodded.

Detective Rodriguez patted Beatrix's shoulder. "Time to let her go, honey. They'll take it from here. You've done plenty."

Beatrix got off the floor as the coroner, a medic, and a doctor arrived. It was routine now, at least for them. They'd take photos and measurements, noting the blood on the coffee table's corner. They would be in charge of the woman as she left for the morgue. Beatrix wasn't able to help her, but perhaps she made her final moments easier.

"Sounds like you either write detective novels and mystery fiction or you are law enforcement," said the detective. "Not many gals in police work, but when I came home from France after the war, they hired me on since I'd trained as military police there. For now, it's just me and one other woman on the force here, and don't know if she counts as she's undercover."

"Neither one of those professions, and I'm encouraged to see the SBPD hiring women. It's about time." Beatrix looked even more closely at the head wound before the medic covered the woman with a sheet and with help, lifted her onto a gurney to wheel her out to the coroner's van.

Beatrix scanned the room quickly, memorizing every detail. A desert wind, a Santa Ana, was blowing toward the coast. Surfers said it was "offshore, " and knew the waves would behave in a certain manner.

Both the detective and Beatrix were acting in ways that had previously encouraged others to talk. The pause might cause someone to offer information that was unexpected because of awkward silence.

Beatrix knew the strategy of silently waiting, and if the Olympics gave a gold medal, she'd have been in the running, so practiced she was at the same waiting tactic when in New Orleans and pretending she was a psychic.

"You notice a lot, Miss Patterson. How come?" the detective asked.

"In the past. It's been a while. Back then in New Orleans, I helped the police and federal investigators solve some mysteries." She moved close to Thomas and linked her arm in his. They both thought how they met, on their first adventure in crime solving, and how that "adventure" could have easily killed one or both of them.

She bent close, her breath in Thomas's ear as she whispered. "Please talk with any neighbors, and Thomas, the dead woman had those connected circles on her breast, which were visible through the sheer fabric of her dress. She was one of them, whomever 'they' are."

To Thomas's credit, he stared at his shoes, knowing that whatever Beatrix whispered, a shocked glance would give it away and the detective would notice, perhaps even follow him. "I require some fresh air," he said, and he did. But there was another reason why he left the cottage- Beatrix's request to talk with anyone who might have seen the event, or anything out of the ordinary at the cottage. He stopped where the road began, then walked directly across the little lane. Another pint-sized Cape Cod cottage stood silently. Not a mirror image, but tidy. Here stood a couple in their fifties, too concerned to ask the police any questions. By their physical bearing, they were already too aware of what had happened, or at least that's what Thomas guessed.

The man acknowledged Thomas's presence with a nod, but didn't take his eyes off the front door. Then he cleared his throat and pointed toward the police cars and the coroner's black van. "This is terrible, right across Butterfly Lane. Is someone hurt?" the man inquired, but he knew already. The answer came with the truth as the three watched the medics glide the covered body to the van, then heard the screeching of metal on metal, as the back door slammed shut.

The woman a few feet away from Thomas pulled a tattered green cardigan tighter across her slender frame, and shook her head. She shivered.

"Did you know the lady of the house?" Thomas asked.

"Seen a few women coming and going," said the woman, now twisting her hands in her apron.

"The lady who died was blond." He looked toward the cottage, police now scouring the gardens, poking under flowerpots and examining the Hydrangeas. "Had you seen her before? Does she live there?"

The man shoved his hands more deeply into his pockets. To hide blood? Thomas didn't know but he wasn't going to move from that spot until he found out, which for a scientist and a timid one at that, took all of his courage.

"I've seen a blond lady come and go, she waved and wished us 'good morning,' just like neighbors should," replied the man, gruff, but with a shaky voice. "I finished weeding these front flower beds yesterday or I would have been out here. Maybe I could have done something, stopped something."

"Oh, Haru," the woman put her arms around his shoulders. "You couldn't have known anything bad was going to happen." She turned slightly to Thomas. "I'm Yuri Nishimoto and my husband, here, is Haru."

Haru scowled. "Been working in my vegetable garden all morning, in the back of the house. Since after breakfast. Just came out front here when we heard the police sirens and cars arrive. Things like this don't happen in this little town, at least not since we moved back here after they let us out of that damn internment camp. Near the end of the war, the government decided in its great and holy wisdom that a gardener from Santa

Barbara wasn't going to do anything treasonous, so they let me and Yuri out early." It came out with a huff.

"Terrible times. My condolences for all that you lost," Thomas said.

"Yeah, lost my job, lost our house, and some friends died when we were in the camp," Haru added.

"Now Haru, we're going to start again," she consoled her husband. Turning to Thomas, she said, "I hope to get hired to cook for a family up on the hill and Haru is an amazing gardener. He can shove a stick in the ground, and it'll turn into a tree."

Thomas knew their stories were shared by thousands who had been incarcerated by the US government for simply being of Japanese descent. Eventually, Haru withdrew his hands and Thomas saw sprinkles of top soil clinging to his nails as the man rubbed them vigorously on the front of his trousers, adding to the layer of dirt that clumped on his knees.

Yuri patted her husband's arm. "We like to sit on the porch in the afternoons, sip tea or lemonade. Like we did. Before."

Thomas understood that "before" meant being rounded up against their will and transported to the prison-like internment camp.

She continued, "Besides, as my husband said, lots of ladies come and go. It must be some sort of club, we figured, although we were never invited. Must be because..." She looked at Thomas and then down to the end of the sidewalk and the Pacific beyond. "But the blond woman, she was different. She even brought us a bouquet of those Hydrangeas. I took her some tea cakes."

There was no need to complete the sentence. Thomas understood. Asians would remain second-class citizens for the foreseeable future. "Did you ever meet anyone else from the house? Did you go inside?"

"No," Haru said. "She seemed pleasant enough. However, last time, when she brought the flowers, she kept looking down the street as we talked. We talked for a few moments, but she was distracted."

Haru interrupted, "Or waiting for someone or maybe even afraid."

"What about other visitors, children, or men?" Thomas wondered if Beatrix was being interviewed about why she was there as she still hadn't left the cottage.

"Once in a while, they had a gentleman visitor, older man, large and always laughing. He'd tip his hat, wish us a good day, that kind of stuff. Probably an uncle or maybe a grandfather?" Haru began to stand a bit more solid as if the initial shock was losing its grip. He scrubbed his hands together again, attempting to remove more soil.

"Come on, honey, let's give the police time to do their work." The wife touched Haru's arm, turning him away, as if they'd seen more than their share of terror before, during, and after the war.

Haru stopped and looked again at Thomas. "Good to see that the police force is hiring more folks like us. If we remember anything, how do we get in touch with you?"

Thomas knew it was perhaps misleading to let them believe this, but would they have talked so freely if he were just a curious stranger? At one point in his life, he would have been horrified that he was impersonating a police officer, but much had changed inside him since he met Beatrix and if he could help her help others, then nothing would stop him. He withdrew a tiny tablet from the inside pocket of his jacket along with a pencil. "Here's my direct telephone number." He attempted to stand taller than his five-foot-six inches and assumed the no-nonsense air of an officer of the law, trying to imagine what Beatrix would do. He nodded with what he hoped was military precision and walked off, anxious to relay this bit of information to his future wife.

There was no opportunity to nose around the cottage, with police swarming at the scene. Picking up her clutch purse, placed purposely and conveniently on a few pieces of mail, Beatrix tucked it all beneath her arm and once outside, put it into her purse. She turned at the porch and said, "You have our contact information, Detective Rodriguez, and our statements. I don't know if it's confidential, but when the identity of the woman is determined, could you telephone me? I held her while she was dying, and I just want to know her name. Perhaps when you find her family and if they have any questions, I could talk with them?" Beatrix was clouded with remorse. If she'd only driven faster before heading to Butterfly Lane, rather than leisurely savoring the coastline, perhaps they could have thwarted the assailant. Perhaps the woman would be alive. "Damn it to hell," she whispered, trying not to focus on what "perhaps" would have meant in the young woman's life.

"Yeah, sure, I can do that, Miss Patterson. You guys can scram. I think you've probably had enough excitement for today," replied the detective, now in an almost-motherly tone, shooing them out of the house with a plump hand. Her eyes, however, were clearly suspicious about the strange couple and what they were doing in a house where there'd just been an accident or murder.

Thomas took Beatrix by the elbow. "Want me to drive home? You look knackered."

Beatrix hesitated, and nearly agreed, but as the detective said, there had been plenty of excitement so far that day, and Thomas's driving was more like a circus thrill ride than a means of transportation. As brilliant as he was, he didn't always realize he was not in Britain, where he only rarely drove a car. Hence, far too often, he veered to the left side of the road. When that happened, she screamed like a five-year-old, and that only caused Thomas to lose more control.

"No, I'll drive. I need to file away, in my mind, all the details of what just happened, and driving will help."

There was more on her mind than Thomas's inadvertent yet reckless driving and the death of the unfortunate woman. They drove along the coast highway and returned to the house. Throughout the day, both Thomas and Beatrix held each other, unable to shake the sadness of the young woman's death.

After a simple dinner of grilled fish, fresh from the market at Stearns Wharf, and vegetables from the local farm north of town, they sat in the back garden. It was a cool, crisp evening, and they held coffee cups close for warmth, still focusing on the possible murder.

"Would you be my wingman tomorrow, Thomas?"

"Wingman?"

"It's American English for someone you need to look out for you, to stay close to you. After today, I need you even more as my wingman."

CHAPTER 17

FINISHING THE BREAKFAST CLEAN-UP for their hungry construction workers, Thomas asked, "You said last evening I was going to get to be your wingman? Where are we going? Istanbul? Paris? Rio? Please tell me it's glamorous and exciting."

She smiled. "I wish. How I long to visit Paris again. Might we take a few days after the wedding to go there? I know the city is in shambles, but to visit the Eiffel Tower or walk the same paths as Josephine Bonaparte on the grounds of the Malmaison would bring joy to my heart."

"Then it shall be so," he bowed from the waist. "By the way, I saw you tuck mail in your purse yesterday from that poor woman's cottage. Was there anything personal?"

"I'd hoped, but it was addressed to 'occupant.' Just pieces of advertising."

"Do you think we could return there, sneak into the house, and do our own investigation?"

She smiled and pulled him close. "Now that's the man I fell in love with."

"We'll take a drive along the coast and just see if there's any police presence there, shall we?"

"We shall, Thomas, and then go onto our next 'adventure,'" she replied. "Before word spreads of the crime on Butterfly Lane and throughout the entire county, I want to talk with some locals. Let's visit the little village of Montecito and look around. I haven't been here in years. If there's a diner or café, maybe their staff will know something. You're a city boy, but these small towns always have a few nosy parkers, folks who find pleasure in knowing everyone's business."

"Isn't that a long shot?" Once he got into the passenger seat, secretly relieved that he wouldn't have to concentrate on the absurdness of driving on the right side of the road.

"Thomas Ling, life is a long shot. If we don't ask questions, we'll never find the answers, and that, my dearest, is true even if we don't know the questions yet to ask." She turned the key and the Woody's engine purred.

They drove toward the sleepy little town of Montecito, which most likely would become popular as it was blessed with the lush rolling hills and the steep mountains beyond. The Pacific glittered with gentle waves. The views of the islands and the crystal blue of the sea at its doorstep looked like Hollywood had created them for a movie set and slowly Hollywood's elite would become residents there, she was sure. She hadn't asked Henry where Mr. Brockman's new villa was located in the town, but she hoped it had an ocean view, especially on a crystal day like this one.

Beatrix slowed the car as they entered the village and turned right onto Butterfly Lane. She stopped the Woody where they'd parked the previous day. "Good, no police cars," she said getting out of the station wagon.

"But that doesn't mean the neighbors aren't watching with their fingers ready to dial the police," Thomas replied.

"How about if we start with the kind older couple you met yesterday? Will they talk to me, even though I'm not Asian?"

"If you're with me, I'm sure they'll be gracious," he smiled. "I liked them, Bea. You will too."

The lady of the house opened the door even before Beatrix could knock.

"Oh, the police are here again," Yuri called out. "You are such a nice young man, and you brought a police woman as well. Come in, please."

"We can't stay," Beatrix began. "Just wanted to make sure that you and your husband were safe."

"Oh, we've seen worse, my dear. I don't know where Haru has gotten to. He putters into the garden and as he's getting deafer by the day, I need to physically drag him to me when I want his attention."

"We won't keep you," Thomas said. "Has there been any unusual activity other than the police at the house across the street? Anything we should know about?"

The tiny lady smoothed her hands on a dish towel. "I thought I saw someone in the bushes last evening. Decided it was my imagination after what happened yesterday. I would have called you folks if I'd been worried."

"Thank you and so glad you're safe," Thomas said.

"Trying to do the American duty," she patted his arm.

"Ma'am, my colleague mentioned that you both were looking for work. I have a good friend who just purchased a home here in Montecito. Would it be impolite of me to mention that you and Haru are seeking employment? Thomas mentioned that you're a chef and Haru is a gardener?" Beatrix thought of John Brockman's need to staff his new home and would reach out to him, with the couple's permission.

"That would be a kindness," Yuri said, and wrote down their telephone number on a slip of paper. "Thank you. It has been difficult to get work now, especially with all the service members returning home, needing jobs."

After Thomas and Beatrix said goodbye and walked across toward the house where they'd discovered the battered woman, Beatrix said, "What is it about you and older women, Thomas? She couldn't keep her eyes off you. She's smitten, just like Bunny. Dazzled by your charms."

"You're far too kind. It's my 'superpower,' just like Superman has in the comic strips."

The door was locked. The police seemed to have finished here. They walked around the house and tried the windows.

"Darn, all secure," Thomas said, about to head back down the driveway and to the car.

"Wait just a moment, Thomas. Just a hunch. Lots of people hide keys outside. Let's look around." Beatrix slid her hand above the door frame. Nothing. She looked under the welcome mat and pots of scarlet geraniums. Zip. She pulled back a clump of ivy that was crawling up under the window. Nothing except a few dead leaves and a fat spider.

Thomas walked toward a small patch of yellow and purple Chrysanthemums. A garden gnome grinned at him. He said, "Hello there, my little friend," and Beatrix expected to see a neighbor when she turned around, but her fiancée was talking to a plaster statue.

Thomas turned to her and cocked his head. "Are you aware, Miss Patterson, that garden or lawn gnomes as we know them today appeared in Germany in the mid to late 1800s and were always made of clay? Gnomes first appeared in the gardens of England in the 1840s and from there their popularity began to take off."

"No, I was not, and are you feeling well? I hope you won't be disappointed that he doesn't respond to your greeting."

"Additionally," he reached down and turned the gnome over, exposing a key. "Gnomes are known as symbols of good luck. Originally, gnomes were thought to provide protection, especially for buried treasure and minerals in the ground. In many parts of Europe, they're used today to watch over crops and livestock, often tucked into the rafters of a barn or placed in the garden. This little fellow was guarding the house, but unfortunately, couldn't save that young woman."

"Oh, Thomas, I love how you have all this pertinent information available at any time," she said, and she unlocked the front door.

The house still felt like death, but they put that aside as much as possible, searching the cupboards, under the bed, in the trash. The closets were bare of clothing, "Probably because the police took it." There weren't even dust bunnies under the bed.

"Do you suppose anyone actually lived here, Beatrix?"

"That's been bothering me since we walked in. It doesn't smell lived in, yet that woman was here and so was her assailant."

She walked into the tiny kitchen and opened the drawers and cupboards. No cups or glasses, no food, nothing to tie anyone to the home.

"This just gets weirder." She walked back into the bedroom and then to the front door. "I need to find out who actually owns the house."

"Would the detective we met yesterday tell you?"

She shook her head. "If I had an excuse to know, yes, maybe. But right now, our best bet is to go into town and ask some questions. Small towns and small-town gossip are a mainstay of any little community."

They locked the door, and replaced the key beneath the guardian gnome. "We must get gnomes for our garden," Thomas said opening the driver's side door of the car for his fiancée.

There wasn't much to the little town of Montecito. It consisted of a gasoline station, a tiny market with rows of vegetables and fruits in boxes that were lined up along the sidewalk, a barber shop, and a café. There was a small church, a school, and what seemed to be a library finishing out the two long blocks.

Beatrix parked the Woody and turned to Thomas. "I think you need a haircut."

"Truthfully? Am I that gormless that I didn't notice?" He skimmed his fingers through the jet black, coarse hair that always stuck out in the oddest directions. He kept it short, yet it grew in thick. "Am I looking like an unkempt dog in need of a good grooming?"

For a split second, Beatrix could see their children. She'd always found her reddish brown hair boring, but there certainly was never anything boring about Thomas's. "Then, just get a trim. Actually, my love, your hair is fine. It's just a way to have you chat it up a bit with the barber. Aren't they always privy to the town's gossip?"

"They are? Not in Britain. At least, my regular barber never says more than the price to be paid when he's done. Apparently, that amount changes depending on the number of customers waiting."

"News of the woman's death will have spread like a wildfire in Santa Ana winds, but because it just happened yesterday, it may not have reached the town yet, unless more neighbors were actually looking out their windows. That's a strong option as I'm sure everyone in this tiny community probably heard the sirens when the police arrived. Tell the barber you are curious about the commotion. Be vague. See if they know anything about the neighborhood there or the residents on Butterfly Lane. With your accent, they'll talk with you rather more freely, because you are exotic, than if I marched into the guy's only domain. They'd shoo me right out the door."

"Am I blushing? You think I'm exotic? Perhaps even a bit glamorous? Oh, Bea, I thought you loved me for my intellect, and now I'm to learn that I'm merely a plaything for you? Oh, be still my heart," he patted his chest and winked, knowing full well his questionably debonair looks were just a small measure of their mutual attraction. "Since we don't need gas in the car and we're well stocked with produce, I assume you are going to the diner?"

"Spot on." She lifted the cuff of her jacket and checked the time. "I'll order a coffee and try to talk with the server or any customers. When you finish with that haircut come over and we'll have pie as it's a bit too early for lunch."

Beatrix made it sound simple, but Thomas wasn't as good at coaxing information from people as his fiancée. They both knew that. He'd prefer the direct approach, always the scientist that he was. Just ask a question and wait for the answer. It was a logical motto. He blamed it on being British, as he always felt he stood far apart when compared to Americans, as if they expected him to own a castle, sprinkle all conversations with quotes from Shakespeare, or be on chummy terms with the Queen. Or something just as preposterous. He felt he let Americans down when he told them he was a scientist, lead a quiet life outside London and, truth be told, hadn't had any adventures at all until he met Beatrix, although he never told anyone that. When he barged into Beatrix's office four years ago, he had no idea that his entire prior, orderly existence would flip forever. Life certainly was never dull with Beatrix in it.

The bell over the door clunked as Thomas walked into the shop, seeing one customer, just one swivel chair, just one barber. "Couple minutes, mister, you're next," the barber said, squinting to see if he recognized Thomas, slightly suspicious of a stranger in town, especially an Asian. Then looked down at the head in front of him when he was caught examining Thomas's face.

"Thank you. I have plenty of time today." Thomas sat in the row of three leather chairs, nodded, and tried to look calm although inside he felt like a herd of buffalos was stampeding in his stomach. Casually picked up the newspaper, he fiddled with the pages as he tried to conjure up a way to start a conversation and ask probing questions of the locals. He knew they were staring at him. At length, he folded the paper in half and realized the customer, a man about Thomas's age with lush, wavy hair and the bald barber were not moving, waiting for him to do or say something. "Um, I'm visiting. My host thinks a trim would be a good idea." He smiled and the barber nodded.

"You're not from around here, right?" the barber asked.

There had been a large Asian population in the county prior to the horrors of the internment camps and now a few, like Haru and Yuri, were resettling back into the area. Whether these locals could tell that Thomas was Chinese and not Japanese didn't seem to matter. Suspicion still ran high. War was an experience that continued to be grappled with. Too many had lost loved ones and now the maimed were coming home and were attempting to live a normal-ish life. War had touched everyone, visited every kitchen table in the country, and for some, the memories were dark, long and complicated.

"Yes, I am from England." He pointed East. "That way."

"Always smart to look nice for the women," said the customer. "Seen you and that little lady with auburn hair get out of the Ford. She's mighty nice looking, if you don't mind me saying so."

Americans constantly bewildered Thomas. Should he be offended that his fiancée was being openly scrutinized by a stranger? Or should he be flattered? He was still dismayed as someone as shy and awkward as he could have such a glamorous woman interested in him, willing to marry him, wanting to have children with him. Any other day he would have pondered this, but with the life of a young woman recently snuffed out, it seemed inconsequential what the two thought of him or Beatrix. Besides, he decided to go with being somehow complimented and relieved to have discovered his opening. "We were out for a drive yesterday morning, admiring the coastline, and saw police cars when we were skidding into town. What a commotion. What was wrong? Has there been an accident?"

The barber finally looked up from cutting the wavy black hair of the patron in the chair. "They headed down that street two blocks west, Butterfly Lane. Saw them, three cars. Ain't been that much excitement in town in a spell." He returned to carefully trim around the patron's ears.

"I tried to talk with one of the officers," said the wavy-haired customer. "The cop told me to mind my own business and then whispered that somebody got bumped off, someone in those little row of beach cottages. They're all renters down that street. Foreigners and the like, I think."

"Yeah, renters," interjected the barber as if it was a swear word or that only renters would bring the police and criminals into Montecito.

"Bumped off, oh, you mean killed? That's shocking. Do you know who died? Or why?" Thomas said and tried to look dismayed, although Beatrix said he was a terrible liar. He was shocked at how quickly the incident's news traveled.

"My wife says, well, that there was a group of ladies coming and going from the house on that street."

Thomas straightened a stack of "Field and Stream" magazines. He liked to hike, but the idea of standing in a river for long periods of time with an objective to catch a fish only to toss it back baffled him. "It is a boarding house, do you suppose?"

Mr. Wavy Hair, as Thomas had internally started to call the customer, just smirked. "Don't know what you call 'em in the Old Country, my friend, but here the well-mannered translation is that some of us thought it was a bordello. Ladies of the Night. That's what I'm thinking, anyhow." And Mr. Wavy Hair snickered as the barber elbowed him and shared the tasteless reference.

"The ladies who live there are tarts?"

CHAPTER 18

THE BARBER AND HIS CUSTOMER bent with laughter as Thomas felt his forehead wrinkle. *Another reason that American English is unfathomable for anyone but Americans,* he wanted to say, yet he forced a small bit of laugh in order to go along with the rude men.

"They run their operations out of a cottage near the beach?" He leaned forward, trying to coax more details, and flashed on one of the movies he'd seen where the hero had used this technique. Yet, Thomas knew he was not suave enough to pull it off and was surprised when the barber blurted out, "Mister, you don't need no other action when you got a looker like your lady," said the barber.

The other two men laughed. Again, Thomas didn't know if he should be indignant or complimented. He sat back and waited.

"Oh, guess you're just being nosey. Right? Nothing really odd going on there, at least that's what my wife says."

"Good for the gossips, but the real action in is Oxnard and Ventura," wavy-hair nodded to the south. "The weird thing is that a few women do come and go to that house, carrying Bibles tucked under their arms." He turned to look at the barber, but that man's attention was focused on watching a black and white police cruiser drive at a snail's pace through the little town. "I've seen them get off the bus right here, at this stop," he nodded outside and all three looked at the empty bus stop bench on the sidewalk adjacent to the barber's front door. "Often a little gray-haired lady, about as big as a minute, comes alone, and struts to the house on Butterfly Lane."

"My goodness," Thomas filed that away. "Have either of you met any of these ladies? The ones from the house?"

"You are a curious guy, mister. I found out in the war, served in North Africa, that you British people like to learn stuff. Brits ask too many questions, I think. Wait? You aren't a reporter, are you? Because I don't want anything about what we just said about the ladies at that house to be in some damn newspaper. Don't want my name in any paper." As the customer huffed, the barber took a soft brush and whisked away dark curls. Mr. Wavy-hair ripped off the cape and bounded to his feet.

"Rest assured, your comments are safe with me. I'm just visiting the city. I am a scientist and simply interested in everything," Thomas said, taking his place in the barber's now empty chair. He turned to the man with clippers in his hand, swiftly becoming afraid he was going to look like a GI with a shaved head. "One moment. Just a little off the back, please."

Mr. Wavy Hair slapped a silver dollar on the counter. "See you next week. And mister," he looked at Thomas, "you take good care of that pretty little filly. Looks like a keeper to me."

Yes, Thomas filed that away, too, and wondered if he'd ever get used to America slang. He would never dare to call Beatrix a pony; it was absurd.

The barber seemed to have lost interest in talking, although Thomas tried with the weather, baseball, and the little he understood about it and the outrageous cost of gasoline at eighteen cents a gallon. He tried to sound American and added, "Why that's highway robbery," not understanding what highway robbery had to do with gasoline. He'd heard the expression last time he was at the filling station and never thought he'd get an opportunity to use it.

It was as if the murder unsettled the barber far more than he let on when the previous customer was in the chair. His shaking hands told the truth. Thomas tried again. "Did you happen to know anyone at that house, I mean as friends, not in their professional capacity?"

"Professional? I got to remember to tell that to the guys at the tavern." He snickered and Thomas's smile froze. He wanted to tell the man to put a sock in it.

Mr. Wavy Hair grinned, but not with joy. "Oh, I get it." He turned and left.

As the door slammed, the barber stared toward the street.

"Have you seen the people who come and go from the cottage??" Thomas asked.

A long moment passed. "Yeah, a couple of the ladies, I think, go to my wife's church in Santa Barbara. Older ladies visited, seen 'em here and there. They got off the bus right here on the corner and then headed down to Butterfly Lane, like I said. I don't think...I can't imagine they could've been hookers, too. I mean, geez Louise, they looked like somebody's mother or like my granny. You're done, and that'll be two bits."

"Ta." Thomas quickly placed two quarters on the counter, pleased that he remembered that the American quarter was "two bits" and the extra quarter was the tip. He stood, waiting to see if more details were forthcoming, as he'd seen Beatrix do.

However, the barber just slipped the money into the till and said, "Come again, next time you need a trim." As Thomas turned to leave, the man picked up the telephone, but he didn't speak. Clearly, he was waiting for Thomas to go so he could spread the news about the British visitor and his nosey questions.

Beatrix was twirling a spoon in an empty coffee cup and smiled when Thomas sat down across from her in the café's last booth in the back. "Coffee? Tea? I could use a refill."

"What are the odds of getting a cup that tastes better than the brown water I've been served in diners like this before? I need some strong builder's tea after my encounter with the barber and his rude customer."

Beatrix nodded. "I'll see what I can do. You could just become accustomed to drinking coffee. It is American." She walked up to the counter. It was mid-morning. The breakfast rush, if there was one, was over and lunchtime customers hadn't arrived. The server wiped the counters. "A cup of tea, please, for the gentleman, and will you please put two teabags in it? My fiancée is from London and thinks American tea is mediocre at best. He's asking for builder's tea, which I've come to realize is black as night and then doused with cream."

"Can do. You know, I was just thinking of what we were talking about before," the waitress poured hot water into a tall mug and plopped in two teabags. "Thought about what you asked, if I knew the ladies in that house. Once or twice a blond one came in for lunch. Seemed pleasant. Think she had an accent, but then that was back when we were at war and I'm embarrassed to say, anyone with any accent seemed to be German to me. Fear. All leftover fear from four years of fighting on the fronts and even here at home. My baby brother didn't make it back after D-Day."

"I'm so sorry. Are you sure she wasn't American?"

"Maybe. Heck, she could've been from up north maybe? Always looked nice and dressed up, too, like she was a bank teller or a clerk or maybe a teacher. Neat, and hair all tidy. Sometimes, she put a daisy stuck behind her ear, which I thought made her look glamorous, like a movie star or someone who wanted to be one."

"Did she ever come with other women or meet anyone? A man?"

"A couple of times with a few gals, like they were on their lunch break or something, which now that I think of it is odd as we don't have any business offices in this little town, except the doctor and I know his nurse. Teachers don't get away and I know most of them, too. Maybe they drove down from Santa Barbara? Yes, there was a man. Think it was last month, no, it was the end of summer. Tall and fat. Seemed friendly enough and she didn't seem bothered when he walked in to sit with her. I remember it, and it sounds rude now. But I was going to a party that night and I wanted to impress a certain marine. She had on a summer dress I would have died for. Oh, the lace collar made me swoon. I thought it odd that a pretty thing like her would have a date with this fat guy, so fat that when he said down, I didn't know if the chair was going to hold. That's it. Sorry. She was a friend of yours?"

"We were close." *Holding her while she died makes her my friend for life,* Beatrix fought back tears. "Thanks, that's helpful." She waited as the server topped Thomas's now inky-black teacup with more hot water.

"We don't get many strangers, tucked away as we are. Just locals. Wait, the man. I remember his hat. It was made of straw, like he lived in the south. I grew up on Biloxi and my gramps wore hats like that in the summertime."

"You didn't by chance hear them call each other by name?" It was a long shot.

She puffed up her cheeks. Shook her head. "Sorry, it's been months."

Now that was a fact which was helpful, and she returned to Thomas with two steaming mugs of tea, one black as midnight. Hearing what Beatrix had just learned, he said, "This is the second time we've heard about a man visiting the ladies." He sipped the tea. "You really must join me and Mrs. Turney for a cup one afternoon. She does make the most incredible blends with herbs I've never heard of."

"Thanks, but sitting with our neighbor sipping herbal teas and discussing migrating birds is your own cup of joy, Thomas. I'll leave you and the lady to spot a bottled-nosed twitter finch or whatever. Now, regarding the man in question, I only saw him dead, mind you, but the deceased Mortimer Ramsey fits her description. The waitress said he wore a Panama hat. I need to get into Ramsey's house or apartment."

"More breaking and entering on today's schedule?"

"Just finish your tea. I have an investigation to run."

CHAPTER 19

ARRIVING BACK AT THE HOUSE, Mrs. Turney waved from her herb garden and invited Thomas, oh yes, and Beatrix for tea, but they both politely declined. "Another time, Doctor? Later today? I've created a blend of herbs for tea that you'll just fall in love with."

"You are so kind, but I'm behind on my carpentry jobs right now, Mrs. Turney. Thank you. Perhaps later, as usual?"

Beatrix waved and dashed inside on Thomas's heels. "That herbal tea is probably a home-grown aphrodisiac so she can seduce you. It's never smart to underestimate a woman of a certain age and I can tell, Thomas, she wants you. Bad. I've known women like that, my darling, so my advice is to not put your guard down."

"Stop teasing. She's a bit odd, sad, I believe. I think she's charming and probably lonely for her husband, I'm sure. The stories of the old days in Santa Barbara around the 1920s are amazing. She seems to know everything about the city and everyone, as well."

"I bet she does know all the gossip in the neighborhood."

"I don't know about that as she mostly talks about her late husband, gardening, and the charities and organizations she's involved with. Complains a bit about the husky workers who help with the heavy garden, but in a genteel way," he said. "Reminds me a bit of my aunties, always baking little treats and drinking copious amounts of tea." He slipped his arms around

131

Beatrix's waist, and pulled her in for a kiss. "Now you go break and enter and I'll try to shore up the front porch if our workers will tell me how. We're going to enjoy it there, in our dotage, with white rocking chairs and a good book, watching the world go by."

Beatrix raised her eyebrows. She pictured the future, running after children, driving the kids to sports and clubs and swimming in the Pacific, enjoying careers in whatever capacity that may be, and traveling, not rocking as their muscles atrophied. Still, she smiled as she sat down in the chair next to the big black telephone and dialed Frankie Ramsey's hotel. It took a few moments to get the guest to the phone as the only telephone was in the lobby.

"Beatrix, thanks for catching up with me. I have been thinking of what to do about my father. The coroner insists that I make plans and they've given me forty-eight -hours to direct them, or they'll bury Morty in the county's potter's field, a charity graveyard at the mission."

"Would that be a bad thing, Frankie? You don't have a family plot or anything like that in New Orleans, do you?"

"Mom is buried behind the church in her hometown of Thibodaux, in Cajun country. It'd be wrong for him to join her there since he was such a crappy husband." Frankie's voice cracked as if he were crying, but why? "At least that was my observation on their relationship. Yet, she stayed with him, until her mental abilities took her away. He was the one who put her in that sanitarium. Life is a mystery and sometimes it stinks to be a grown-up."

Beatrix imagined over-sized Frankie Ramsey filled with emotion as he spoke the truth with the final comment in about the past. She'd felt the same, confused and alone. "I'm sure the coroner can supply you with a list of mortuaries and cemeteries. Might you consider having him cremated and scattered at sea?"

"No, never. He avoided mass, but still called himself a Catholic. They won't allow cremation."

"Then ask about the graveyard at the mission. Frankie, I called for another reason, but let's talk it over when we meet. This is hard for everyone, yet in your case, and with the tumultuous relationship, it's got to be tougher."

The phone line was quiet. "Thank you, Beatrix. I am lost right now."

"I need to go to wherever your father lived, need to see his house. I've got the address."

"I've seen it, on upper State Street, I've never been inside. It's weird, but I had to go there after I got here in Santa Barbara. It's just a twenty-minute walk from here. Will you meet me there?"

"I'll pick you up in front of the hotel, Frankie, in about ten minutes?"

State Street, as always, streamed with traffic, but luck was on her side and Beatrix parked the chunky Station Wagon in front of Hotel Santa Barbara. Before she could turn off the engine, Frankie got in. He asked, "Mind if I inquire why we're going to Morty's? Must we? I could barely tolerate his office. You were watching as I nearly dropped that fancy glass vase that Morty had on the shelf."

They inched along in the traffic. "I need to learn more about him, who he might have invited into his apartment, and even what books or magazines were lying around. You can wait outside if it's that uncomfortable. I want to look around. It'll help me figure out, just maybe, who your father really was and what he was doing in Santa Barbara." She didn't tell him that if there was a Panama hat among Morty's things, then he certainly had a questionable reason for being in Montecito. Those style hats were just not that popular in California.

They wove through traffic and arrived at the address. Beatrix made a few more suggestions about Morty's final resting place, but she knew that Frankie wasn't listening. His fingers drumming on the dashboard seemed to consume all of his thoughts. *He'll ask again when he's ready,* she thought as she parked the car in front of a neat, single-story stucco apartment complex with Spanish-style red tiled rooves, individual casitas that were perhaps part of a motel in earlier years. "Any chance you have a key?" She grabbed her messenger-style purse from the back seat of the car and slipped the strap across her chest.

"No." He opened the car door and unfolded his long legs.

"Okay, we'll see how public the place is. You might just need to break a window this time for us to get in, unless there's a manager on site and he believes that you're Morty's son."

There was, in fact, an apartment near the back marked with a sign that said manager. The small, wiry man didn't blink when Beatrix explained why they were there, and that Frankie was his son. He put out a hand and Beatrix placed a $5 bill on the palm, which was enough to buy a lavish dinner. He extracted a key from a nearby closet and handed it to Beatrix, only to turn away, apparently not caring to venture from the kitchen table and the bottle of beer that was his only companion.

Number seven was in front with a view of the street. Beatrix twisted the key in the lock and stepped aside. It seemed right that Frankie should go first. Instead, he flung the door wide, however he'd turned to stone, almost as if he expected his father to jump out from some hiding place and confront him. Beatrix walked around him. She pulled back the curtain and the light seemed to chase away Frankie's hesitation. He finally stood on the threshold, and latched on to the door frame for moral support.

Beatrix peeked around and underneath the furniture, inside a much-painted built-in cabinet, looking like an archeologist surveying a potential dig. The front room was tidy, shabby, but smelled fresh, as if the windows had been just recently shut. *Morty died weeks before, it should be stuffy with the smell of too many occupants,* she thought. *And stale cigar smoke.*

She didn't touch anything, but read the spines of the books stacked on a side table. There were three: *Cannery Row, Gone with the Wind,* and *Brideshead Revisited. Animal Farm* was on the floor next to an overstuffed chair. From what Beatrix had learned about Morty, these seemed to be an odd selection and not light reading. *Perhaps they were left by a previous tenant,* she thought. A recent copy of *Life* magazine was on the coffee table.

She glanced down at the newspaper, folded and stuffed into a corner of a somewhat worn wingback chair. She followed the olive-green patterned carpet into the small bedroom revealing a perfectly made bed with two pillows. She got on her knees and scanned under it. There was one large pair of slippers tucked to the side. She opened the small closet, finding business attire for a large man and yes, a woman. There were no Panama hats, but when she picked up a small box from a corner, there were two, one straw and another in black with a veil and feathers. Trendy for women.

She looked into the minuscule sparkling bathroom. A heap of towels was in a hamper. She touched the top one. It was damp. The sink was clean of any shaving stubble. She opened the medicine cabinet. There were two toothbrushes, a tube of Colgate, and a half-empty bottle of aspirin. A bottle of hot pink nail polish, Burma Shave shaving soap, a razor, and a comb. A hairbrush was balanced behind the faucets, with a few strains of blond hair. She glanced at the trash can and saw a crumpled tissue with hot pink lipstick.

She used her photographic memory to mentally record everything in Morty's apartment, categorizing and filing away information in her mind.

After leaving New Orleans, she'd thought that would be the end of her investigations. Yet, as she moved through the apartment, she wondered if life as a private detective who could depend on her education as a psychologist, might be in her future, although she couldn't imagine her future husband, the scientist that he was, agreeing to be her man Friday. And when they had children, could she put her life at potential risk and possibly harm any little ones?

Beatrix continued toward the kitchen. It was compact and orderly. As she stepped toward the stove, she stopped. She moved toward the two-burner hotplate and gingerly felt it. Warm. As was the tea kettle.

"Frankie, you can do this. Come to the kitchen. We need to talk," she called over her shoulder, knowing that he'd retreated from the tiny apartment to the front steps. She turned and watched him stub out a cigarette, exhale the smoke into the breeze, seemingly needing the smoke to muster courage and enter the flat.

Finally, Frankie made it inside, but now, before he visually inspected the dark corners of the apartment, Beatrix said, "Someone's been here. Been here in the last five minutes."

"Morty's killer?" his face paled and his eyes searched the little kitchen as if a killer might be hiding in the curtained area under the sink.

"A woman, if my instincts about following the clues are correct. She left traces of herself including not removing all her makeup before she went to bed as a bit of foundation remained on the pillow. The little wastepaper basket held only a tissue with a lipstick blot. Since the single cup in the sink is empty with a ring of lipstick on the edge, she wasn't scared off by our arrival. We've just missed her."

"I can't do it, Beatrix, I know one of us has to stay and wait for her to come back, but, but I'm just..." He had moved to the front door, as if being in the former home of his late father was too loathsome to linger even a second longer. His already pale face became the color of soured milk as he backed toward the front door.

"Uncomfortable? I get it. You go on, Frankie, if you don't mind walking back to the hotel. There are a few more things I want to look at, including re-checking the closets. I'll leave her a note, telling her we're trying to help find who killed Morty and ask her to contact me," Beatrix said as Frankie stood on the front steps.

"Wait. That's outrageous, Beatrix. If she had something to do with Morty's death, will she actually contact you?"

"Never misjudge someone who is trying to cover their malicious deeds." Then she explained that she'd relate any news to him later in the day, wanting to be alone in the apartment.

He nearly ran down the sidewalk, clearly wound up. *Scared? Of what. Morty's dead.*

Beatrix was stopped by that thought. *John Brockman said Morty was a tough person to like, but how did the man really treat his son? I only have Frankie's word. People lie all the time, to make themselves seem more important, to cover embarrassment, to win favor, or to conceal information.* Those options puzzled and troubled her. Plus, it was curious as to why Frankie hadn't yet claimed his father's body. He could well afford to have the remains shipped back to New Orleans or buy a burial plot in the city. Yet he did not.

She settled in the wingback chair and stared toward State Street. Pedestrians dotted the sidewalk, some waiting for the bus at the corner stop, some heading to only they knew where. She had started analyzing people as a child, seeing their expressions change when they were happy, sad, and lying. It was a game from her childhood, which she'd perfected over the years. It served her well, as now she could tell much from clothing, hand gestures, and micro-facial changes. Now she did it out of habit.

She closed her eyes, trying to form a picture of the occupant. *Who is the mystery woman living here? What did she know about Morty's disappearance? If they were cohabitating, as it certainly seemed, why hadn't she contacted the police or claimed his body? Unless, as Frankie thought, the tenant has something to do with the death, that only resembled suicide.*

From all Frankie had said about his father, the anger ran deep. If Morty had abused and ignored the boy, the feelings were quite understandable. While Beatrix's adoptive parents had died in a terrible car crash when she was just twelve, her life had been one filled with love and support. She couldn't imagine what the opposite felt like.

Then her eyes flicked wide. *What if he's psychologically unable to experience empathy? Or what other reason could contribute to his acting this way? Or...yes, or perhaps he killed Morty.* That thought stopped her and she knew as soon as she got back to the house on Anapamu Street, there were phone calls to make. Someone had to know the truth and she pondered if Frankie was not who he seemed. *We all have our own truth,* she thought, and had Frankie slanted his to ensure he was a victim rather than the abuser? She had quickly been swayed by his story becoming sympathetic to him and his relationship with Morty. *Frankie is an actor. Is he playing me? Is he really this grief-stricken?*

Beatrix rambled through the apartment once again, looking for clues into Morty and his housemate's personality. More important, why were they in Santa Barbara? Again, she searched the closet. As she'd expected there was men's clothing in XXL along with trim-fitting women's outfits, like one would wear as a teacher or secretary. The suits and dresses were the current style of proper, cover-the-knees-completely hem length and the colors were in grays and browns, as were fashionable that year. There were cotton blouses with good labels like from Saks Fifth Avenue and other shops she didn't recognize, so the woman may not have been a resident of the coastal city. On a hook on the back of the bathroom door hung a flashy, black silk kimono bathrobe with elaborate embroidery. It looked like something a soldier might have brought home when returning from war and for a special girl. This woman was classy in her business wear and the fabrics and designs were expensive. The heels of two pairs of shoes were in good shape and the bathing suit in the top drawer was for someone who was modest. This seemed in direct contrast to Morty Ramsey, wheeler and dealer big shot from in New Orleans. From his reputation, one would expect he'd be romantically involved with a glitzy showgirl or one of the girls in his organization or talent business, whichever it was.

She pulled out more of the drawers. Things were neat and folded, and obviously, a couple had been living there for a while. As her hand reached beneath a pile of jumbo-sized white boxer shorts, she felt a corner of paper. She dug down and discovered a faded black and white snapshot. Beatrix fingered it, turned it, and wondered what stories it would tell. She walked to the window for more light. It was of a slight blond boy, about five, and a scruffy dog, a small terrier most likely. The boy was smiling and appeared to be waving. She flipped the photo over. Yes. In neat upper-case script, it said, "Frankie. First day of school."

Why did the supposedly obnoxious Morty Ramsey keep a photo of his sweet little boy? This is totally out of character, unless, well, somehow Morty had changed. Could the woman who he's been living with be encouraging a reconciliation? John said that Morty could be problematic, but was he really that way with his own son? Beatrix again kept circling back on Frankie's words about his father's cruelty. She picked up the folded newspaper from next to the chair. It was dated the previous day. She blindly read the articles. There had been a house fire in Lompoc, and according to the report, the family's dog barked until everyone woke up and got out of the house. There was a county judge weighing in on widening the coast highway to two lanes on each side of the road. The hospital was adding beds to accompany the wounded soldiers and sailors returning, and there was to be a ward just for those with mental health issues. A "John" was arrested for solicitation on Main Street in Ventura. The weather report predicted a dry winte and water shortages as voters had decided against building a dam north of the city.

Beatrix smoothed the paper and folded it back as it was, placing it on the floor.

Once the woman who was living there returned, would she contact Beatrix? Did she even know that her gentleman friend or husband was lying stone cold in the city's morgue? Would it be up to Beatrix to break the news? Or would the woman simply skip town when she learned that her massive meal ticket was dead?

Beatrix stood in the middle of the room, turning slowly, and as usual, memorizing the details. While she'd hoped to meet the occupant, when she heard the back door in the kitchen open, she felt fear grab her stomach. She'd faced down killers before, but not in a tiny apartment, not when she wasn't ready. She folded herself quickly behind a wingback chair. If the tenant was a murderer, what would happen she found Beatrix snooping through her dresser? Beatrix held her breath and felt her heart pound in her ears.

CHAPTER 20

"BEATRIX?" came the masculine whisper. The light footsteps could only be made by Thomas, who because of his martial arts training, seemed to be able to control the weight of his body. "Are you here?"

She stood up, and sighed. "You are not whom I was expecting, Thomas, and I'm relieved it's you. I thought maybe Morty's housemate was returning or someone who did him in decided, like I did, to investigate the apartment."

They hugged briefly. "He has a woman living here or a partner of some kind?"

"A woman. Wait, you followed me?"

"Naturally. You never fired me as your bodyguard, from our time in New Orleans. Now that you're going to spend the rest of your life with me, I have an even greater vested interest in your safety."

"Then look around with me." She waved her hand. "I just have the feeling I'm missing something that would tell me about why Morty is here in Santa Barbara."

Thomas's forehead crinkled. "Other than wanting to establish sex trafficking and run a prostitution ring along California's Central Coast?"

Beatrix picked up the newspaper. "We only have street gossip to confirm that. I know John said that, but what if it's not true?"

She retreated to the bedroom and came back with the tiny black and white photo. "It's tattered and looks like a treasure."

"Morty kept this? I'm confused."

"There's a lot more to this mystery than we know, Thomas. I need answers to the questions I don't even know to ask."

"Who do you want to ask? Can't really stand on a sketchy street corner in Lompoc, Oxnard, or Ventura, and question every call girl we meet, can we? Could he have already taken over the sex traffic 'business' on the Central Coast?" He saw her raise her eyebrows. "Beatrix, that's not what you're thinking?"

"You once believed I could read minds, and now you've read mine." She pointed to a small news article about Ventura prostitution. The details briefly covered that information on a police operation to curtail prostitution.

"I don't like this," he said flopping down in a chair, rubbing his temples.

"Here's the plan," she replied. She explained to Thomas how they'd approach those who might have information about Morty. "Please give me the little tablet you keep in your pocket, and the pencil, too. I want to leave the woman who is living here a note, asking her to contact me to learn where Mortimer Ramsey is."

"You're not telling her he's dead?"

"Not in a note left here after I've broken into her house." That information would be better said in person if the woman contacted Beatrix. She finished the note and placed it in the middle of the kitchen table, placing the salt and pepper shakers on top of it.

Beatrix slipped her arm through Thomas' and closed the front door, making sure that it was locked. For now, she'd keep the extra key. She leaned in close, breathing in the scent of him. She would have stayed like that, expect she caught a quick movement, a dash, from the alley to the left. She dropped his arm and quickly rounded the corner. "No one. Nothing. Must have been a cat."

She felt the unease of being watched again. *Why?*

Late that afternoon, Beatrix drove to a downtrodden section of Ventura, near the train depot, close to the ocean, dotted with rusty tin cans and empty beer and wine bottles, all the debris tossed aside by humanity. Shacks with corrugated metal roofs lined the coast highway. Some looked like shops, and others were ramshackle homes. In a few spots, there were signs of construction sprouting up. She smelled the briny sea, with the distinctive fragrance of dried seaweed that always lined the beaches, and heard waves crashing on the shore. Fog now encased the Channel Islands, putting them away like precious jewels to be revealed the next day. In a few hours, it would blanket the entire shoreline, cool and damp as late fall always was.

She wasn't there to take in the sights. She was looking for someone special, someone she didn't know.

Beatrix sat behind the Station Wagon's steering wheel, keeping her eyes on the street. In the distance, perhaps two blocks south, a woman slowly walked near the street, got to the stop sign, turned, crossed the roadway, and walked back along the same route. Beatrix saw her do this four times. With each passing car, she bent toward the vehicle, waved, and looked as if she wanted to ask for directions. She made eye contact with the driver, and only did if there was a single male in the car.

Beatrix waited. Every once in a while, a car pulled to the curb. The woman went closer and talked with the driver, but it seemed there were no takers for the services or price tags for whatever services were being offered.

Now or never, she thought. Beatrix hustled down the street, trusty notebook and pen in hand. "Excuse me, miss?"

The woman looked Beatrix up and down. Shook her head. "Sorry, honey, I'm not into girls. Find someone else for your thrills," she replied and walked in the other direction.

"Wait, just a moment. Oh, no, I'm not looking for a hook-up. Can you wait and listen just for a moment and then if you don't want to talk, I'll leave you alone. Promise. I'm harmless."

"Nobody's harmless, honey." She smirked and smoothed down the snug, black silky dress, something Beatrix imagined would be worn by an actor who wanted to play a hooker in a movie. Her makeup was slathered on and there was a fake beauty mark near her mouth, a full mouth heavy with lipstick the color of Merlot. Oddly enough, Beatrix smelled expensive Chanel Number Five perfume, or so she thought.

"Just listen for a second, please. I'm a mystery novelist and one of the characters is a hooker. I'm doing research as I want my book to be authentic. Can I buy you a cup of coffee, a drink, or dinner, and interview you? Can I offer you twenty dollars to spend a half hour with me?" She quickly read the woman's face and wondered, *Her make-up and clothes are over the top, but she doesn't seem frightened or angry. She's confused by a bizarre stranger's request, yet still composed.*

"I can't tell you much, really. It's all business for me. However, I missed lunch, and I am hungry, so if you throw in dinner and not just coffee, you've found the right girl. Give me a moment," she disappeared into a tiny grocery store and returned moments later.

If she were the undercover officer and involved in the sting Beatrix had read about, the woman would have told her to get lost. Or would she? "How about that diner across the way?"

"Works for me," she said, yanking up the bodice and furtively tugging down the skirt of the skimpy dress, and in doing so revealed a whole lot more cleavage than Beatrix wanted to see.

They sat in the rear of the diner in a booth, and the woman chose the side to face the door. Beatrix joined her.

A food server flopped down two somewhat greasy menus, and asked if they wanted coffee or were they planning to eat or just do business. She smirked and Beatrix gritted her teeth. *Just walk in someone else's shoes for a few miles,* she wanted to snap, remembering the comments and slurs thrown at her during her tenure as a psychic. Whatever this woman was guilty of, the reasons were hers alone.

"We're eating, thanks," Beatrix said, but the waitress had already turned her back. "She knows you?"

"Naw, it's the dress. It's me. It's typical. A girl gets used to it, doesn't like it, but it's always happening. I've become immune. Maria's the name."

Beatrix studied the woman and imagined her without the theatrical makeup. The skin on her arms and upper chest was smooth, she was a bit plump and soft, and then like a magical jigsaw puzzle, the pieces found their right location. Beatrix said, "You're too healthy, too well rested, too, right for a hooker. You are the police officer arresting Johns."

The statement made Maria's eyes widen and then narrow as a mask stopped her emotions. Her eyes grew hard and focused, and she scowled. "What's your game, lady? You a reporter? Going to blow my cover now just to get a headline for tomorrow's paper?" She started to get up.

"Wait." Beatrix put out a hand, but didn't touch the woman. "No one informed on you. I'm well practiced reading people and remembering details. You don't give the impression of a woman who could be pushed around by any man, especially a pimp. I just have a couple of questions." She reached into her purse and pulled out a twenty-dollar bill, which was enough to feed a family of four for two weeks. "I am not going to disrupt whatever you're doing. Maybe you can help me. I'm Beatrix Patterson and you are Mary Davies."

"What? You're a sharp cookie." Instead of becoming upset, Maria's face relaxed slightly, and she shoved the bill back toward Beatrix. "Okay, I'll bite. What'd you want to know?" Slowly she unfurled the cloth napkin containing the silverware, and inspected each utensil as if she were concerned with germs. However, she was just buying time, considering what she wanted to divulge to this odd woman across the table.

Beatrix's memory never failed. Here was the major's wife, who happened to be an officer of the law.

CHAPTER 21

BEATRIX FACED MARY DAVIES, who now called herself Maria, and was posing as a whore. And waited, knowing that silence often produces the truth.

"Herb told me about you, back when we were all in New Orleans and since you know the old ball and chain, what can I say. He lusted after me when I was a shy Latina, then we married, and he decided to Anglicize me in front of his White friends. Maria is my name. No, I'm not about to be pushed around by some lowlife who hires out women for sex. I know you as well. You're renovating that monstrosity on Anapamu Street near the high school, right?"

"Yes. That's me," Beatrix thought she'd kept a low profile in the town, although discovering the battered woman early the previous morning and being interviewed by the police wouldn't have been exactly considered low. If the woman across the table knew things, could she know Morty's killer too? Had she really been under surveillance when, the other day, she felt watched?

"Honey, word gets around. This is a small town and small towns always have grapevines that relish sorted news. You visited the morgue the other day. Morty Ramsey is one of their guests, in their refrigerator. It's going on two or three weeks now. Son didn't want to see the man, but did, and then identified that wallet found on the body belonged to Morty. Heard that the son's not claiming him, and I bet that's a story worthy of a boatload of gossip.

"Word's out that Ramsey was a small-time opportunist, yeah, a crook from the South, but nobody seems to know why he landed in Santa Barbara. No arrests, no run-ins with anyone, rented a place on upper State Street, office in the El Paso. The curious thing? It's too quiet."

"Yes, I visited there with his son." Didn't mention that she'd left a note for Morty's housemate or any of the details she's discovered.

Maria continued, "As for you? You checked out reference books at the library trying to get intel on some locals. You and your fiancé's names were called in to SBPD when you came upon a murder scene in Montecito. We are a small town, Miss Patterson, and that means news, among those who care to listen, travels like lightning. I care to listen. Never know when you might meet someone or how some knowledge can be useful." Maria studied Beatrix, tilted her head slightly and waited.

Beatrix sat back. *Two can play this game.* She sipped the coffee that the waitress had plopped down on the plastic tablecloth after taking their orders. It seemed the server was about as happy to wait on customers as the customers were to have her condescending attitude.

"You go first," Maria said. "I don't have much time."

"Okay. Did Morty Ramsey come to Santa Barbara to take over some territory or open his own pimping business?"

"Maybe you can tell me. The state-wide task force has been working on this sting for about two weeks, but putting it together for a year. Lousy as it sounds for the women involved, this type of operation takes time to organize. I've been working the streets for the entire time, and on the sting. Then in waltzes good old Morty, whose reputation followed him halfway across the country. He was here in town for four months and he didn't make a move, well, any that we can find or with any of the established girls. I've asked. My guess is that he was going to inch his way in, and then import some beauties from New Orleans, or maybe refugees from Europe, playing up the exotic role, then offering their services to Hollywood's not so moral population.

There are a lot of rich folks right here in Santa Barbara, and while these little towns look all sweetness and light, don't let it fool you."

"Could he have been taking his time, scouting the competition, waiting to discover a weak link?"

The waitress slid two Denver omelets on the table and flopped down a tall stack of lavishly buttered white toast. "Want anything else? You do, just yell." She didn't wait for a reply which suited Beatrix perfectly.

Beatrix was shocked that the food looked and smelled delicious. "Was Mortimer Ramsey here to fight for turf rights?"

Maria picked up a piece of toast and bit off a large chunk. "Since I know you're not going to leave this alone and I heard from some sources that you have helped the government and police at times, especially during the war, I'll be frank with you, Miss Patterson. The taskforce and Santa Barbara police selected me to answer an ad for a talent agent, which I did."

"Maria, that's how I recognized you, from your photo. I've reviewed Morty's files. Why did you use the address on Butterfly Lane?"

"That was Morty's idea, and he said for those of us who didn't have a permanent address, we could use that one. Since I certainly wasn't going to give him info as to where I really live, I agreed. Yeah, we on the force thought that was the pimp's newest scheme, too. The guy, which I learned was Ramsey, had me get those headshots. He made an elaborate deal of telling me about his connections with MGM and Warner Brothers. Said they needed women of a certain age, which made me steam as I'm just forty-six. He kept telling me, 'Doll Face, those eighteen-year-old girls are a thing of the past. You're going to be gold in Hollywood. Big-time movie studios need girlies like you, with your, you know, experience and proven sex appeal. They'll look at you and know you like making love. Waifs are so last year. Today, they need sexy women. Why there'll be parties every night. Lots of cash. Hollywood wants women who embrace their sexuality, like you'. Or something close to that bull. He said he'd just take a small commission, twenty percent. Which is on the low side."

"It seemed legit?" Beatrix forked a mouthful of omelet.

"Not to me, not at all. Look at me. I'm a middle-aged police officer in a skinny silk dress with the 'girls' here long past their prime if they were ever perky," she patted her breasts and pushed them up a bit, which they ignored.

"How long have you been in law enforcement, Mrs. Davies?"

Maria blinked. "I'm Maria."

"Do you know that your husband is trying to find you, offered to pay me to locate you?"

"Now you can collect the money if the rat actually pays up. You found me." She picked up a slice of toast and shredded it into dime-sized pieces.

"Only if you want that," Beatrix replied sipping the coffee and waiting.

"Why not buy a new hat and get back to your fancy high-end life? My life and job aren't some silly diversion or girly hobby, you know. That why you're here? To get Herb's finder's fee? I grew up in Santa Barbara. Your folks were one of the wealthiest couples in the city. Remember they liked to help out at the reservation, and as a teenager, I thought that was charitable and unusual for the rich folks. Did you go too, taking library books there for the children? Listen up. If you don't need the money Herby is offering, I know a lot of charities that could help." She barked, anger making her dark eyes even darker. Then she blinked and once more became the police officer that she really was.

Beatrix nodded, admiring Maria's ability to tamp down the anger at her husband. *What else is she that angry about?* she wondered.

Beatrix smiled at the memory. "Yes, as a child, Mother would load me and boxes of books from the library into the bed of our old Model T truck. Then we would trek out to the Chumash Reservation. I remember playing games with the boys and girls and those were some of my happiest childhood memories, running wild through the groves of Eucalyptus trees along with the other children. At home, I was secluded and only played with my imaginary friends, as my parents had received threats to kidnap me from a disgruntled former employer of my father's."

"Your parents died in an accident." Maria sat back in the booth, now frowning. "Sorry, didn't mean to lash out at you because Herby is a thoughtless, egotistical idiot. And my condolences about your family. How cruel to be orphaned liked that. My biological family is opinionated and mostly nuts, but I cannot imagine maneuvering through life without them."

"Yes, old news, and a tragic end of to my childhood. Now Thomas, my fiancé, and I are going to be residents here in the city and maybe I'll resume some of the work that Mother started on the reservation, and no I don't need your husband's money. He was actually gracious to us, hard to believe, and I hoped I could repay the gesture by finding you. That said, Maria, I'm not here to give away your whereabouts, although that's what your husband wanted me to do. I won't unless you tell me it's okay.

"I'm here to find out what I can about Mortimer Ramsey. You probably know all about it since the SBPD is as big as my front pocket. His son, Frankie, hired me because of my reputation in New Orleans. It's more of a gut feeling that I have, but something is wrong. The answer seems to be there in front of me, but I don't see it.

"Still, meeting you is opening a door that I never thought was connected to this case. I support what you do if you are saving young women from a tragic downward spiral that will be impossible to climb out of. Not just punishing them and letting the guilty men and the pimps go with a slap on the wrist. That's flat out inappropriate.

"What happens to the women involved? If you'll answer that perhaps I can share some facts with you that I've recently uncovered." Beatrix was surprised that the coffee was bitter, but drinkable. She finished the omelet and nibbled a slice of toast.

"Since we're a small law enforcement agency, things can get done faster than, say, San Francisco or Los Angeles. Not as much red tape or palms to grease. There's a place in LA, sponsored by actresses like Dorothy Lamour and Ingrid Bergman. It's not a perfect situation, but the ladies who live there get three meals a day, clean rooms, and medical help if they need it. It's the only facility I know about for women who truly want to get out of the trade. It's all done under the radar and not connected to any governmental agency. I heard that box office leading men like Ronald Coleman and Cary Grant are involved, at least financially. Don't know if that's true. It is funded and supported by the studios and Hollywood's elite; I've been told. Some folks are trying to do good in their community."

"Don't these same studios exploit young women, especially by paying a fraction of the salaries as their male counterparts?"

"Yeah, that's pretty crappy, and all true. God willing it'll change, but until then, a few people do care. This safe house and the staff have signed documents so that everything is secure and confidential. These gals might be walking Sunset Boulevard, or here, or in Oxnard, one day and then the next, they just disappear from their pimps and from the streets. They emerge as middle-class women with marketable skills. They give the girls classes to boost confidence and help them get clean and sober if they're willing, through a program called AA. The girls, some as young as twelve, are victims. These younger kids can stay at the safe house until they're of legal age or the group finds them loving foster homes.

"There is a seventy-five percent 'graduation' rate and that's why I got mixed up in this. I haven't been there, don't even know the name of the place. Don't want to. I'm just damn thankful people care."

Beatrix finished the coffee and knew another cup would just make her jittery. "Do they have professional therapists for the women to talk with?"

"Doctors and nurses come regularly, like I said. There are teachers so the women learn basic math, typing if they want, reading improvement and how to budget. Even basic cooking skills. What are you saying? There should be psychiatrists that put them on drugs? The women aren't crazy, just made tough and bad choices. Every one of us, if we're honest, has done stupid things. Yeah, look at me and Old Herby. These gals are just like us in that way."

Beatrix believed everything Maria said. "I'm not suggesting that they have mental health issues, although that could play into their situation, Maria. Instead, since the mid-thirties, and most importantly now that the war is finally over, group therapy is being practiced among prison inmates and those with neurosis, alcohol dependence, and issues that are curtailing a productive life. You might want to recommend that the staff check out the work of Paul Schilder and Louis Wende, respected colleagues I met before the war. I would be honored to talk with the staff there if they're looking for volunteers."

"To help with what?"

"With group therapy, Maria. I have studied psychology for years, and passed my California state board exams, yet, honestly, I have ever so much more to learn. I may set up a practice here in town, but that's in the future." She laughed, "It'll probably take me a lifetime to learn everything I need to know about the human condition."

"Good luck on that score. Okay, I'm really nobody in the organization, so I can't make recommendations, you understand, right? I'm just a cop. Not a psychologist."

"I am," Beatrix responded.

"Can I count on you being discrete?"

"Absolutely."

"Say, the next time we pick up a girl and I take her to a contact who transports her to the safe house, may I give the liaison your contact info?"

Beatrix withdrew a business card from her purse and put it on the table. "That'd be great. Let them know I'm volunteering and would be happy to give my references. Before the war, before so much death and destruction around the world, it was my goal to become a psychologist. I've now achieved that. The dreadful fighting stopped the process for a while. I got my master's degree, and I'm planning to start my doctoral program at the university this fall." Beatrix sipped the now cool coffee.

"You certainly do care." That empathy was written on Maria's face and Beatrix hoped that the officer would give her contact information to the staff at the safe house, thinking, *Is this the reason I've gotten mixed up with Morty, Frankie, and even the major?* She realized with a start that the answer was yes.

"Care? More than I'm supposed to, more than the bosses at headquarters tell me to. Stella, Detective Hernandez, who's my lead, is quick to say how I'm a bleeding heart. That's why I backed out of the FBI."

Beatrix's eyebrows shot up.

"Ha, you didn't know. Why would you? Some of the stuff I had to deal with tore my heart to shreds, especially when it happened to kids, and those were the good days, mind you. As an agent, you lose your edge if you feel too much, and then you're done for. Feelings get in the way of matters that need to be done, and that's how I knew it was time to resign. I left before I screwed up something really terrible."

"Maria, does your husband know about your career?"

"Herbert?" She chuckled, but there was no joy in the sound. "He doesn't know squat about me, and I believe he's happy about that. He's ten years older than me and met me as a teenager, a country girl from this backwater town of Santa Barbara who wanted frilly and fluffy things. Maybe hard to believe, but Herb was a looker, especially in his uniform, all fresh and sexy, straight out of West Point. A real catch, my mother kept telling me, and my girlfriends drooled when Herb escorted me to senior prom. Call it peer pressure, that's why I let him chase me. What does an eighteen-year-old know about love?" She laughed again and shook her head at the memory. "I felt like Cinderella at the ball, as I'd been the other Cinderella, who scraped and cleaned. I knew positively we'd have a house with a white picket fence and a big shaggy dog, oh and kids, lots of kids. That, Beatrix, was far from reality. Okay, the kids I did get, and I'm blessed for that. They're fine, hardworking adults with families of their own now. Yep, I raised the children while he was off saving the world from various evildoers, including that nut job Hitler. Early on, I realized I needed to finish my bachelor's.

"Herb apparently was good as he rose up in rank, but if you've known him for a while, and I believe you have, he's quite the chauvinist. Herb thought it was charming when I enrolled in graduate school the year our youngest learned to walk. By then, we could afford a fulltime nanny. We were living in D.C. Got a job with law enforcement there and when ugly, black clouds of war were gathering over Europe, in '38 and '39, I was recruited by the FBI. I just didn't bother to tell him that my 'little vacations from the family' as he liked to call them, were part of the job. He thought I was a meter maid, checking Washington's cars that were violating parking meter times. Although after that fiasco in New Orleans, the you-know-what hit the fan for me as well. That was my breaking point."

"He's ill. Did you know that?"

A flicker of surprise dashed along Maria's forehead, but she was good at keeping her face neutral. "Heard. Care? Not much anymore. It's complicated. We have history. Lots of ill-suited couples stay together for that. I decided it's not enough and should have left twenty years ago."

"He wants you back, he says." Beatrix tilted her head and noticed, briefly, a softness in the woman's mouth.

"Does 'fat chance in hell' seem the appropriate response to his years of skirt chasing, betrayal, and infidelity? He just wants an adoring female to be at his beck and call, to be his nurse. That ship has left the dock and won't return. I'm done with him, fed up with the philandering, and one-night stands. Mostly lies. I'm just embarrassed at myself, Beatrix, because I should have put on my big girl panties years ago and left the bastard."

"I am not married, but will be right after Christmas. I do know, however, since I've had a couple of romantic relationships, which were soured by mutual stupidness, that communication is the key. Might you at least tell him to his face?"

"No promises."

Beatrix could tell that Maria was at least contemplating this.

"I don't owe Herb anything and I'm not about to give up yet another career because some man can't care for himself." She folded the paper napkin in a perfect tight square. "Now, how can I help you with Morty? Still having doubts that his talent agency was a front for pimping? I need to get back on the street, as my job as a hooker waits for no woman."

"I need to ask Frankie, his son, more questions, and connect with a few others who knew Morty in New Orleans. Something fishy is happening. I went to the address on Morty's death certificate and two people are living there, a couple, one a large man, and a smaller woman. You wouldn't know who she is, would you?"

"No." Maria folded her napkin.

"I am still working on that, but it doesn't make sense. Mortimer Ramsey is in the morgue and yet someone, two people, are cohabitating in his apartment. Frankie gets weirdly uncomfortable even getting near his father's things. I know this was probably off base, but I left a note for the tenant in the apartment to contact me."

"Good."

"I hinted that there could be money involved. Morty was a rich man, yet the apartment isn't classy. However, the woman's clothing certainly is. And then, actually, I only have Frankie's word that his father was so horrible."

"Wow, I thought my life was complicated. I'll ask around if there's any gossip of a woman hanging out with Ramsey. He's not invisible. Had to leave traces of his life, where he ate dinner, where they partied, where he bought a newspaper."

"Maybe he came here, not to pimp, but to actually open a talent agency. People do turn their lives around, Maria. I have, and sounds like you have, too."

"Are you saying I should forgive Herbie for years of infidelity? For being a world-class cheating, double-dealing, unprincipled, sleaze-bag rodent of a husband?"

Beatrix tried to process all Maria had been through and then said, "Tell me how you really feel about him, Maria."

The woman stopped and stared at Beatrix and suddenly, deep from within came a huge laugh. It was long and hard. "Thanks, I needed that. Being a cop, a woman cop, doesn't give me any opportunities to have girlfriends to talk about throwing, even metaphorically, our boyfriends or husbands under the gossip bus, at least once in a while. It always seemed that Herby couldn't share feelings, and near the end, talked to me like I was some underling. You ever feel like Thomas and you don't speak the same language?"

This time Beatrix laughed. "Oh, Maria, you cannot imagine. The man speaks British English, tries and botches American slang, and I absolutely do not get him at times. You don't want to know about his driving either," she reached across the table and patted Maria's hand. "As for contacting your ex, I can't address that, but I know from my experience that the weight we put on ourselves, with issues that could be resolved, gets heavier by the year. I did that with my birth mother and only through talking, not just once, but to build a relationship, did I learn how she felt completely unprepared for motherhood because of depression, which of course wasn't diagnosed, and, it gets problematic here..."

"And?" Maria asked.

"My birth mother is able to tell the future." Beatrix sighed. It was the first time she'd shared this with a stranger and somehow that brought the women closer. "Parisian to the core, Maman wanted to believe she was eccentric, yet confided that she knew she was deranged, as those who were 'normal' didn't have her gift. Most of the medical professionals who were consulted thought she was deranged and told her so, putting her away in a mental hospital before she escaped. I cannot imagine the psychological cost of giving up a child and knowing that that little one would be better with others. Maman is one of the bravest women I know. We have made inroads to a relationship and for that I'm glad."

"Yeah, well," she sighed. "It never hurts to talk."

"Can we, then, talk again? Could you let me know, unofficially, if any of the women you meet on the streets were connected to Morty? Or to the young woman whom I found on Butterfly Lane. She died in my arms, Maria. I need to find out why and who did it."

"Best leave this nasty stuff to the cops, honey. Killers often have a reason for murdering that only they think is reasonable. Or sometimes they kill once and to cover that up they continue to kill."

Beatrix sighed. "Were you alone when you met with Morty?"

"When I signed with the agency, it was just Morty there, the two of us in that tiny office in the El Paseo. I mean, the ad and his flattery shouted crime all over it, and like my boss said, it screamed as a front for prostitution. He never tried to put the moves on me or anything."

Beatrix paid the bill, and they headed out of the café. Maria looked up and down the street. "No competition today. Good thing for the sting, busy evening for me. Back to Ramsey. I actually got a call from Morty Ramsey weeks back saying that MGM wanted me for a screen test, but the boss wouldn't let me off. A scam? It had all the ingredients, for sure. If I weren't busy pretending to be a hooker, I'd stake out the apartment to see who comes and goes, see if you can find his flat mate."

"The person will be curious, I'm hoping," Beatrix replied.

Maria laughed and shook her head. "You are one determined woman, and I'm betting she will. Let me know if there's anything that the police can do. Right now, as I understand it, Morty took his own life. Done deal." She got up, smoothed the bodice up, and pressed down the skirt of the silky black dress, "I like you, Beatrix. You've got spunk. If you ever want to think about a career in law enforcement, it's not a bad gig, good benefits, crazy hours, weird people, and the job of a lifetime that I missed when I tried to play mother to Herby and the kids. We do help people you know."

"I will, Maria. I'll let you know when I track down anything. Figure you know how to find your husband if you want to talk."

"I'm still wrestling with that."

Beatrix watched Maria scan the street, sway her full hips, and head back to the block where they'd first met. Then she returned to the café as the waitress looked up. She placed a five-dollar bill on the counter, which was three times the cost of their meal. "Here's some extra. Do something nice for yourself."

The waitress's face lightened and sighed. "That's really kind, thanks, Miss. Maybe I'll buy my kids some ice cream along with groceries. Things have been tough."

Beatrix walked to the curb. She opened the Ford's door, tossed her purse across the red leather bench seat, and only then saw the note folded and placed under the windshield wiper.

Beatrix got out, and looked both ways, but could not see anyone seemingly interested in her movements. "What do we have here?" she asked, got back into the car, and locked the door. Fear tickled her arms, and she did not like that sensation.

"I am watching you." The words had been cut from a newspaper and precisely glued onto a piece of lined paper.

Her first thought was: "Oh, Thomas, how dear of you to watch me," then uneasiness clutched her throat. Goosebumps doubled their size on her arms. The initial bravado evaporated. They only had one car and she was in it, twenty miles from home. Beatrix inhaled sharply, turned on the key, and finally breathed as the engine came to life. "Why? Who?"

She checked that both doors were locked and headed north along Highway One to Santa Barbara, all the time sensing she was being tailed. By someone who knew what they were doing. She went past the regular turn on Milpas Street, which would bend and end up at their home. She turned right on State, left on Cota, drove a few blocks, made a right, and when she felt sure that her feeling was wrong, no one was following her, she headed to the house on Anapamu. Her palms stuck to the wooden steering wheel as the evening closed in. She was about to turn into their graveled driveway when a dark sedan pulled out from a side street, stopped, hugged the curb, and waited. Either the driver was ducking down to conceal him or herself, or the person was short. Beatrix put her foot on the accelerator and drove by quickly, not daring to stop at their house.

CHAPTER 22

BEATRIX HAD BEEN STALKED BEFORE, knew the reaction of being so vulnerable, and hated it. She purposely slowed to twenty, turned down a few side streets, stopped at Milpas Street grocery store, and waited. A full five minutes. Then she waited for another five. *I'll go into the store, use their phone and call Thomas,* she thought.

"Evening, Miss Patterson," called out the grocer, a woman of considerable size and muscle. Beatrix was no fragile flower, yet she felt absolutely petite next to the lady.

"It's rather important. Might I use your phone, please?"

"Right on my desk in the back, my dear. Help yourself, Miss Patterson. By the way we got some really nice pineapples in from Hawaii, if you and your family want some tropical fruit. Apples are local, too."

Pineapple was the last thing on Beatrix's mind as dialed the five-digit number for their house and listened as it rang. Again, and again. *He's probably outdoors.* No answer after ten more rings.

"Time to put on your big girl panties, Beatrix Patterson," she told her reflection in the shopkeeper's unusually frilly mirror that was hung over the desk.

The grocer was helping another customer as Beatrix waved goodbye. The parking lot was empty. Traffic moved sedately on Milpas. She double-checked the car door, and it was locked. She turned the key, the engine started, and she drove out of the parking lot. She longed to believe it was her overactive imagination, yet the truth was someone wanted to frighten her and has following her. The crumpled note now in her pocket was no illusion.

The construction crew was tackling the wobbly windows on the east of the house, replacing them with the reclaimed ones from the demolition across town. They waved and returned to work. Their foreman, Giuseppe, looked like he wanted to say something, but just nodded and started on the banister, which wobbled frightfully.

"Thomas, I'm home," she called. No response. She was certain he'd want to hear all of the coincidence of meeting hooker/undercover officer Maria Hernandez Davies. She walked around the house believing she'd find him engrossed in a delicate painting project. He really got into the detail work, and she smiled, thinking how the carpenters probably managed to give him plenty of these projects, ensuring he always was busy but away from the real carpentry that he enthusiastically wanted to do and constantly seemed to botch.

Beatrix re-checked the kitchen table, which was the spot where they'd leave each other notes. "Hm," she said. "He always jots something down if he's headed out to get supplies."

Beatrix stood at the counter and thought of what to do next. She changed into baggy jeans and a lightweight black sweater, and wrote out her notes. Circling in her mind were thoughts of the girls and women at the safe house, of those who were forced into the trade, or even felt the street was the only solution. She contemplated the tragedy of the dead woman, lying in the city's morgue. She grabbed her purse and plaid red wool jacket and picked up the keys from the credenza in the front room. She dashed a note. "Off to the morgue."

The city building was quiet. It was late in the day so that made sense. Unfortunately, the door to the morgue was locked. She bent down to peer through the small window, spying the young coroner inside, feet up, reading an "Archie" comic book. He blinked and recognized the visitor, waved, slowly put down the comic book and came to the door. "Lunch time. Wouldn't read during working hours," he said, as if Beatrix needed a reason to care about his material. "Surprised to see you again, but it's a small town."

"Small towns can be dangerous places," Beatrix replied and walked into the room reeking of chemicals. She didn't even want to think about what they were used for. It was cold inside the room. "The woman found at Gaviota Beach? Was her body claimed?"

The young man tried to set a masculine pose leaning on a steel examination table. It worked until his hand slipped and he tumbled to the gray, scarred linoleum, where chemicals had spilled, and white spatters made patterns of their own.

Beatrix pretended she was looking for something in her purse, pulling out a notepad and pencil, to avoid adding to his embarrassment that was burning his freckled face as he got back to his feet, with the grace of a newborn colt. "The woman?"

He scrambled to his feet. "She's not here. Still writing that book? Or are you just one of those morbid types of dames?" Again, he tried to look macho. Again, he failed when his voice suddenly hit a high note.

"Yes." It was an answer she could live with and just maybe both were true. "Do you have any documentation after the autopsy?"

"Autopsy? She took her own life, lady. Why spend the county's money?" His forehead wrinkled.

"But isn't that suspicious? Was she even examined by the coroner?"

"I work part-time. I don't ask questions."

"She's been buried?"

"Quick and easy. No need for extra paperwork or attempts to find next of kin. We have it in the file if someone shows up asking. Besides, the department doesn't have a big budget and frankly, I don't think the coroner cares for anything except when he can get to the tavern in the afternoon." He picked up the comic book and flipped to where he'd apparently stopped reading. He sat back down, and put up his feet.

"Which tavern?"

"You're kidding, right? Hey, more power to you. It's Garcia's on Anacapa. Sometimes he frequents a joint on Haley, unless one of those bossy types from the Women's Christian Temperance Union drags him out by the collar." He laughed at that image. "Don't think he's choosy. I can nearly understand how this job would cause a man to drink." He got up, walked close to Beatrix, and she had the feeling he was smelling her perfume, which gave her the creeps. He opened the glass door to the hallway and waited. He looked at his watch, "Since it's only two I'm betting he still might be sober. Or at least close to it. Good luck."

Beatrix left the car at the courthouse and walked the blocks to Garcia's Bar and Grill, light on the grill and heavy on the bar. It took too long for her eyes to adjust to the darkness and the place smelled of stale beer, sour cigarette smoke, and melancholy lives. Later, she imagined when the jukebox was flush with coins, and the music vibrated against the patrons and the walls, it could be a local pub where neighbors came in to release some stress and find a friend. Then, it simply felt alien and sad.

In the back of the bar sitting alone at a table was a man twisting a shot glass in his fingers. He was in his fifties or so. The coroner was said to be old. Still, when one is maybe twenty-one, just about everyone who's an adult looks old. She walked up to the bartender. "I'm looking for the county coroner."

The man behind the bar shook his head. In his mid-thirties, Beatrix guessed, his face was rugged and smile lines were evident around his mouth. There was kindness in his eyes, too. This was definitely not a man soured on life and that seemed odd, as if he were playing a part in movie. "Not today, ma'am. Get you a beer or a soda or coffee? Can I help? Quiet here this time of day."

"Coffee. Thanks. Does the coroner come in most late afternoons?"

"Why him?" He put a steaming mug in front of the woman. "You're a classy lady and he's an alcohol-addled public servant. What gives?"

"I'm gathering research," she said, which wasn't a lie, but didn't reveal that she felt determined to discover why and how another young woman died. "A follow up about that woman found on the beach with the Chumash totem strapped to her arm."

"Tragedy."

"You're Chumash. What's your take on it?"

His pupils dilated. His chiseled features didn't change.

She waited. Sipped the coffee, which was surprisingly fresh and good. "What do you think happened?"

It wasn't just a good guess. Beatrix had years of practice reading microfacial expression. This time, it was easy to determine his heritage and that he'd have an opinion on the recent death. The bartender's crisp white shirt sleeves were rolled to the elbow and on his muscular forearm, there was the Chumash tribal symbol of an X encircled by a scalloped ring tattooed there.

The man glowered and shrugged his shoulders. He stepped back as if whatever she was about to say was going to be a slur against his tribe or at the worst some veiled racial slur against indigenous Americans. "You one of those newspaper reporters who needs to feed the juicy details of horror to add more readers to your rag? Have to share it with the readers, the great unwashed of Santa Barbara? Just leave." The final sentence came as a growl.

She took a slow sip and met his angry eyes. "I care too much for others, or so I've been told. I grew up in Santa Barbara, I love the city, and am just trying to unravel the mystery, maybe even find the woman's family. They have a right to know she died and where she's buried. While I am not proud of the second-class citizen status for indigenous people through the city's history, since the times when the padres and Conquistadores ruled the people and the land, I'm not here to argue with you or upset you. Keep in mind, as a woman, I've been a second-class citizen my entire life."

He backed up and leaned against the shelves containing dozens of liquor bottles. "Old habit, unfortunately. Jumped at the obvious conclusion with you asking pointed questions." He poured himself a mug of coffee and his features softened.

"I do know she's not the first to have 'fallen' from the cliffs at the beach, close to the reservation. It's time this cold-police case was solved. What was she? Number five or six. Maybe fifteen or thirty or more. I've wondered, as I've looked into this, how long it's been happening. I'm good at finding answers and finding people. Did you know the woman?" Beatrix twisted the coffee cup on the bar and waited for him to respond.

"I'd seen her at a few tribal gatherings. She looked as white as you but with blond hair, and nobody in the family believed she had any of our blood when she just showed up one day. We can tell. When she told an elder she was Chumash, I thought the guy was going to bust a gut laughing. Yeah, laughed at her and she didn't even flinch. Think her name was Linda or Lillie or something like that. She came dressed to the last powwow in buckskin and beads and the ceremonial red headdress. It looked like she bought the outfit at a Halloween costume shop. A lot of the elders were quietly horrified, but they were kind and gracious and smart. They wanted to learn about whatever game she was playing."

"Was it a game or could she believe, in her mind, that she was indigenous?"

"It was an act, ma'am. That was the word passed between elders. Why, she even had a turtle tattoo on her leg, way up there. If you know what I mean. I'd never seen a woman so willing to expose it to anyone. It was hard to swallow. I didn't know whether to laugh at her or get her some help. The elders are more polite than I am with outsiders. My take? She was delusional. Nuts, but not dangerous."

"Do you believe she was ingesting peyote cactus or something else, another mind-altering drug or plant?"

"She totted around a tiny, beaded Sioux peyote bag, but I didn't see any sign of the peyote's hallucinator button. That stuff doesn't grow well around here, too foggy, but one can still buy it if they have sources, especially through a few of the lesser ethical folks in the community. I didn't actually look in the bag. Didn't want to get that friendly with her, if you want to know the truth. I did see lavender and rosemary twigs sticking out of it. Some were weaved into braids in her hair. I tried to look away. I saw her talk to some of my family, rub the sticks of herbs together, smell her fingers and then she rolled her eyes back. It didn't look like any hallucinogenic plant that I know of and I'm a shaman. I steered clear of her. Could have been she was just not stable. She kept trying to share some herbs she kept in a leather bag tied around her middle. But no takers."

"Hey, thanks. My name is Beatrix Patterson." She pulled a business card from her clutch purse. "Here's my phone number and address if you hear or think of anything else."

He held out a massive hand. "You working for the cops? Wait, a reporter? I never talk with your kind, can't be trusted."

"I've been known to consult with law enforcement, but I'm not with law enforcement and never worked for any newspaper, still don't." She opened her wallet and started to place a dollar on the bar, but he shook his head.

"Coffee's on the house. You'll find, Beatrix, that the tribal leaders and elders aren't that chatty about stuff that happens on our reservation. However, these girls that die on our cliffs, near our homes, frighten everyone. The police think it's all Indian mumbo jumbo, that's what one cop told me, and a few don't give a rat's ass except maybe to close down our meetings and force parents to send our children to those horrendous Indian schools. We wonder if there's someone out there who really wants to get rid of us."

"For your land?"

"Why not? It's prime beach property. Not worth a lot today, but in the future, it will be as there's just so much along the coastline. Besides, this would is just history repeating itself. You need any answers, come to me." He grabbed the mugs and began wiping the spotless counter. "You wouldn't be related to a Mrs. Jennie Patterson, would you?"

"My late mother. Why?"

"Just remembered her bringing boxes of books and leaving them in the tribal school building, asking the teachers to give them to children. She changed lives, you know? I was one of those kids. I remember a little red-headed girl coming with her. Of course, I was about five at the time."

"Then we have met." She laughed. "Yep, small redhead, now all grown up."

"Small world. Be careful, whatever happened to those women could be a sign of something eviler to come. The elders have warned me, the ones who have seen the past and know the future."

CHAPTER 23

BEATRIX DIDN'T LOCATE THE CORONER at either of his favorite drinking holes and resigned, strolling east toward the house.

It was breezy and cloudless, and she smiled at the feeling of coming home. There were so many times when living in New Orleans that she couldn't imagine a future. Now, she was restoring a Victorian house on the same street where she'd grown up. Her handsome fiancée was the brawn and brains behind the renovation, and she was to be married in just over a month, acquiring a large, and she heard loud, Chinese family. And she thought, driving more slowly, about the family that she and Thomas would create. She'd never experienced such longing for the future. After the grimness of the war where death shouted from every newspaper and radio, the thought of their future was a profound joy. She recalled with new affection meeting and knowing, finally, her biological mother. *We'll visit. The children must know their history and grand-mère.*

Reaching the house, she gently coaxed the bulky Woody into the skinny carport, strolled the stone pathway around to the back and entered the now-finished kitchen. One of the workers was slicing a long loaf of crusty bread, another pouring a ruby red wine into a jelly jar. The rich aroma of coppino made Beatrix's mouth water. It had been years since she'd tasted the Italian fish stew and it smelled spicy and succulent.

She asked Giuseppe, "Could you save me a bowl? Have you seen Thomas?"

"He is in the room with the piano, Miss B." He frowned.

"1 hope he's not ripping out that carpet. 1 rather like the puce color," she laughed, but the worker didn't join her. "Is he alright?"

"1 do not think so, madam. He was talking to us, then fell to the floor," Giuseppe replied joining the others, shaking their heads in unison. "He sleeps now. That's good. We put him in the chair, and he didn't wake up."

Beatrix lobbed her jacket and purse at a chair, and both fell to the floor, as she dashed to what they jokingly called the music room, since the only furniture there consisted of an antiquated grand piano with missing keys and two ancient wingback chairs that faced the windows looking out on the side yard and Mrs. Turney's home. Thomas was sprawled in a chair, his arms sagging over the sides. He'd been covered with a blanket and his feet were propped on a lumpy leather ottoman, that had tuffs of horsehair sticking out and spilling to the floor. Now pieces clung to Thomas's jeans.

Beatrix knelt before him, grabbing his icy hands. His chest moved up and down. "Thank God, you're breathing," she exhaled the words as she shook his arms. There was no reaction. For a second time, she watched his chest slowly rise and descend with each breath. "Thomas, darling, what's wrong, wake up," she smoothed a hand over his cheek. No fever. He was not sweaty. His color looked good. "Darling, you're frightening me. Why can't you wake up?" The words caught in her throat. Her body quivered. Still, no response came.

"Stop bothering me," Thomas wanted to say, refusing to pay any attention to the voice even if it sounded vaguely familiar. "Go away," he wanted to shout, but words couldn't form. He would not do as this strange woman demanded. Absolutely would not let that American tell him what to do. *I am British,* he tried to tell her, yet once more, words failed to reach his mouth.

Furthermore, he was far too busy. There was work to be done, calculations to triple check, notes to be reviewed, and the woman kept yelling. *How dare she interrupt me?*

As if watching a movie, he saw himself pacing back and forth in his lab at Cambridge. He looked down and saw he was wearing his favorite boyhood pajamas with cowboys and horses printed on the flannel. Instead of being dismayed, he smoothed his hand over the soft fabric and felt more relaxed than he could remember.

The touch of the flannel reminded him of Saturdays in London. He had gone off to a respected boarding school later, but at that age, five or maybe six, he was still at a local school, and Saturdays were for fun. Mum would make a lavish breakfast and the family would gather around the table, with his grandmother doting on him, the only son. In Chinese cultures then, the son was supposedly the favored one, but his three older sisters never let that go to his head.

He had been smitten by anything American, especially the cowboy heroes Tom Mix and William S. Hart. Saturday afternoons, Grandmother and he would take the bus to central London and indulge in the silent movies that she said were just for him. Even as a boy, Thomas knew his grandmother liked them as much or more than he did, and throughout the next week, they'd talk about how brave the cowboys were, and how daring the bandits were to try to cross these great movie stars. Sometimes on the way home, they'd stop for tea and cakes. He was sworn to secrecy, promising to eat all of his dinner, even if he was full on sweets.

Then something clicked deep within his brain, not about how silly it was to be wearing little boy PJs in a grown-up man's body walking around in his laboratory. He froze. He blinked. He stared at the blackboard with white chalk calculations. Quite without warning, the answers to all the work he'd put in for ten years were there. The equations were correct, and the solutions were written in a precise, clear hand. His own. Directly in front of him. But he'd never seen it before. He snapped up a tablet and pencil and ran through the calculations again. They made sense. His heart raced and it felt as if it were about to jump out of his chest. "No, no, no. Can it be? Wait. This is impossible," he frowned and madly erased the scribbled calculations, only to scratch them once more on the blackboard. It was true. *So simple. This will revolutionize the entire world. No, I'm an idiot. It will save the world. It's the ultimate answer to renewable energy. Finally, I've got it. Crude oil and filthy coal will never be needed again. It is so magnificently basic. Safe. Straightforward. Everyone in the world will have electricity even in the most remote location and this source will drive industry and cars. There will be no more polluting of our environment. Cities will be smoke-free, and people will breathe without fear, rivers will be clean, the oceans pristine, hunger will be history, and worldwide health will improve.* He could barely believe the discovery, but the answers were right there in front of him.

A wave of joy exploded in his heart, and he threw his arms in the air and danced around the lab, shouting and singing a tune that he remembered from a childhood dream:

> "The moon is bright, the wind is quiet.
> The leaves hang over the window.
> My baby, fall asleep quickly.
> Sleep, dreaming sweet dreams.
>
> "The moon is bright, the wind is calm,
> Gently moving cradle,
> Mother's baby, close your eyes,
> Yeah, sleep, sleep, dreaming sweet dreams."

Thomas yanked off his lab coat and twirled it around over his head. It didn't matter that he was now dressed in boxers and a t-shirt. He cranked open the creaking window and tossed out the coat. It took off like a kite and sailed into the distance. The campus, as far as he could see, was shrouded in a mist, lovely and wet, until in a heartbeat, it turned into something alarming, straight from a horror movie. Images far below seemed to now be watching him and he attempted to close the window, to keep them out, but the crank would not work.

He counted to ten in an attempt to calm himself and breathed deeply of the foggy air. He sang the soulful lullaby in a whisper. Fear dissipated. Joy enveloped him as the English morning vapor clung to his face and moistened his lungs.

He rubbed his face and glanced at his hands. Red. They were streaked with red, not moisture. *Blood. Gushing from my wrists, palms, fingers, oozing out, dripping on my bedroom slippers.* Fear gripped his body as he attempted to wipe the red mess onto his white t-shirt. Quite unexpectedly, he was suddenly wearing a stiff black, formal suit, something he was certain one of the Queen's butlers would wear. He'd worn tuxedos to his sisters' weddings, but this was like out of a Victorian photo. He scrubbed his hands on the sleeves of the tuxedo and it was as if the blood was glued to his palms. *I can't breathe,* he tried to scream, but no words came from his mouth.

All at once, he focused on the blood, but it wasn't blood at all. He was looking at particles. Atoms. They were wearing ballerina tutus while dancing in circles on his palms, twisting and dipping as if they were Ginger Rogers and Fred Astaire. Then they actually became the famous dancing duo, all decked out in fancy costumes just like in the movie he'd seen a decade before called *Shall We Dance.* They twirled into the room. He flopped down at a desk exhausted, and one by one, a big band with the Dorsey Brothers leading the parade crowded the laboratory. Ginger and Fred were life-size. "Thomas, come join us, old man," said Fred.

Ginger waved. "We're going to have so much fun," she said beckoning him to join them on the dance floor. The swing music of trumpets and trombones vibrated off the walls and the lab equipment swayed, bubbled, and pulsated with the beat. The sounds pulled him onto the dancefloor, and he blinked wildly, his eyes unable to focus. His mind had given up trying to make sense of it.

Just as abruptly, Beatrix was in his arms, dressed in a floor length sapphire-colored gown with diamonds dripping from her ears. Her hair was gleaming and shimmering on her shoulders and his heart melted. He wanted to tell her that he'd discovered the formula for saving the planet, but the music was too intoxicating. He kissed her neck and the essence of old country roses swirled around him.

As she bent close to his chest, the sweet scent nearly made his knees buckle. He'd never imagined a love like this, so thrilling and passionate and easy. Yes, easy, honest, and good. He could dance with this woman for a million years and not tire.

She whispered and he tried to pull her closer, but his arms wouldn't cooperate. He felt her slipping away and instead, someone was yanking on his arm. He wanted to swat the bothersome person and grab Beatrix back. Yet his arms felt as if they were made of stone, and he could barely lift them. Beatrix was trying to tell him something, vitally important, and whatever she had to say, he'd remember it forever. He'd have it engraved inside their wedding bands. Yet, he felt himself being pulled farther and farther away from her words. They began to echo as if they were lost in a great tunnel, black at both ends and he was adrift. He shuttered violently. Then, the cold damp fog of England assaulted the room and he wanted to run away, get away, before the fog attacked his lungs. He had to stop breathing or it would kill him. He knew that for certain.

CHAPTER 24

BEATRIX HELD ONTO HIM, rubbing his arms, patting his hands. He could feel her touch but couldn't see her, it was so dark in the tunnel. If she'd just stop, step away for a second, he could return to the chalkboard and make notes of the computations. The future of the world depended on him.

"Thomas Ling. You must listen to me. You must wake up." His shoulders were being aggressively shaken. It couldn't be that his tiny bride-to-be was assaulting him, right there on the dance floor in front of Ginger and Fred, inside his laboratory with the entire Dorsey Brothers' Band watching? Impossible, but the shaking didn't stop, even as he tried to pull away, tried to run and get a tablet and pencil to copy the notations, but his feet wouldn't budge.

"Wake up. Right now. Open your eyes. Listen to me. I know you can hear me. Wake up." There was nothing gentle about the demands and Ginger and Fred looked as confused and frustrated as he felt. The woman's voice had made the vicious fog disappear and everything in the laboratory squealed to a halt when she spoke.

He couldn't stop this domineering; harsh and outraged voice allow him to ignore from the most valuable work of his entire career. Then he felt hands rubbing his face and everything turned the color of wet pavement, a brownish gray. He squeezed his eyes tighter, trying to hold on to the feelings, sights, and sounds that he'd experienced.

He flinched when he felt a slap. Not hard, but definitely a smack on his right cheek. "You're frightening me, Thomas." It was Beatrix's voice and it cracked. Only then did he realize she'd grabbed his shoulders and was shaking him. Once more, he squeezed his eyes shut, trying to hold onto the music and dance alongside the couple twirling across the floor and out the door. Then everything was gone. The music. The chalkboard. Gone.

"What's wrong? Are you ill? Why can't you open your eyes?" He heard a sob.

Then, as if of their own volition, his eyes focused. His vision cleared but his brain felt too big for his skull. Beatrix's fingers dug into his shoulders before she examined his face and hands.

It took all his strength to say, "Hello. What are you doing here?"

"Here? This is our house," she sniffed, pushed tears off her cheeks, and flattened her body to his. There still was a faint smell of roses, which was impossible as there were no roses in bloom in England in November.

Her voice quivered and the demanding questions resonated through the tunnel that occupied his brain. There was something definitely amiss with his beloved. She was breathing hard, as if she'd been running or something was terrifying her. Unexpectedly, he realized that she was afraid for him.

"Beatrix, what's wrong? Why are you crying?" He rubbed his eyes. They fluttered closed and then he squinted as if the sun was shining straight at him which it wasn't. He grabbed the arms of the chair, struggling to sit up and didn't make it. Once more he tried, only collapsing back against the chair. A poof of dust billowed from the cushion. The third time he grabbed the arms of the chair and propelled himself forward, nearly plummeting on the carpet face first, and he would have if Beatrix hadn't stopped the motion.

"Whoa," he scrubbed his eyes once more and then his neck. "My head doesn't feel attached to my body. Have I been drinking? I can't focus my eyes. How did I get here? My sweet love, tell me why are you crying? What have I done? What's happened to you?"

She wrapped her arms around his torso and squeezed her hardest before she could reply. "Thomas, try to relax. You're not going anywhere until you're steady on your feet and then we need to see a doctor."

"Doctor? I'm fine, I just feel, well, muddled, and my thoughts are tangled like a spider's web." He picked up her hand and kissed the palm.

"Can you remember anything? You were not on the roof fixing the shingles, were you? Did you fall? I felt your head and there are no bumps." She pushed up the sleeves of his chambray work shirt. "You are not scrapped or bruised that I can see. The men brought you in, thought you needed a nap, and said they had checked on you. Before you collapsed, they were talking with you, and you just crumbled to the floor. What do you recall?" She smoothed her hand over his forehead, pushing back the prickly black hair that constantly refused to do anything but spike.

Thomas shook his head, "Could you get me some water? Could I have fallen? My head hurts a lot. Do we have any aspirin?"

"I'll get you water and then we can talk about what's next. Whatever happened, dearest, we'll figure it out together. We are a couple now and forever."

Returning with two large glasses of water, she watched as he gulped down the first and then reached for the second. Beatrix inched a chair toward her fiancé. His skin was now clammy, and he looked tired. Could it be a stroke? He was strong, trim and fit, yet she knew that guaranteed nothing in life. *A heart attack? She felt chilled at the idea.* "Do you feel any pain? Does your left arm hurt? Your shoulder?"

"No, just the headache and it's subsiding. The water helped. Can I have more?" He downed it and stood, gingerly at first and then straightened his shoulders. "I believe it was the heat, but it's cooler today than it has been. Something I ate, perchance?"

"We had the same thing for breakfast, oatmeal with raisins and honey and hot tea. I'm fine. And it is cool today. It could be dehydration, I suppose. Please, sit for a few more minutes." As she described her trip to Ventura and the seedy side of the area, Thomas seemed to grow stronger.

He took long deep breaths and turned his attention away from her, not listening or truly concentrating on the report. He needed to think, but first he had to know, "What did you find out, if anything. about Morty? What he was up to?"

"Okay, Thomas, but lean back. I'll make it short, or as short as I can. And then we need to talk about whatever happened to you." She told first about meeting Major Davies' wife, Mary – Maria, whichever. Of the sting operation. Of the supposed talent agency.

"Would you like a cup of tea? Something to eat?"

"Just watch me closely, don't let me leave your side, and I'll be fine," he promised, but then closed his eyes for the briefest of time. He longed to return to the laboratory conducting experiments and revising the notes in the ever-present journal on his desk.

"You are certain you have no pain?" Before her adoptive parents died in the car crash, and even in past relationships, she'd never agonized over anyone. Now she wondered if the worrying would ever stop if you truly loved another. For a moment, she thought, *is love good if it hurts this bad?* But of course, it was.

With a cup of inky English Breakfast tea in his hands, Thomas watched the droplets of steam dance up from the hot liquid and disappear. He relayed what he remembered of "the dream," as he called it. "We were in my laboratory in Cambridge. We were waltzing. Have we ever waltzed, Bea? You were magnificent in a bright blue ball gown and diamond earrings. And the Dorsey Brothers' band was playing 'Getting Sentimental Over You'. Ginger Rogers and Fred Astaire were dancing and even the Bunsen burners and the lab equipment were bouncing with the beat. There was blood on my hands, sticky and gushing and I felt an urgency to stop it as if the flow was the sum total of all the bloodshed in the world. Then, from far away, came the song Grandmother sang to me as a child." He closed his eyes. "It was extraordinary and lovely and frightening. I know there is a mammoth meaning to all this. I just know it. But I cannot put it into words."

"There's something more?"

"Well, this is the peculiar part."

"Crazier than Ginger and Fred and the Bunsen burners swaying with the horns and instruments of the Dorsey band?"

"Earnestly, Bea. I know that it sounds irrational, and it feels that way when I relate it to you, but as surely as I'm sitting here, grabbing your hands, longing to hold you and take away my fear, I was there. Truly. I looked at the blackboard and I'd calculated a formula for clean energy, abundant energy, from the sun." Tears sprang to his eyes, and he shoved them away with a fist. "I promise you. It was all there. It was not like the toxicity of coal or the petroleum fuels we depend on. It wasn't hazardous like atomic energy. It was just so blooming simple, and I knew it would change the world for the better. Maybe even save the planet." He swallowed the remainder of the tea. "No, I know it can change the projection of our planet from self-destruction and the greed of wars to harmony."

Beatrix was stilled by the fierce emotions showing on Thomas's face. She let her mind play for a moment with the revelations of his dream, of the ramifications in a world without contamination, soot, belching filth from factories and hope for those in desperate areas of the globe that didn't have access to power to run machinery and pump clean water. "Thomas. Do you remember the calculations? The formulae? Any of the exact details?" Was it right to encourage this when it was simply a freak accident, and he could not have possibly solved the world's shortage of fuel? *Or could he have?* She was afraid of either answer.

He snatched her hand once more. Linking his fingers in hers. "I feel in my heart if I do not pursue this, I will have failed as a scientist, but more so, as a human being. If I do nothing,

I'll have the blood of millions of people on my hands, Beatrix."
Once more he wiped tears from his eyes.

"You didn't answer the question, though. Can you remember what was on the blackboard?"

He paused, the line of his mouth straight, then exhaling, rubbed his temples. "Yes. No. Maybe. It's foggy. I know you're depending on me to help assist you with the house. You need my help to find out what happened to Mortimer Ramsey and even the women who fell to their deaths, but I need time to deliberately ruminate on it, and work it through. Maybe it was something I ate or dreamed or maybe it's a physical ailment, but I need to comprehend what happened."

"Are you trying to tell me you need to return to England? To your job and the lab?" A pain of regret pierced her heart, yet if it was true that Thomas could create clean, affordable energy for the entire world, could she stop him?

"Let me think about that, too." He pulled her on his lap. "Would you be willing to leave here, this crazy ramshackle house and go with me to Cambridge on a fool's quest that might just have been a bad dream? Or even food poisoning?"

She wanted to scream: "Absolutely not. This is our home, for ourselves and our family. No. You cannot leave. I will not let you and I will not go."

Instead, the words didn't come out and her heart sank knowing that she'd lost Thomas to science, a fear that always had lingered deep that it might happen someday. Now, that day had come.

CHAPTER 25

IT WAS EVENING WHEN BEATRIX WALKED into the foyer, sat at the scruffy leather chair, and with fingers trembling, knew she needed to call her friend John. She picked up the heavy black receiver and then replaced it. With all she'd been through in the last few days, from finding a battered woman on the floor of a pristine cottage and feeling the life force leave her, to Thomas announcing that "with or without you," he was returning to London, it shouldn't have been a surprise that stress had devoured her spirit.

Her heart ached. Thomas was unwavering, so clear on the visions from his dreams or hallucination or whatever it was of that afternoon that as she sat staring at the telephone, he was packing a satchel and planning to catch the morning train to New York. Without her.

"I'll take the first ship, no matter what kind, to Liverpool and get to Cambridge however I need to. I can always hire a car, if necessary. Need to make some calls and reservations." He added, "I love you, my darling. Nonetheless, I must be true to my vocation. I must investigate the truth. This breakthrough is even bigger than our love. I am not deserting you. If you truly love me, you will try to understand."

Beatrix stood up. Dazed.

Before she'd left the house earlier, and just for a few hours, he'd visited with Bunny Turney for tea and bird watching as he did quite often when Beatrix would retreat to a quiet place and read about the human mind. Later that day, she tried to piece together what happened. When he woke, all he could talk about was the vision, a delusion caused by whatever happened in her absence. Her fiancé was the epitome of rational and analytical. In Webster's dictionary, after the word logical, the definition was Dr. Thomas Albert Ling. "How can this be happening?"

She tried to tell him that in a few weeks they'd both be traveling to Britain for the wedding. "Just wait. Ten days from now, we'll go together." She tried to pat his hand, but he pulled it away.

"This cannot wait, Beatrix. Do you even comprehend the magnitude if I could discover clean energy?"

At that second, her world crashed at her feet. All the plans for the wedding, their plans, visits with his family, the honeymoon, and even the house so close to being habitable evaporated. Everything she'd thought was true and clear and joyful vanished in a matter of hours.

Beatrix gave up, gave up being brave and strong and optimistic. If she had a box of chocolate, she would have jumped in. Alas, there was only fruit on the kitchen counter, and she didn't bother moving for that. She crumbled in the chair near the phone, grabbed the table for support, gave that up as well, slipped to the shabby carpet, and wept.

CHAPTER 26

SOMEWHERE ABOUT THREE the next morning, Thomas slipped out of bed. She'd heard him get dressed, running water in the bathroom, and heard him grab the satchel from the armoire.

She didn't breathe as he kissed her forehead.

They had barely talked the previous evening. Their conversation was as intimate as a boring dinner exchange among strangers who had nothing in common. "I expect we might get some rain in a few weeks, after all, it is November," he said helping to clear dinner dishes.

"The garden can certainly use it," she replied shoving her hands deeply into the soapy water, adding one dish after another, being extra careful not to take her grief and anger out on the tableware that needed scrubbing, which she did with a vengeance, nonetheless.

"If there isn't more rain, we may have to water the fruit trees in the side yard. The apple will need it, as will the orange trees," he added, wiping the countertops and placing the chairs squarely beneath the table. Twice.

"It would certainly seem that way."

Later in bed, they pretended that everything was going to be fine. "You'll come before the wedding, right?"

Finally, she kissed him on the cheek. "Good night, Thomas. As for the wedding, well, we'll see." She rolled over so she didn't have to face him, and thought of the most dreadful things to say, recounting the crazy dream and how utterly thoughtless he was. Yet, she never spoke..

That was it. That was the goodbye after four years of intense exploration of their relationship, of passion, of partnership, and of plans for the future.

Then he was gone, the train would leave the Santa Fe station at five, and punctual to a fault, Thomas left an hour and a half early.

Beatrix punched his pillow with such force that her hand hurt. Then she kept at it for another five minutes. Fearing she'd bruise was the only reason she stopped, and the vengeance did make her feel somewhat better.

At about nine, she got out of bed, readied herself for the day, and explained to the work crew that Thomas had an urgent need to return quickly to England, but to be assured, the work would continue, and they would be paid. "Henry, whom you met previously, will be here each day, once I ask him, to help with the logistics of the renovation."

The men watched her make the typical huge breakfast, although normally Thomas would have been the chef. All married men, they didn't make eye contact with her as she slammed pans and broke eggs into sizzling plans. A few eyebrows were raised, but Beatrix didn't notice them, or refused to respond. If they wanted to shake their heads or ask questions, her angry demeanor blocked any inquiry.

The men's ability with English was improving every day. They were not naïve, however, and all had seen a scorned woman before. These men could read between the lines, even if their native tongue was Sicilian. Hence, not one asked a question. They quietly polished off breakfast with gallons of strong coffee, starting their day by scraping ten layers of paint off the front porch railings and repairing the porch's floor where a visitor had tumbled through.

Beatrix cleaned the kitchen, changed into comfortable jeans and a sweater, covered her hair with a red bandana, and headed to the rear of the house where the steps leading to the porch needed to be sanded.

By eleven, her muscles ached, and she was still livid with Thomas. She'd rehashed their conversation, remembering every detail, every possible alternation in his personality for the last month. "Whatever happened to cause that dream, Thomas knew it was real, or felt it so, even if it is preposterous," she said, sitting on the stoop, flicking paint flakes off her jeans. "There's nothing logical about this." *I'm a psychologist. How could I have missed this grave defect in his personality,* she thought for the tenth time.

She repeated that sentence as she walked through the house to the tiny alcove where they'd had the telephone installed and she got the nerve to dial John Brockman's number. No answer. It was his private line, and those who worked in the gambling hall, right by his office, would never have dared to enter his personal domain without an invitation, surely not to pick up his telephone. It was one o'clock in New Orleans and he'd probably left for lunch.

She fumbled through the telephone and address book that she kept on a shelf near the phone and dialed Henry, John's assistant, and now the caretaker of John's new villa in Montecito.

Ever positive, Henry told her how he would just keep trying that private number, and eventually, Mr. Brockman would pick it up. "The boss doesn't want anyone to mess with it but himself."

"Thanks, and by the way, Henry, did you ever have any personal contact with Morty Ramsey? Or see him interact with John?"

"Yes, plenty of times."

"You're a wise person, Henry. What is your take on him?"

"He was gruff and loud. Unlike some of the boss's visitors, he was never condescending to me. I wouldn't say that he and the boss were friends, just did business deals together, I think. You'd have to talk with Mr. B about that. Didn't like or dislike him, just another of the men coming and going from the office."

"Ever see him with Frankie, his son?"

"Once, and I remember it because I was pretty close, as a kid, with my own dad. They'd come into the office for some reason and there was Frankie. Bean pole, never moving closer than six feet to his father, like the guy had something contagious."

"Remember Frankie's face or mannerisms?"

"You ask the most detailed questions, Miss Beatrix, and if it hadn't been that the visit was days after Daddy died, I would probably have forgotten. The kid alternated shoving his hands deep into his pants pockets and then weaving them in a death grip across his chest. His face had two patches of bright red on his cheeks. and whatever had happened before they arrived at the office, there'd been fireworks. His eyes were shooting daggers like he wished his dad were dead."

Had Frankie wished his father dead? Had he hired someone to do it? Why kill the missed man, all these years later? She fingered the tablet next to the phone. *Why not?*

CHAPTER 27

"LAST OR ONLY TIME you saw Morty and Frankie together?" Beatrix asked.

"Did see both of them a few more times, and son and dad seemed to always be in the middle of an argument. The kid never said two words to me, never even looked in my direction." There was silence and then Henry cleared his throat. "You know Frankie dresses up like a lady, right?"

"It's okay, Henry, I know all about that and his theatrical life."

"Well, now, that's a darn smart way to say it," he chuckled. "Is there anything you don't know, Miss Beatrix?"

"Yes, Henry." She paused and then it began to spill out. She told him how Thomas had passed out or fainted and he got the ridiculous notion that he'd discovered the formula for clean energy and by proving it, he, alone, could save the world. She didn't cry, which was a miracle, as she relayed what happened. "It's a big, crummy mess, and I have a mind to tell him to jump in a lake."

"Want me to go after him and break his arms, Miss, or at least his pinkie? Or, better yet, Mr. B's got people in New York that could stop him when he gets off the train so he can be fitted with cement shoes. Isn't that how it's done in those gangster movies? How about that?"

There was silence and then Henry laughed. Then Beatrix laughed. Then they laughed together. "You are a wise man, Henry."

"Your doc told me that, too, when he was flying around New Orleans trying to find you after you'd been kidnapped. The man's a lunatic sometimes, which is weird, because he's supposed to be a scientist, right?"

"He does seem to lose control and then focus on tiny elements of a problem."

"My mama always said that a marriage works when two zany people come together and create an odd relationship that turns two into one. I think he'll come to his senses, but if he doesn't, I'll make sure to have the guys with the concrete ready."

"Come over Sunday afternoon, Henry, please? Nothing special, tea and cookies. We'll sit outside and catch up."

"I'd like that, Miss, and as for the doc, he'll come to his senses, or you can take me up on that offer for a gangster friend of Mr. Brockman's to remind him that he's got you right here."

Beatrix sat in the alcove and heard the sounds of construction, felt the breeze through the window, and saw Bunny puttering in her herb garden and picking up the binoculars to stare at the trees. "Birding," Beatrix said. "Not bird watching." She'd made the mistake of using the wrong term and the neighbor scolded her as if she was a naughty child.

Her chin rose and her shoulders squared. "What have I become? I didn't need Thomas for thirty years of my life, why am I miserable and morose? I don't even like myself right now.

"If there is a wedding, and that remains to be seen, then before that I've got work to get done." She took the stairs quickly, tossed the soiled work clothes in a pile, and put on a navy gabardine, full-legged, high-waisted slacks, slipped into a crisp cotton shirt, and added a red boiled wool jacket.

She picked up her oversized leather messenger-style purse with the notepad tucked inside, as a prop for her being a writer. "Why haven't I done this before?" *The Women's Christian Temperance Union had been mentioned three or four times when interviewing people. They were powerful in the city and Santa Barbara was on the brink of voting to be a "dry" or non-alcoholic city before Prohibition was the law. Now that is influence,* she thought.

She found the telephone directory that came with the phone's installation and yes, there was an address for the organization. It was just a few blocks away from the house on Garden Street. She covered the distance in ten minutes, again assured that she must find the answers as to why young women were jumping from a cliff along with the symbolism of the Onus Organista, reported to be a sister group to the WCTU. Finally, were the two connected?

She had walked this peaceful way often rather than along busy State Street, yet never once looked in the back of a small business office to see another home tucked at the end of a long driveway. The entrance was dotted with pots of rust, yellow and purple mums decorated the front door, and tidy roses lined the edges of the garden. Above the door was a wooden sign with the letters WCTU. She walked to the door, knocked, and twisted the handle. It was locked. "Darn." Beatrix felt compelled to learn if there was a connection. It was a gut feeling. There was far too much of a coincidence that the WCTU wouldn't somehow be involved or at least know something about the women who died.

She knocked again. A small voice made her turn. "You need something, ma'am?" A boy of about four pushed a tricycle up the drive, "I think you want to talk to Mama, right? She's probably out back. I'm Sammy, 'cuz Dad's Sam, and that way Mama can tell us apart." His chocolate-colored skin tone and smile was infectious.

"Hello, Sammy. I'm Beatrix. You live here?"

"Yep, and it's Saturday, so Mama'll be hanging laundry." He motioned. "Come on. Mama loves company." The child's chocolate-brown skin and black wild curls melted Beatrix's heart. She struggled, refusing to listen to her biological clock. But the steady banging was starting to ignore her intentions.

That was frightening, and unexpected, something she'd only heard whispered from other women.

The mama he referred to was a petite lady jumping up and down, trying to catch hold of the clothesline with one hand and a bright white sheet with the other.

"Here. Let me help you," Beatrix said, dropping her purse on the back steps and reaching out to snap up a corner of the sheet to clip to the line.

"It's a challenge being short, so I normally grab the kitchen stool for this chore. Think that man of mine must have taken it to work."

Together they hung the sheets, put towels on the line and finally, added three pair of sturdy large men's working overalls. "Sam Sr. works for the Southern Pacific, a railroad laborer, and does that man get dirty. Think sometimes he rolls in soot at the end of the day just to see if I can get his overalls clean." She laughed; it was the contagious type that make a person feel up lifted. Beatrix liked the woman on the spot.

The breeze picked up and fluttered the clothing as they finished together. Every item on the clothesline was spotless.

"You look like a nice person and not an angel sent from God to help me hang laundry, although you blessed me," she said. "I'd still be bouncing like a jack in the box if you hadn't come along. How can I help you, Miss?" She smoothed back her hair, tucking a black curly strand into the bun atop her head. "Sammy, don't go far. We're visiting your grandmother for lunch. And try not to get muddy. Oh, that child. He's never found a mud puddle that he hasn't loved, 'course I was the same way."

"Yes, Mama," he called over his shoulder scooting down the sidewalk on the trike.

"I have some questions about the WCTU," Beatrix said sharing the cement stoop with the woman.

"That'd be me, then." She shot out a hand. "Josephine Conrad. Call me Jo. Most friends do. I'm the president, secretary and well, most of the time, the entire staff, but we do get a lot of good work done. We're not busting up saloons anymore, you know."

"Beatrix Patterson, and I have a feeling we could be great friends, Jo. I've done some reading about the organization and know you're focused on helping women in domestic abuse situations and from being exploited. Those are principles I can truly support."

"Then join us, Beatrix. The first Monday of each month we have a meeting. You'd like the other women. We're beginning a campaign to stop human trafficking. I fear it's going to get worse, and nobody wants to talk about it. Sorry." She squinted and looked at Beatrix. "Sorry, when did we meet? Was it at a city event? You aren't a reporter?"

"I certainly must look like a reporter as I've been asked that question a lot in the last week. It was a few days ago. You were trimming that extraordinary rose bush and gave me a fragrant pink flower. I tucked it into the pocket of my jacket, and I swear, its scent was there all day long.

"That'd be Cecile Brunner, oh, and it can get monster big unless I trim that rascal each fall. Yes, now I remember you."

"The reason I'm here is that I'm helping to solve a mystery." Now with Thomas on a train heading to New York and then on a ship to England, she was alone again. She felt more determined than ever to find out the truth of the girls who had died and the two lying in the morgue waiting to be claimed, if they ever would be. She'd been alone once, not that long ago, and wondered if anyone would have reached out to claim her if she'd died, if that happened before she'd met Thomas. She'd searched her conscious as to why she'd become so focused on discovering why they'd died, and it was because they were alone. *No, that's not true. Now I have John, Henry, and my birthmother.* She smiled at the correction, yet knew she would not stop her "investigation" as she called it until the reasons, as horrible as they might be, for the death of three young women were explained.

She looked at Jo and knew that whatever she shared would be kept between them. She told her everything, from Morty and Frankie to Thomas's erratic departure. Then she told her about the dead girls. "So that's why I'm here," Beatrix said at the abbreviated summary of the women with the concentric circles tattooed on their breasts. "And I don't like coincidences. Life isn't that organized. Too many have mentioned the WCTU and something called Onus Organista, a group affiliated with your organization."

"Claptrap and rubbish," she spit the words out like a bitter pill or swearwords. "Who told you that? That lie has a way of circling back like carrion or Satan, grabbing the blind, defenseless and uninformed."

"Does it matter?"

"Might. Honey, the OOs are fruit cakes, to be polite. See, I grew up on the wrong side of the tracks as Daddy worked for the railroad too, and I could be far more explicit."

"Could you tell me anything about them, the OOs?"

"A group of women here in the city founded it. Think it was around the time of the crash on Wall Street and definitely at the beginning of the Depression. Apparently, from what I remember Mama telling me, they thought our WCTU 'values,' an interpretation of their misguided Puritan moral code, was far too liberal and they thought the WCTU was far too broad-minded and splintered off. While they had been members of the WCTU, helping us pass legislation and eventually Prohibition, they came up with this gosh-awful set of rules. They were not welcome with our members, but that didn't stop them from preaching a code worthy of Saul before he found Jesus and became Paul." She laughed a bit and Beatrix nodded, imagining the militant members in girdles and feathered hats.

"With violent consequences?"

"Never proven. But I'd bet my best Sunday dress on the fact that they would have done whatever it took to stop the ethical decline of our city. Had nothing to do with alcohol, and it was all about sex and pagan rituals, and drink probably had to have been a part of it."

As the sheets, towels, and clothing billowed in the breeze, Beatrix felt peaceful, and the heartache of Thomas's abrupt departure diminished. Being with Jo made her feel more like her old, independent self.

She liked it. "What were their objectives, if you can remember, Jo?"

"Do you have time for a story?"

"About the OOs? Absolutely."

"I was a kid, but my mother was a force in the WCTU, so I've grown up with this in my blood. The OOs wanted to expose sexual impropriety across the board, with everything from listing sexual deviants, according to their own code, in the newspaper, and plastering photos of the degenerates on every flat wall in the city, all the way to illegal means of trapping them. The perverts, as they were termed, Beatrix, might have been a husband who smoked a cigar or got too close to a female at a church, three feet distance was the rule. Why, they were said to accuse a teenage boy of impropriety when he ogled a girl. What teenage kid doesn't do that? The OOs, at one time, took out huge ads in the newspaper and put photos of the men and their addresses right out there, for everyone to see, without regard to the consequences to the males' families, or their careers, or standing in the community."

"Without proof?"

"They were sued, and the lawsuits were typically dismissed, but the men and their loved ones still suffered as you can imagine. That kind of notoriety can ruin people. This was in the late 1920s."

"The group didn't care?"

"Seems not. The leaders recruited young women as much as pimps would for the poor women in the profession. As far as I remember, they were actually paying a finder's fee for dirt on public officials. Then they'd trap them. These were some of the most righteous-looking church-y ladies, mind you, singing in the choir on Sunday and then insnaring and exposing men on Monday, all according to their own truisms."

It was a long shot, but she had to ask. "Was their symbol two entwined circle?"

"How did you know?"

"Yes. I saw it tattooed right here," she placed a hand on her breast. "One of the tats looked irritated as if it were fresh. I saw the marks on two of the women who'd recently died, yet interestingly enough, those two circles were the symbol of a quasi-cult, the Guardians of Light."

"A fluke, Beatrix?"

"Could be. Do you remember any names connected with the OOs ?"

Jo smoothed her hand over the flowered cotton house dress and flicked grass clippings from her shoes. "I don't like to say. Our work is to help humanity, not toss them into the gutter and stomp on them."

"You've lived in Santa Barbara a long time?"

"My entire life, why?"

"Does the name Bunny Turney ring any bells in your memory?"

Jo took extra interest in pulling up sunny yellow dandelions shooting from the crevices between the back steps and the sidewalk. "I've never been one to point fingers."

"You don't have to, Jo. Just let me throw this out and you can comment if you want. Would Bunny have the ability to persuade young ladies to do the OOs bidding and expose lecherous individuals or other men who could have sexually harassed women? Would she be the type to go out for revenge against a reprobate?"

"Boy, Beatrix, you nailed that one. Why yes, that's syrupy little Bunny. Is she in it again?" She seemed to try to make light of it, but the chuckle was hollow.

"I take that as a yes. I'm really good at reading people and Bunny's persona seemed to have holes in it. All goodness and light, but I've seen her verbally rip into the gardeners who help her weekly, and she's got a mouth. A sailor would blush, but I don't think she knew I was in the garden, under that clump of bamboo when she harangued them, berating them even in Spanish and English so they'd be sure to get the message."

"No surprise to me, Beatrix. I try to be a good role model for Sammy, the community, and members of the union. I avoid folks like Bunny who are all goody goody on Sunday, and criticize someone because of who they are or where they were born."

"Could she be working with others on a self-proclaimed moral ministry to rid the city of lusty males?"

"Can't argue with you there. There could be one or two other ladies, and I use that term loosely, who might assist her. They're all pretty old now, and younger women, those under the age of eighty, prefer to join us or some of the other worthwhile charities in the city. But let me think, Bunny must be in her late eighties now. My mama and I used to go to her church, but when it was decided, by this holy group, that people of color needed to sit in their own 'special' section of the sanctuary or even better yet, have their own service. Holy heck broke out."

"No. No?"

"It was quite a spectacle," Jo snickered. "One Sunday, Mrs. Turney got up after the first hymn and pushed the frail little parson out of the way before he could get to the sermon. She had the audacity to tell the congregation about this cockeyed 'separate and equal' seating program. Previously, and each week, she and a handful of self-important and self-appointed saintly ladies all sat piously in the front pews, their backs ramrod straight. I remember her saying something like, 'Everyone will be happier when we are with our own kind.'

"Mama shot up like a firecracker on the fourth and I'll never forget it. She said something like, 'Ladies and gentlemen, that was what Kaiser Wilhelm had in mind and the result was wholesale genocide. Have you forgotten the Great War? Remember seeing our boys come home in '19, broken and without limbs? They fought for equality and peace and now these ladies are trying to divide our church. What's next? Our city, county, state, and finally the nation? The Civil War was just a little over sixty years ago and I remember my grandmother telling me of the horror of that one. Every one of us has been touched by war, or worse, lost loved ones. Every one of us knows the price of freedom. We're still paying it, with our boys and gals battling war wounds, physically or mentally.'"

Jo smiled at the memory of her mother, sturdy and tall, standing ramrod straight as she continued. "'Talk like this of separate services is hypocrisy and has no place in Christendom. Stay here, my friends, and follow these white supremacists if your conscious agrees. As for me and my family, we've heard enough.'

"Oh, the parson wailed and begged, in a squeaky voice that could have broken crystal, so that Mama would come back, excusing Mrs. Turney's notion of a separate service. All except the ladies at the front looked at one another, everyone else followed Mama and us kids right out of that church. We marched straight across the street, opened the doors to the First Baptist Church, and never looked back. Think the Baptists were startled, but they embraced us wholeheartedly."

"Has Bunny always been on this moral crusade with questionable absolutes?"

"That's an excellent comparison. She's definitely a crusader for her cause. She's in the middle of the pot and stirring it up. You have a lovely way of putting things, Beatrix. I'd call her cracker jacks. I think her moral compass got mangled after Mr. Turney returned from the Great War. Neither were ever the same. Mama said he didn't talk, didn't leave the house except once a week. She whispered to me that he'd come home smelling like cigarette smoke and perfume. Mama was the help. After the explosion at church, Mama quit. We ate a lot of beans that year, until Mama got another job.

"Heard Mr. Turney drank. Heavily. I was a kid so don't quote me on that. Thinking back, it had to be battle fatigue, shell shock, whatever. Then in the mid thirties, I heard he took his own life by jumping off the cliffs straight into the sea, just north of town."

"Near Gaviota? On the Chumash reservation? That's where there have been a few more deaths of young women that happened right there near the ocean and above razor-sharp rocks below." Beatrix visualized the rocks and the sheer cliffs.

"I can't be sure. It's been years. I read the newspaper, but sometimes, I skip the brutality of human against human and just go to the comic pages. Oh, my dear, I'm sorry, lemonade or water or something to eat? Where are my manners? You helped me hang the laundry and I've repaid you by telling you stories that are old and sound like gossip."

"This is just what I needed to know. You've been really helpful, Jo." The notion that sweet neighbor Bunny Turney was in some way connected to the murders made sense in a perverted and frighting way. Beatrix thought of the old woman. *She can barely walk. I've seen her trotting around in the garden with her cane. How could this be, unless she has accomplices, maybe like the workers she had in the garden?*

The pieces, like a 1000-piece jigsaw puzzle, didn't look like they should fit, but perhaps they did. *Truth is not always logical,* she knew.

"The American poet James Whitcomb Riley once said, 'When I see a bird that walks like a duck and swims like a duck and quacks like a duck, I call that bird a duck'. You know, Jo, that 'duck' seems to fit Bunny's moral plans." Beatrix focused on a cluster of crows. "One more question, Jo. Do you know anything, any history, about the Guardians of Light?"

Beatrix watched Jo's face. Her new friend's forehead wrinkled, and she stared into the distance as if organizing her thoughts and words. "That's an organization I haven't heard of in years. Oh, back in the day, maybe the 1920s or early thirties, before the crash of Wall Street, it held wild parties and practiced weird rituals. Mama never shared any of that, so I learned about it when I joined the WCTU, but as far as I know, it's not active."

"Not even with Bunny Turney's circle of do-gooders?"

"I don't think so, but I'll ask Mama. She was the secretary for us, for the WCTU, during those days and Santa Barbara was a place for the rich and infamous to let off steam of, I guess, being rich and infamous. Wait, is that your house on Anapamu that's being renovated?"

"Guilty," Beatrix said with a laugh. "It's a work in progress."

"That was the house where all the high-end mischief happened with the Guardians of Light, you know. Oh, what stories those walls could tell. I don't blush anymore but hearing them might raise the color of my cheeks."

"Thank you, and if your mother thinks that the Guardians are alive and well, but underground, could you please let me know? Same with the OOs?"

"Sure enough."

Jo got up from the cement stoop and Beatrix stood as well. She smiled at her new friend. "Would you, Sam, and the boy like to come for a visit tomorrow, after church, say about two?"

"You are so kind; however, my baby sister Louisa is arriving by train later today all the way from Chicago. Going to medical school there. She's the brains in the family. I don't want to inconvenience you."

"I have others coming, and a dear friend from New Orleans who is on his own right now, and if lemonade, coffee, tea, and cookies are okay, nothing fancy, please come. It's not far. Sammy can ride his tricycle over, too, as my patio is large, perfect for a boy and a bike. As long as the weather is this good, we'll sit in the garden." Beatrix said and reached out to hug the woman.

Jo returned the hug. "Yes, Beatrix, we'd love that. You say that Bunny lives next door to you? It'll be interesting to meet her again."

"The WCTU and the old guard of the OOs don't travel in the same circles?" Beatrix swung the strap of her purse over her shoulder.

"Now that's a hoot. You know why it's the Onus Organista? Onus refers to having to do something out of duty and the organista is a songbird, so they are singing their own truth out of a duty. But to whom? Odd, right? My colleagues with the WCTU are appalled at the stories about the old days and the OOs. Do you really think that the organization is alive and well and up to its old misbehavior?"

"I'm going to find out. Those women are in the city's morgue, and I need to learn who they were and why they died. I need to do that for them, Jo."

"Promise me, Beatrix, that if you need a friend to help, or someone to talk with any time, you come here. I'm always home, working in the office in the front of the house, or hanging laundry out back here. If the OOs are killing girls for some outrageous moral code, then they need to be brought to justice."

"That's my plan."

Walking back home, she did not have even a hint of a plan. She was so caught up in trying to work one out that she missed the ocean breeze and the jaunty "hellos" from a string of those passing by. She only saw the face of the woman who'd died in her arms and the other one who was lying on a slab in the morgue.

CHAPTER 28

THE REST OF THE DAY, Beatrix needed to be in the garden to organize her thoughts and put them in order. She remembered every detail of the morning, yet, it required mulling over.

The garden had been screaming for attention, and she could no longer ignore it. She pulled weeds and hacked the lilac bush that was about to encapsulate the rock-lined flower garden. She took sharp clippers and dead headed a Sally Holmes single petal white rose, currently the size of a small house, and cut a handful of late blooming tiny flowers with their happy yellow centers. The shadows were long when she stretched, and her back felt tight, but she knew in her heart that the truth of Morty Ramsey's murder had to be exposed, as well as why these young women had to die.

She'd just filled an old pickle jar with water for the flowers when she heard Giuseppe calling. "Miss? Miss? Grande uomo in the front porta."

What in the world is an uomo and why is it at my door? She thought, rinsing dirt from her hands, and placing the bouquet in the middle of the kitchen table. Her Italian was poor, but she thought he was saying "big man." Maybe Frankie Ramsey had come to tell her some news.

Giuseppe blocked the door with his stocky form.

"*Grazij,* thank you, Giuseppe," she entered the front room and he stepped away from his position as a guard.

A petite woman with hot pink lipstick stood on the porch. "Good afternoon, Miss Smith. Thanks for coming," Beatrix said, wishing for a moment that she wasn't dusted with topsoil, but her appearance hardly mattered.

"You were expecting me?" came the quiet question and her smile quivered.

Expecting was a stretch. Beatrix hoped the woman would be curious and contact her. "I did leave you a note at Mr. Ramsey's apartment and yes, I knew you were cohabitating with Morty when I smelled your perfume there and knew it. It was the same fragrance as you were wearing when we met at the library. Also, it was the color of your lipstick.

The woman stepped back and gestured to a man who could have been Mortimer Ramsey's twin, or a doppelgänger. Just who was this man who moved into sight from a corner of the newly renovated front porch?

The large man didn't smile but stuck out a hand. "Mortimer Ramsey, alive and kicking, ma'am. And with a long, obscene story to tell. Hoping you can and will help me and my wife."

Beatrix blinked. "Miss Smith and Mr. Ramsey?

"Yeah, it's me. Call me Morty. This is the former Miss Smith and now lawfully wedded to me. Darla told me you'd come to the apartment. I was out of town, but she said you'd also been to the library, so we thought we'd visit you." He held Darla's elbow, as if to stabilize himself, and it reminded Beatrix of how a tugboat guides a jumbo cargo ship into a safe harbor.

Mrs. Ramsey smiled adoringly at the oversized man who gripped a Panama hat with his other hand.

"Before you tell me your story, who is that poor soul is who has been identified as you? But wait a moment. We need to go through the house, and you can tell me, in detail, just who is lying in the coroner's morgue." Living and breathing, there stood the New Orleans opportunist, crowding the front of the house, with the librarian hanging on his arm.

Beatrix led the couple through the house, so that if Bunny was spying, and Beatrix felt certain of that, the neighbor would miss out on the rest of their conversation.

Settled in the garden, Morty and his wife on the wrought iron settee, and Beatrix on the opposite side of the little table where the workers always lunched, she looked at both, more closely now.

Darla held his arm. "Morty, want me to explain it to Miss Patterson?"

Whatever "it" was had to be complicated. Beatrix was patient for them to explain, because their truth would explain it all, or at least she hoped that.

"I'll start and you let me know, Darla, if I have forgotten anything."

She nodded and yet still looked like a bird waiting for a cat to pounce on her.

"I know you've met Frankie, Miss Patterson," he began.

"Beatrix."

"Beatrix. I know you're a friend of John Brockman. Heard about you in New Orleans and how you know the truth and worked with the government to oust the Nazi spies and such, so I'm going to be as truthful as I know how. Thing is, I get some of what happened, and I deserved it. But why now?"

"Why exactly did you come to Santa Barbara?" *She wondered about the human trafficking and prostitution theory. Wondered why in the world Morty was confused since this situation was all of his making. Or was it?*

"Lived in the South my whole life, and then I took a trip here to California, decided if I was ever going to make a fresh start, this'd be a good place to do so. You can't get a do-over when everyone assumes you've got an angle, a scheme, a racket, or were going to try to cheat them."

"Why now?"

"Ever since my first wife died, I've been trying to make amends. I stepped away from the rackets and scams, sold flaky businesses, tried to clean up my mess. That said, folks in New

Orleans just assumed it was a new type of swindle of sorts. The property I own there is free and clear, above board. I also tried to be a better father after being a crappy one for most of Frankie's life. The kid had it tough and being caught up, as I was, in the business, he was tossed to the sidelines. He's shunned me each time I've tried. In all honesty, I can't blame the kid. I would have done that to my father if I were in the same situation. I'm ashamed of that, Beatrix. Dead ashamed."

"Why come to me now?" The breeze swayed the Eucalyptus branches on the hillside behind where they gathered as she asked another question. "Who exactly is the dead man impersonating you, dead, in the city's morgue?"

"It's complicated," Morty said knowing he'd have to tell it all. Darla patted his hand.

"The man in the morgue was Frankie's brainstorm, Beatrix," she said. "Frankie showed up at our apartment on Upper State, where you left the note for me. It was three days after we returned from our honeymoon. Bold and demanding, itching for a brawl. I was afraid for Morty, terrified that Frankie might have a gun."

"Can't tolerate guns," Morty interjected. "My daddy was shot in a union workers' strike just after the end of the Great War. Terrible time down at the docks. I promised my mother I'd never touch one. I may be a lot of things, but I am not a liar."

"Then why is there one in the desk in your office in the El Paseo?"

His eyes stretched in shock. "What? No way. Never touched one. Never will, doesn't belong to me."

"Okay, we'll return to that later," Beatrix said, already seeing a pattern and waiting to hear the entire unfortunate story.

"Hired a private yacht for a week cruise along the Mexican Rivera, warm and relaxing, and the Mrs. and I talked about moving to Ensenada, still might now with the law after me," Morty squeezed a smile.

"Frankie shows up at the apartment and pushes me aside to barge in," Darla looks to Morty and then continues. "He's ranting and beating a fist into his other hand."

"I sat down in the living room," Morty continued, "And he let me have it with his demands. He needed money, big money, and he needed me to die. I thought he was going to kill me for that insurance policy I took out., I thought it would eventually give him a nest egg or independence from the people who control him in Chicago. Maybe get away, make a new start like me. I never expected him to want to kill me for it."

Darla pushed a tear off her highly made-up face and Beatrix realized that she was older than it seemed. "Frankie gave Morty a choice. Either pretend he's dead so he'd get the cash, or Frankie would kill him for it."

"The kid was desperate. I tried to reason with him. He let it slip that he'd gambled himself into debt and the guys in Chicago were not going to play nice anymore. I never doubted that was true. He was sweating bullets."

"But, Beatrix," Darla added, "He had this irrational plan. He'd been to some bar the day before and there was a fat, old wino sitting on the pavement in front it. He gave the guy a dollar, went in, had a beer. Apparently, he went to use the toilet then walked to the alley for a smoke. Frankie said there was the same geezer, propped against some trash cans."

"Frankie told me he checked for a pulse, found none, and hatched the plan. He brought his car around to the alley, loaded the unfortunate soul in the trunk, and drove off with him, no one the wiser," Morty said. "The plan, as he yelled at us that morning, was to clean up the gent, dress him in my clothes, string him up to look like a suicide, and knock a chair over. He went straight to my closet and pulled out a suit fresh from the tailor. I hadn't even touched it. Guess he dressed the sad old guy to look like me and then strung the dead body up in my apartment's garage.

"Then he drove straight back to Louisiana, after anonymously tipping off the police. All I had to do was disappear. I was happy to, anything to get my kid out of trouble, even if I thought he was making it worse for himself. Payback is ugly, but I accepted it. We accepted it." He looked toward his wife and they nodded in unison.

Beatrix listened carefully, "Why go along with this mad scheme, Morty?"

"You're an eye-catching lady, high quality, and I'm guessing had respectable parents who cared about you," he said. "Who would you have become if no one wanted you and every time you tried to ask a question or attempt anything, you got slammed down, even figuratively? That's what I did to Frankie. Darla and I talked it through. I figured I owed him this and a whole lot more. I have plenty of dough, tucked safely in banks in Mexico and the Caribbean. I closed the talent agency because it was a long shot at best, although I got a couple of nibbles on would-be movie stars. Our idea was that we'd disappear, Darla and me. Frankie'd get the goons off his back, the wino was dead anyhow. What could it hurt?"

"Sounds like a foolproof scheme, Morty. What happened?" Beatrix asked.

"Frankie. He wasn't satisfied with the million bucks; he wanted all of my estate, or he would tell the police that I'd killed the wino. He'd say I hatched the stunt, and I forced him to take part. Who would the police believe? A calculating quasi-gangster from the Big Easy, or a budding actor trying to make a name in Hollywood? He had more dirt, about some dirty deal's way in the past, said he'd throw those in, unless I agreed. When he found me yesterday, hiding in a dump hotel in Lompoc after he threatened Darla to get out my whereabouts, he forced me to write a suicide note. Needed that to give to my executor in New Orleans to get the money from the policy."

"You know the police report clearly states it was death by hanging," she replied.

"They've got it wrong, then."

"No, Morty." Beatrix frowned and shook her head.

"Impossible. The guy was dead when Frankie hung him. He told us. He promised us that."

"Sorry, Morty and Darla, that's just not true. The victim might have been in an alcoholic stupor but that's not what caused his death. He was alive when he was hung."

Beatrix connected the dots in her mind. "Would you be willing, later today, to come to the police station with me and tell the detective your story?"

"No, Beatrix, I can't," he gulped.

"Would you rather be tried for murder, Morty? Would you let that happen, Darla?"

Silence stretched. They looked at one another and then Morty whispered, "What do you want us to do?"

"Okay, I need to get your fingerprints on a piece of paper. Then I'm going back to your office and gathering the files on the shelf that I saw Frankie touch, and he fingered a cobalt blue glass vase when we were there the other day. I'll take them to a detective I have spoken with at the Santa Barbara Police Department, and we'll see whose fingerprints are on the jacket buttons of that suit. You promise you didn't touch it, Morty?"

"Yes, ma'am, I didn't have a chance to."

"Darla, is that true?"

"I brought it home with me from the tailor shop, after I finished work at the library and hung it in the closet. It was still in the paper package when Frankie grabbed it," she said.

"Give me a few hours. I think you and Darla should stay here, Morty. Make yourself at home. My workers are busy, but I'll let them know you're a guest. I'll call the house after I talk with Detective Rodriguez. Promise me you'll answer my telephone when it rings."

Beatrix drove the old station wagon to the El Paseo. The door to Morty's talent agency was still unlocked. Out of curiosity, she looked into the middle desk drawer. No gun, as suspected. She put on the cotton gloves that, years back, she'd worn to church, and quickly grabbed a few files she'd seen Frankie thumb through, and the bright blue vase. With the finger print sample from Morty already secured in her messenger bag, along with the new evidence, she walked the block to the police station.

At first, Detective Rodriguez laughed off her theory, excused herself for less than ten minutes and returned with a serious face. "I just talked with some people in New Orleans. Honey, you are the real deal. Said to listen to you even if the theories seem hairbrained."

"Thanks, I think." Beatrix asked her to have the lab do a fingerprint test on the buttons on the suit of the person, previously assumed to be Mortimer Ramsey, and then take the fingerprints of the person in the morgue. She gave her the papers and the vase with Frankie's fingerprints, hopefully clear, and the ones that Morty provided, asking that they all be compared.

"This is going to take a bit of time. Fancy some Chinese food? Good place near Ott's Hardware," she suggested and then yelled across the large room, "Maria, company's here, Beatrix Patterson. Have some dinner with us."

The restaurant wasn't busy, and the women felt they could talk above a whisper, but only on mundane topics, definitely nothing to do with the murders. The vegetable stir fry with shrimp that Beatrix ordered was fresh and delicious. It reminded her of the meals Thomas had cooked. Then she silently snapped at herself for thinking of being jilted by a crazy scientist, even if she loved him.

How could I have been so wrong about his devotion? The women were chatting and didn't see her, or ignored it, when Beatrix pushed a tear off her cheek.

They were having a second cup of Jasmine tea when the young coroner that Beatrix had met previously came into the restaurant, asked to speak to the detective, and they walked outside. Hands were waved, the young man flinched, and Detective Rodriguez returned.

"Damn if you weren't right, Beatrix. The fingerprints on the stiff's jacket buttons are from Frankie Ramsey. There are a few others, but we assume they're from the tailor. Definitely not the guy on the slab in the morgue.

"This is murder, in my opinion, since the coroner, who might drink a bit too much but still knows his stuff, said for sure that the death was from the rope around the guy's neck. I sent a squad car to the Hotel Santa Barbara. Most likely, we'll charge him and hear Frankie's version, but it feels water-tight to me. You said Morty would come in and give his statement? We won't be charging him with anything. As it seems, from what you said, Frankie was blackmailing his father."

CHAPTER 29

IT WAS NEARING MIDNIGHT when Beatrix pulled the Woody back into the driveway. Darla and Morty were still at the police station, Frankie was in custody, and the police were trying to find out who the unfortunate man lying in the morgue might be, as he certainly was not Mortimer Ramsey. The only reason they'd assumed it was Mortimore Ramsey was because Morty's wallet had been tucked into the man's back pocket. A few heads would roll for that one, yet perhaps, lessons would be learned.

When Beatrix finally left the station, she'd been informed that Frankie "sang like a cannery," according to Detective Rodriguez. Morty would be asked to stay in the city for the court arraignment and perhaps the trial. He just kept saying, "I'll stick by the kid, that's my justice for what happened to the drunk."

Beatrix had tried to disagree, but thought maybe in time, Morty and Darla would realize that Frankie was an adult and while his upbringing was unhappy, they were not to blame.

She walked through the house, touching the places where work still needed to be done, wood replaced, or ancient paint removed, like the banister. The built-in cabinets in the dining room had the glass that was original to the house, with flaws and bubbles, and she loved the imperfections. "Imperfect like me. Some judge of character," she said out loud. "Good to know that Thomas is the kind of man who will flee like a bat out of hell with the slimmest and silliest excuse ever. A dream. He left me nearly at the alter because of a stupid dream."

She opened the window craving fresh air, which did not help. Her resentment was too hot to be inside. She walked through the moonlit garden, smelled a Sally Holmes rose, and touched the dew on the Shasta daisies still in full bloom. The stars twinkled and the moon looked like a slice of cantaloupe. A million stars twinkled, and she thought, yet again, of Thomas, now probably on a ship heading to Liverpool and back to his stupid, precious laboratory in Cambridge.

She walked toward the front, meaning to sit on the front porch steps, listen to the crickets, and feel the breeze from the sea and put the events of the evening into some type of order, when she heard a voice.

"You whoo? Beatrix? Is that you?" Mrs. Turney's squeaky voice echoed in the night, and she waved enthusiastically from her porch, her binoculars strung around the neck of her bathrobe.

There was no possibility for Beatrix to hide in the box hedge or dash behind the sprawling oleander, still with a few clusters of hot pink flowers and visible in the scant moonlight.

"Good evening, Bunny," she called back and hoped that would be the end, but in reality, she knew that she'd been caught, would be offered herbal tea, and would find it hard to extract herself from the elderly lady's chatty presence. "You're up late." She didn't move from the three-foot-tall box hedge that separated the properties. If she crossed that line, she would have been entrapped for heaven knows how long, and she unexpectedly felt too fatigued to manage much conversation.

"A bit chilly, but you know, I never tire of waiting for the bats to fly by," she waved the binoculars.

Beatrix had the feeling that she was spying on her neighbors rather than nocturnal creatures. "See you tomorrow then," she called out.

"Oh, dear, would you mind terribly moving my trash bins to the street tomorrow? Your precious husband always does it for me, the dear, but now that he's traveling, well, I don't know what I will do without his help."

"I'd be happy to," she said. *She never misses anything and obviously saw Thomas leave early yesterday.* Beatrix never corrected the lady that she and Thomas weren't married yet and didn't then either.

"Oh, and my dear, why not come for tea tomorrow afternoon like your husband always does while you're studying those dull, old psychology manuals he's always going on about?"

What in the world was Thomas doing, telling the nosy neighbor their life stories? If he was here, instead of being out in the Atlantic Ocean, I'd give him an earful. There were so many unanswered questions about the neighbor and her involvement in the Onus Organista, even if it was circumstantial. It made her feel naked with her personal life up for examination.

"Bunny that sounds, um, interesting. However, I've invited a few friends over for an informal garden party." She thought back to what her new friend Jo had shared.

Bunny stood and covered a yawn. "How lovely of you to invite me, and I'll bring tea. I've been working on some new varieties, and we could have a tasting of sorts, like I've heard is done out in Lompoc at the vineyards with wine. Although I wouldn't know about that as alcohol has never touched these lips."

Beatrix wanted to scream, "Noooooo." Yet then an idea began to emerge, sketchy at best, but perhaps it could work. "About two, then?"

"Why you are such a dear and so gracious. Especially for someone with your colorful history."

There was nothing courteous about a comeback fitting someone with Beatrix's colorful history, so she just said good night. She dropped the possible insult and instead thought of entrapment. Maybe when Bunny was sipping tea with the others, she'd let something slip, or the friends would make her uncomfortable in some way, and she'd reveal her role in the splinter group of the Women's Christian Temperance Union.

Beatrix's new friend Jo, president of the WCTU, hopefully, might make Bunny uneasy and possibly edgy, if Bunny did have anything to hide. She smiled as she slipped on her nightgown, crawled into bed, and slammed her fist a dozen times into Thomas's pillow. "I am feeling better," she said out loud and clobbered the pillow another half dozen times.

CHAPTER 30

THOMAS WASN'T QUITE READY TO FLY aboard a commercial plane, one of his phobias, and opted for the long train journey between Santa Barbara and New York City. He was stoic about it. He ate stale sandwiches on dry bread, forced down tea that should have been tossed in the sink, and slept badly every night, hearing other passengers in the Pullman cars partying, snoring, or making love to their partners. Unquestionably, crying babies didn't help, nor did the occasional disagreement between those who had too much to drink in the club car and rambled and bounced along the narrow passageway toward their own accommodations. The train was either hot and stuffy or cold and far too smoky as everyone and their aunt were puffing on cigarettes, something he loathed. *I will have to discard these clothes when I get to England. I'll never get the stench out of them,* he thought and nearly growled at a young woman in the compartment with him, smoking one Camel after another.

He was glum. He felt stupid. He was angry at himself, which is the worst kind of irritation as there's no one to reproach but oneself.

Sleet met him when he disembarked at Union Station in New York. People around him swirled, and he stood in the middle of the huge depot wondering how he could have been so stupid, so self-centered, so ludicrous. *You've made your bed and it's without Beatrix, Tommy boy,* he told himself, using the name that a teacher at his childhood school had named him to embarrass the child. It had worked. He felt humiliated, disgraced, and laughable. Except it wasn't funny.

He looked around the station. There was a long row of telephone booths against a well. Service members, returning from overseas, lined up, possibly to call a sweetheart they hadn't talked with since being deployed by the War Department. The men and women smiled and joked, nudged a shoulder, and shared a smoke.

Thomas studied his fancy British shoes, sat on a bench, and looked at his watch. "It's four in the morning in Santa Barbara. Beatrix will be in bed, our bed, and she will have forgotten all about me by now." Knowing that wasn't true, he whispered it just to make himself feel worse. It succeeded. Thomas was stunned at his rash behavior, although thinking back to his time in New Orleans, he'd gone off the rails before. He would have blamed it on love, but without love, would he be happy? Could he be happy without Beatrix as his wife? That's exactly what he was jeopardizing by dashing across the country and the Atlantic because of a dream. He sat stunned, unable to move or make a decision.

Then he saw a small man with a woman and two children, all carrying bulky suitcases. He saw they were Chinese, and they looked exhausted, confused, and frightened. Thomas understood what it felt like to be lost, much like himself, but they were literately lost. They seemed unable to move and crowds flowed around him. He'd felt that way in a strange land when he'd traveled before the war and empathized with the fright, confusion, and dismay they had to be feeling.

He walked up to them and first in Mandarin, then Cantonese, introduced himself. They looked at him, tried to smile, and the children hid behind their parents.

Finally, he tried English. The couple and the children continued to stare until Thomas said, "Welcome to America. I am Ling," in the Wuhan dialect. It was going to be his last attempt after a few other linguistic dead ends. The dialect, also known as the Hankou dialect, belongs to the Wu-Tian branch of Southwest Mandarin spoken in Wuhan, Tianmen, and the surrounding areas in Hubei, China. The Wuhan dialect had limited mutual intelligibility with Standard Chinese.

The husband and wife bowed and nodded, and told him how great America was to send someone to the train station to help them. "We are lost, and we do not know how to get to Pittsburgh." Pittsburgh sounded a lot like the noise one makes when gargling.

"Yes, America is great, but I am merely a traveler too, from London, but my ancestral homeland is China."

They'd arrived by ship that morning, an arduous journey through the Panama Canal. Their directions, written in English which the man handed Thomas, were to help them get to Grand Central Station and then on the train to Pennsylvania. Thomas checked with the ticket clerk and there would not be another train for Pittsburgh until noon the next day. When they heard this, the wife's eyes widened, and Thomas could only imagine her thinking that the family would spend the day, and the entire night, in the chaos and crowds of the station. The directions assumed that they'd go to the station and immediately get on a train. However, it had taken hours for the ship to clear customs, hence they were late to the train depot.

"Do you have American money?" he asked.

The husband said, "We only have English money. I can give it all to you."

"No, no, no," Thomas said. "That's not what I mean. I was hoping you could stay in a hotel until boarding your train tomorrow morning." He looked at the tired faces of the boy and girl, not more than three and four. "You need a clean and safe place to stay where the children are comfortable, and you can relax. Let's go to my hotel and we'll get you settled there."

Thomas loaded the suitcases in a yellow taxi and the family in the back seat. He sat next to the cabbie. "Waldorf Astoria, my good man," he instructed, having booked the hotel before leaving Santa Barbara. It would be just one room and one bed, but the family would be content. He could not, would not, leave them to their own devices in New York City.

At the hotel, a doorman opened the taxi door and the family spilled out, their eyes wide with amazement at the sounds and smells of the city. On the drive from Grand Central Station to the hotel, Thomas learned that the husband was a Chinese historian of importance and was going to teach and do research at Carnegie Mellon University.

It took a matter of minutes for the clerk at the desk to check them in, Thomas paying for it all, and then they were shown to the room. As the family peeked into every corner of the luxury room, Thomas wrote a note for the husband to give to a taxi driver the next day, and another for anyone at Grand Central Station to ensure the family would get on the 7:30 am train to Pittsburg. Finally, he called room service and requested meals be sent up to the room, and explained it all to the exhausted family in their own dialect.

Something stopped Thomas from leaving as he'd planned, although he felt intrusive, viewing this close-knit family. He sat at the desk, hands folded on his thighs, and looked at the joy on the little boy's face, playing some kind of word game with pad and pencil and the father encouraging him, finally hugging him. The mom sat on the bed as the daughter cuddled on her lap. He'd seen the Mona Lisa and this mother was more beautiful than that painting as she sang to her little girl. He'd seen affection like that from his mum and grandmother. He had hoped to see that adoration on his own beloved's face while she cradled their little ones.

His own father was complex and smart, yet, he always had made time for Thomas's endless questions, reading books to the boy far about his level and explaining every detail. It was like that with Thomas's sisters and their father. Thomas always imagined he'd be the same kind of dad. One that was available.

Except now, he'd screwed everything up that was good and pure and lovely in his life based on nothing more than a preposterous dream. Or a nightmare. *Silly, stupid, stoic Brit,* he scolded himself. *What have I done?* But he knew. *I'm gutted now. Forever.* He'd ruined his chances to be in an intimate relationship with the smartest, sassiest, and most intelligent woman he'd ever known along with never being able to have a closeness with little ones, one that could carry their children safely into the future, whatever the times ahead might hold.

His body and brain felt heavy as he left. He'd never forget this sweet family.

The frown was bitter on his lips. Thomas had planned and yes, hoped that once he'd concluded the work at Cambridge, he would make it all up to Beatrix. She'd be so proud and thankful that clean energy could be accessible to the entire world. Even places that couldn't generate electricity, or so the dream indicated, would have it. He stood in the lobby, unable to make a decision on where he should go or what to do next. He focused on the snatches of what he could remember about the dream, of the chalkboard with his calculations, of the realization that the work he'd done with atoms could be transposed to this energy source, so novel, so powerful. Yet, each time he tried to see the blackboard, even with his eyes tightly shut, pieces of the numbers and letters, and at times the entire formula wiggled, evaporated, then returned, as if teasing him, taunting him. In reality, it was all scribbling, all gibberish. *Bloody dodgy,* he thought and wanted to scream it.

Would it be too late when he returned? How long could it take him to complete his work? If, in fact, any of what he'd conjured up were true, which became less and less valid as the minutes stretched. He didn't seem to be able to move from that spot on the hotel's carpet or get out of the way of the swirling crowd.

More importantly, would Beatrix be waiting after his abrupt flight from their house? He'd spent his entire life working, shuttered away in a dreary lab, and this was the ultimate goal: to save humanity. *She'll have to listen, she'll have to understand,* he argued with his subconscious. Yet, if he listened to his heart, which was an entirely new concept for a scientist, even one madly in love, doubt was written all over these notions.

Some mistakes can be ignored in an intimate relationship. He ticked things off like when one partner likes a full English breakfast and the other only wants coffee, fruit, and a croissant. Or if they're pledged to opposing football teams. Yet could this be ignored?

He was still preoccupied when he went to hotel registration, where previously he'd changed his reservation from his own to the names of the Chinese family. The young clerk behind the desk shook his head. "My deepest apologies, Dr. Ling." The young man tried to get the attention of his supervisor, a matronly woman, but with the posture of a prison warden, who was explaining the overcrowded situation to a sailor and his girl, practically draped across his shoulders. "Well, sir," he swallowed. "It's the end of the war. You see with all the returning G.I.s, we're sold out and that seems to be the story with every other hotel in the city."

Thomas felt empty. "Now what? I'm homeless and clueless as to what to do," he said out loud.

The clerk looked aghast as if he should be able to pull a rabbit from a hat, or close to that. Thomas nodded, turned, and walked out to a frigid November gust of wind. Park Avenue, as always, bustled even in the brisk breeze. The doorman offered to get a cab and Thomas handed him a tip.

"To the wharf, if you would," he directed the cabbie. He tossed his satchel into the backseat and obediently followed it. With luck, the staff of the ocean liner he'd take the next day would find him temporary accommodations. It seemed the only solution unless he wanted to sit the night in the lobby of the Waldorf Astoria among happy couples, brimming with the thrill of being reunited. That was not a heartening thought. Through the agonizingly long and congested drive, Thomas pictured Beatrix and the last time he'd seen her, snuggled in their bed, her forehead warm and soft when he'd kissed her goodbye. She smelled of roses. Was it her perfume or a breeze from the garden? Her hair was tangled in a mass of auburn that begged for his fingers.

He swore, which never happened to the emotionally impassive scientist. Although lately, he realized that emotions had gotten the best of him, so he fought the urge. Yet, recalling that moment, Thomas felt certain that Beatrix had been awake. "Playing hedgehog? Or is it possum?" he thought he'd been getting clever understanding American slang. He stood at the door and there was nothing more to say about his decision. It would have been wrong to push the issue, as he had to go. Instead, he grabbed the satchel, walked out, and did not look back. What if he had? What would have happened? Would she have opened her arms to him or tossed him second-story story window of their house?

All at once, Thomas knew what he had to do, and it would take more courage than he thought possible to muster. He yelled, "Damn it to bloody hell." He slammed a fist into his palm. "Stop this cab right now. Stop, I say. Are you deaf man? Stop."

The cab screeched to a stop and the cabbie hopped out, cutting the engine, and grabbing the keys. "You're a screwball, mister. Get outta my cab right now or I'm calling a cop."

"Wait, no, we need to go to the airport at once."

"No way. Get out of my taxi and find another schmuck to take you." And the driver pulled Thomas from the cab and threw his valise at him, before driving away.

CHAPTER 31

BEATRIX BUSIED HERSELF organizing the garden, moving pots of Jade plants, and sweeping the patio. The November day was fit for Goldilocks, not too warm, not too cool, and she wore a light white long-sleeved cotton shirt and her favorite denim jeans, a cowboy-inspired belt around her middle. The sun felt safe and reassuring on her shoulders. The workers took Sunday off, lounging on the beach, or enjoying the city. She liked being the only person in the house. "My house, all mine, and darn Thomas to Jupiter and back. I am fine without him. I will be just fine without him and his crazy, wild and reactionary emotions," she said raking a pile of liquid amber leaves into a trash can. She knew it was a lie, but it made her feel better declaring it to the trees and scrubs.

By two, the garden planters were pristine, the walkways were swept, and Beatrix had taken pots of hot pink geraniums and placed them around the courtyard in the back of the house. She dragged out an ancient coffee table from storage, added a red checkered calico tablecloth, and gathered a few wild yellow daises, and put them into a fancy cut-glass vase she'd found in the attic. She'd taken a break and walked to the Danish bakery on Milpas Street, loading up on an array of cookies and delicate opera cake with its many layers.

Mrs. Turney insisted she would bring tea, but Beatrix preferred coffee, hence, she'd make a pot for those who were like-minded. Although in her heart she knew the neighbor was somehow complicit in the death of the two women in the morgue, feeling never would stand up in court.

Beatrix fussed, arranging the plates of cookies, until Henry showed up. "You've done a bang-up job, Miss Beatrix. No Thomas? The fool will be back. He'll come to his senses."

"I wonder."

"No wondering, miss, he's a fool, which I established a few years ago in New Orleans when he would not let heaven or hell stop him from finding you, nonetheless he's a first-rate guy. I might not have his fancy degrees, however, I know people and I've seen the good ones and the bad ones. He'll come to his senses, and I just hope it's not too late. Or is it already?" Henry inquired quietly.

"Yes, that's a good question and right now, my friend, I don't have an answer. Wait. That sounds like the rest of our company coming around the side garden as I'd asked them to."

Detectives Stella Rodriguez and Maria Hernandez Davies strolled up the path, and Beatrix came down the front steps to meet them. "So glad you both could make it, and I think you'll enjoy the company. We're sitting in the back garden, and I'll bring the lemonade and coffee out shortly. Just follow the brick path around to the side."

Then came Jo and Sam, with Sammy on his trike. Following them was a tall woman who commanded attention. Jo introduced her, "Beatrix, this is my favorite sister Louisa."

Louisa grinned. "That only sounds like a compliment, Beatrix. We're the only two girls and there are five brothers who constantly included us in their adventures and games. Give me a basketball and I can show up all of them, and I played tackle football since I could walk. We girls had to stick together, or they would have created a revolt."

"Sammy takes after all of our brothers put together," Jo said. Her husband, obviously not the talkative partner, just laughed and hugged the child.

For a second time, Beatrix showed the friends to the rear of the house and returned to the kitchen to gather glasses and plates, when banging against the front door echoed through the home. "Someone's impatient," she said, leaving the dishes and dashing through the house.

"You called to say my wife would be here. I demand to see her, my Mary," former Major Herbert Davies puffed out his chest, clenched his fists, and scowled, making his bulbous nose seem even more protruding. "I hid in the bushes across the street, watching her arrive, with another woman. Miss Patterson, I command you take me to her at once. I need to see Mary. Now."

"Now, Mr. Davies, when we talked on the phone you assured me that you'd keep your temper under control. Yet, here you are shouting. Your promise that you'd stop these outbursts was the only reason I told you she'd be here," Beatrix lifted her right hand placing her palm out, and stood straighter. "This is a garden party, a gathering of friends, and I will not allow you to rush at her, browbeat your wife and shout ultimatums. We are not at war. You cannot command me, nor your wife, to do anything. Should you make a scene, well, there are two police officers among my guests and either one of them would be happy to arrest you. I will not be bullied. Ever."

"Well, you can't talk to me like..."

"Yes, I can. Those are the rules, sir, and follow them, or turn and leave." She saw his eyes and the glint of anger faded.

She didn't move and she watched the man step back as much of the braggadocio seeped out. He looked smaller, older, grayer.

"Now, if you can be civilized and polite, and I warn you I will not tolerate anything but that, then you may join our party."

"Thank you, ma'am," he nodded, and as Beatrix stepped aside, he walked through the house.

It took her a few more minutes to gather the glasses and plates as Jo and Louisa had already brought the lemonade and coffee to the table. Standing at the back door, Beatrix looked at the tableau. First to Louisa and Henry sitting aside from the others, but just by a bit, and talking and laughing. Beatrix never thought of herself as a matchmaker, but they did look like they were enjoying the introduction.

"Get a move on, Silver. High ho, Silver," Sammy bellowed with sheer, four-year-old imagination, as his tricycle became the cowboy sensation Lone Ranger's trusty stead. "Giddy up, big fellow." He made the "horse" maneuver in circles around Davies' legs and the man became rooted to the middle of the patio, just staring at his wife, somehow unable to speak until she said, "Herb, sit down."

"Mary, my dearest Mary," he swallowed the emotions that nearly burst into outrage again. He moved toward her, and Beatrix watched Henry begin to stand, ready to settle any marital dispute. Then less than a foot away, he knelt and steepled his hands, almost in prayer. "You have every right to slap me or worse."

"You're right, Herb. For the millionth time, my name is Maria. Not Mary. Maria. Got it? I'm glad you're here because we do need to talk. I know you've been following me and that's got to stop. You're getting in the way of my profession."

He gulped as if he had to swallow an entire watermelon. Whole. "Your profession? Your job? You've got to be kidding me. This is ludicrous. You are too, Mary." He bounded to his feet and instantly Henry was by his side, a massive hand on the man's shoulder. It was a warning not to act out the aggression that was all over his face. Davies shouted, "You're a hooker. What kind of occupation is that?"

"Herb, you need to take a deep breath and listen," Maria's palm came close to his face, a gesture that stopped him. "I've always calculated that eighty percent of the problems in our relationship was that you did not listen. Do you even have any clue as to why I'm here in Santa Barbara?"

"Selling sex," he spit the words, but in a whisper, aware, apparently, that there was a child present. However, the boy was now coaxing his trike up and down the sidewalk toward the front garden at a breakneck speed for someone who was four.

"Do you have any idea that I used to work for the Federal Bureau of Investigation? Or that I've been an uncover police officer for the last four years?"

Now Davies did sit and might have fallen on the patio if Henry hadn't glided a sturdy wrought iron chair close to him. The man, if anything, seemed more bewildered. He pulled on his necktie and ripped it off as if it were choking him. "Police? FBI? You couldn't. Why are you lying? You were home with the kids and never held a job. I would have known. I knew everything about you. Then when we left Washington and we were in Louisiana, you had the house and committees and little trips with your lady friends."

"Herby, I tried countless times to explain what I was doing. You were so caught up in the military and your own ego that you rarely listened and then pushed off my opinions and thoughts until I gave up." She stood and faced him. "Then I gave up on us."

"I'm sick, Maria, and I need you," came the whine.

"No, Herb, you need nursing care or a caregiver to live with you. You only want me to fill in that void, and quite honestly, that ship left the harbor about ten years ago."

"You can't do this to me. Please, Mary," he begged.

"Again, listen to what you said. My name is Maria. Oh, come on, Herb. I'm not ruthless or hardhearted as you seem to believe. I'm going to help you find some comfortable lodging for now. I know you've been staying at a dump of a studio apartment in Hollywood. I've already made arrangements and I'll help when I can."

"Then you will be with me?" he asked.

"I'll be with you. As a longtime friend. I'm still legally your wife, but I will never be your nurse, nor will I be there to care for you as this disease gets worse. You need professional help for that and after all these years of neglecting my career and myself, I plan to do that in the future."

"The doctors say it'll be bad, Mary, um Maria," he quietly corrected himself. "Do the kids know about how you work in law enforcement and as a hooker?"

"Yes, Herb, they know. They know I'm a cop. Look at me, Herb, and try to remember. I am not a prostitute, not a hooker. This is a job. It's an undercover sting operation. When it is over, I'll go back to being a regular policewoman. I'm a detective with the Santa Barbara Police Department."

He looked more confused. "Will you explain that to me again? You work for the police?"

The group longed to help or run from such an intimate glimpse of a relationship crumbling. It felt too private to watch. Then Detective Rodriguez joined Maria, and together, they bid everyone goodbye, escorting the confused ex-army officer out of the garden, each holding him by the elbow.

"What'll happen with them?" Jo asked.

"Maria is incredibly resourceful. She told me, when I invited her here after asking permission to tell her husband she'd be at the party, that she's arranged accommodations at a care home near the beach. Their adult children have pledged to assist her for whatever happens next."

"It'll be okay, then?" Louisa asked, shaking her head in dismay. "I'm just finishing my residency to become an internist, yet before that, I briefly studied the effects of dementia. It's cruel."

As the threesome turned the corner of the house to leave, Mrs. Turney waddled up the path, balancing two jumbo teapots, jingling on a large silver tray.

Sam and Henry jumped up to help. "We'll take that, madam," Henry said, and Sam moved the fragile tea pots to the middle of the table.

"Oh," she swallowed. "I didn't realize you'd have so many, um, people here."

Beatrix watched as the elderly lady's eyes went from one guest to the next and then the next, and obviously, finding

Beatrix was the whitest person in the group, focused on her. However, she seemed frightened and started to step back.

Beatrix was faster and took her arm. "Please, sit down everyone. It's time to enjoy the cookies and company. Dear friends, this is Mrs. Turney, my neighbor, and she is known for the unique herbal teas she makes. Thomas," she took a breath, "Thomas always shared a cup with her right after lunch while I was studying. It was rather a ritual."

Sam moved away, sensing, Beatrix knew, that the woman was not comfortable encircled with people of color. Beatrix continued to introduce her friends one by one. *There's always a tell*, Beatrix thought so experienced at reading microfacial expressions and body language, *when a person believes that their skin color makes them superior*. A pang of pity for the woman touched her. *What else is in her heart, like convincing those women to kill themselves, if it's even true?*

"We've met before," Jo said. "But I don't think you've been introduced to our Sammy."

The child's trike squealed to a stop, inches from Bunny's brown, button-up shoes, not fashionable since the 1930s. "How do you do, ma'am?" he asked and stood as tall as the little boy can, sticking out a pint-sized hand.

Beatrix watched closely as Bunny was caught making a decision. Instead of shaking the child's hand, she patted him on the shoulder. "What a sweet pet," she remarked and then reached across and took a lady finger cookie from the table, placing it in the middle of the ornate gold-trimmed dessert plate that looked like Limoges. Beatrix had salvaged them from a box of broken plates before the kitchen renovation.

"He's a sweetie," Jo said. "Are you still active in all sorts of organizations, Mrs. Turney?"

"A few, mostly from the old days, Josephine. There's so much good work, good Christian women's work for me to do, although now that I'm getting older, those who were committed to the core values of morality along with me are not as vital as we once were."

"I have not seen you at a WCTU meeting in a few years," Jo cocked her head. "What of that other group you were involved with? Were they called the AOs?"

Beatrix would forever be grateful for her friend's determination and bravery. She waited, but Bunny did not. "My goodness, no. It's affectionately called OO, you might try to remember that, my dear. The Onus Organista is active and still doing God's work," she sat up straighter.

Beatrix noted that Bunny used the present tense for the splinter organization.

Bunny smiled, but her tone was condescending. "I doubt you'd understand our mission. Briefly, our goals are to recruit young women, well, of a certain type of young woman," she waved a hand dismissing Louisa because she wasn't white, at least that's what Beatrix, Jo, and the group assumed.

"Please tell me, Bunny, about the Onus Organista. I really want to be involved in helping our community grow in the right way," Beatrix said, lying, as there was no way she'd join the contemptible group.

Bunny quickly nibbled yet another lady finger cookie followed by three spritz cookies heavy with apricot jam. "We only select a few candidates a year, all women, of course, as men cannot be trusted with these mandates." She didn't even blink with that statement. "Nonetheless, Beatrix, I will keep you mind. Our work is to protect the moral conduct of the city, make known those who favor living an unscrupulous life." She huffed.

Beatrix smiled and asked sweetly. "Do all the women in the group have those circles entwined on their breasts?"

Bunny's right hand flew to her chest, and she pulled up the lacy blouse around her throat. "Whatever are you talking about?"

"Thomas told me all about your little chats and mentioned that you were wearing a rather low-cut blouse one afternoon and he remarked about the tattoos. I saw your tattoo the other day, as well, when you were leaning over in the garden. I've seen that same tat on the breasts of others, girls no more than twenty."

"I say cheers and amen that these young women have taken up the OOs battle cry of virginity, of the highest moral conduct, and obedience."

Beatrix shook her head. "I am confused, Bunny. If being a virgin is a requirement, and you're a widow, does that mean that you've never had intimate relationships with a man?

Bunny's spine straightened and indignation etched her words. "Someone like you could never understand. However, I am happy to explain. You see, with my widowhood and years of celibacy, I am now regarded as a born-again virgin. That's part of our code of conduct. Why I had the pleasure of writing it into our manifesto."

Beatrix sat still. Bees visited late-blooming flowers and clouds scurried overhead, but all she could think about right then in the garden was that every inclination she felt pointed to the fact that Bunny was behind the deaths of the girls who had jumped off the cliffs in Gaviota. Proving it was a different matter. As she pondered her next question, from where she was sitting, she saw Detective Rodriguez once more behind the side gate waiting to see what would transpire. Waiting to see if Bunny Turney would become vicious.

"I'm afraid that will leave me out, Bunny, as Thomas and I plan to have a big family." She turned to Jo, "He says we have to fill up the bedrooms. I'm sticking with three kids."

Jo grimaced. "How do you recruit young women, Bunny, as we could certainly use some inventive minds and hands with the WCTU?"

The older woman squirmed. "You could take some lessons. I personally visit with ladies who are new in town, give them a place to live as we own a cottage in Montecito, and then help them find employment, as long as they're willing to follow the OOs rules, which are to be moral women."

It's now or never, Beatrix thought. "I met one of your ladies the other day, at that cottage. She had fallen, had been pushed by someone, and before she died in my arms, she said 'the pimp' did it to her. Truth be told, Bunny, aren't you a pimp getting girls to attract men and then you entrap them and blackmail them, or you'll expose them, just like in the past?"

Bunny flew to her feet. "How dare you? How could you ever call me a pimp, why, they do it willingly, and they want to be good Christian women in our city."

Beatrix grabbed her arm. "And if they're not, or if you find they've lied to you about their virginity, what then?"

"Let go of me." She tried to yank away. "If they go against the OOs rules, there are certain protocols. There are ways they can redeem themselves through ritual cleansing."

"What? Like jumping off the cliffs on the beach? They are released from your so-called iniquities if they jump and don't die. Are you saying they're then absolved of their misdeeds?" Beatrix felt her face get red, and her anger toward the silly, obstinate, and morally deviant woman soar.

"I have no comment and you are rude to even ask. Shame on you. You all couldn't possibly understand how to live a good and moral life. You are included, Beatrix. You're just like them," she waved a hand and scowled. "I knew your mother, Jennie Patterson, and I know a huge, unfortunate thing about the likes of you. If your mother wouldn't tell you, well, I will. You're not white. You're Mulatto."

CHAPTER 32

BUNNY WAS SHOUTING and her fury appeared in blotchy red spots on her face. "You're no better than the rest of these people as your mother was illegitimate and promiscuity between a black man and a white woman. You are no better than them and would never, could never, be a part of the OOs or any virtuous part of society."

"I'm proud of it, Mrs. Turney. I'm honored of my heritage and the mix of my ancestors. You may have known Mother, but apparently, not well enough that you realized she'd never have kept anything from me. She told me, finally, about my adoption and my heritage when I was ten."

Beatrix towered over Bunny now looking somewhat like an elderly angel in the chair on the porch. "Now, please go. I'll leave your tea pots on your front porch and my friend here, Detective Rodriguez, will show you out."

The silence was intense until Henry cleared his throat. "Think if you sell the house right now, Miss Beatrix, you won't have to tell anyone about the fruitcake lady next door. Bet you can get some good money now that a person can actually live here, well, almost live here."

"Wish it were that easy, wish she'd confessed with Stella standing there looking all police detective."

Stella returned. "You're right, Beatrix. I'll go have a word with her tomorrow about this outburst."

They tried to laugh and enjoy the warmth of the afternoon, but the party mood fizzled. However, Louisa and Henry did seem to be deep in conversation about the Brooklyn Dodgers chances of winning the pendant in 1946.

Beatrix wondered if anything could come of the information that she'd discovered. Would they ever know why Bunny Turney hated men and formed a vigilante group to bring down males she felt were immoral. It had to be something from her past. "Hurt people, hurt people," she explained as the group disbursed. She avoided thinking of why the old woman had such amorous feelings for Thomas, her former fiancée, which was odd, as Mrs. Turney seemed to be downright nasty to anyone of the male gender.

"Sam, where is that boy of ours?" Jo walked back from the front sidewalk, expecting to see her son dashing along at the speed of light.

Her husband looked around, and peeked under some bushes. "I don't like this. His bike's over there, Jo, under the hedge."

Beatrix felt as if she'd been kicked in the gut, with a terrible fear that got larger by the second. "I'll check the house. Louisa, could you come with me? Henry, please walk up the hillside. Maybe he's playing in the Eucalyptus forest. He could have climbed a tree and gotten stuck there."

"Sammy? Sammy?" His name rang out as each searched only to return to the back garden without any signs of the boy.

Jo sat down, and her sister consoled her. "We'll find him, honey, he's just walked away and got too caught up looking at an insect or a worm. He'll be back."

Then her husband knelt at her knees, his breathing heavy. "I just ran back to the house, thinking he was there, but there's no sign of him."

Beatrix's mind raced through the conversations of the afternoon. There was one word that jumped out at her. "Pet." She said it again and out loud, "Pet. I'll be right back. I'm going next door. If I'm not back in twenty minutes call for reinforcements."

Sitting in the rocking chair on her front porch, Mrs. Bunny Turney looked the picture of tranquility and old-fashioned charm. At first, her eyes focused across the street Then, seeing Beatrix climb the tall front steps, she gave a companionable wave.

"Where is he, Bunny? Where is the child?"

She giggled, exposing crooked, yellow teeth. Then in what sounded like the voice of a schoolgirl's voice, which made it more frightening, she said. "Ah, my little pet. Why he's perfectly comfortable and you don't have to fuss about him."

"His mother and father are worried. Where is he?"

"Everything is well taken care of. You can go back to your party and those shabby folks you call friends. My little pet seemed tired. I gave him some tea with lots of honey. Tea always helps me to relax. A good, long sleep works for everyone," she said, but her words were softer than usual. Slurred.

"Is he in the house?"

"If you go in there, you'll be sorry, my dear." She giggled again. "Or do you like surprises?" I will find him and he is not a pet. He's a child and the child of my dear friends."

"Why can't I have him?" her voice now gruff. "They can have other children. My husband never had time for children. Or time for me. When he returned from the Great War, well, that part of our relationship was over, yet he found pleasure in the arms of whores. I saw it with my own eyes. Oh, the filth of it all. That's why I established the Onus Organista. Someone had to."

Beatrix was afraid to move. Had she murdered little Sammy out of spite or thinking that way they could all be in heaven together, according to the bizarre doctrine?

"You asked about the woman and the others? Yes, I helped them to transcend this life and finally, they are pure. I never hurt them. They made their own decisions and chose to have a warming up of tea before they jumped. You see I never really harmed anyone. Maybe a slight push or shove, but I never hurt them, I'm certain."

"Bunny, tell me about what happened at the cottage."

"Oh, my goodness. You know about that as well. Aren't you a smarty pants? That was an accident at the house. That woman wouldn't agree with my plans for her. I grabbed her as she stepped back, tried to stop her from falling. She was so much larger and stronger than me. She fell. No court could condemn me, an eighty-five-year-old lady from a good Christian background and president of the OOs."

"Don't be so sure, Bunny. Justice will be served."

Bunny picked a teacup in front of her. "All that said, please say goodbye to Thomas. He loved the afternoons we spent together, until I used too much peyote in a mixture. Please apologize to the darling for me. The mixture, I've since learned can cause odd dreams. I meant no harm."

"You drugged him?" Of course, she did.

"Not drugged. Herbal tea. It was for love. I wanted to entice him into my bedroom. What a surprise when I returned, after slipping into my nighty. Why, he was gone. Somehow, he made it back to your house, and I really couldn't go there to seduce him, could I? That would have been immoral."

Beatrix swayed slightly. Her whole happily ever after future was changed by the sexual desire of a bizarre old woman who had the hots for her fiancée.

Bunny yawned. "I'm going to finish my tea now, I've decided, as I also feel like a nap."

Beatrix looked at the teacup with light-colored liquid filling it to the brim and a foxglove flower decorating the saucer. But she didn't stop the lady from sipping the liquid.

"This world is so complicated." Bunny took a deep swallow then and smiled. "It's a new brew I've just developed just for an occasion like this."

Beatrix understood what Mrs. Turney was implying and she'd made her choice. The lady was drugged, but not going anywhere.

Storming into the house, Beatrix called. "Sammy? Sammy, where are you?" she called, praying that the crackpot neighbor hadn't drugged the little guy with something that would kill him. She flung open the doors to cabinets, bent to search cupboards, hurled furniture, and peeked behind the heavy drapes that shrouded the windows.

She dashed to the back of the house, to what possibly would be another bedroom, yanked open the door, and stopped dead. Her knees buckled. Bile was in her mouth.

Serial killers, Beatrix had read in her studies of the criminal mind, sometimes keep treasures from the people they kill. Trophies. Beatrix gulped at the sight. The walls of the bedroom were decorated from top to bottom, in a frightening collage of trinkets and jewelry.

Bunny Turney had trophies. These were bits of jewelry and trinkets from the women she'd ensnared to do her bidding with the OOs, and with each was a handwritten card with the person's name and the date that they jumped from the cliffs. It all formed a tapestry of ornaments, a collage of horror on every wall. Beatrix froze. After long, deep breaths, she managed to walk to a wall that seemed incomplete, or at least not fully covered with earrings, bracelets, baubles, and costume jewelry.

She turned to another wall. Dozens and dozens of keepsakes glittered in the light from the only window not covered in brown velvet drapes, as if Bunny liked to see the sun sparkle on her trophies.

Beatrix vomited. Her head swam; it was too bizarre to process. Then she saw something that startled her even more. There were the names of three women and their recent days of death. They had to be the ones Beatrix knew about. This confirmed it all. There was the evidence. Hung with a name and date there among the hoard was a tiny shamrock with a little green stone, the exact charm that the coroner had described.

And lastly, a tiny gold cross, the same as she'd seen on the young woman who had died on Butterfly Lane.

"No," her hand flew to her mouth. Death was all around her, every decoration screamed it. She staggered back and held the door frame. This was a frightening collection, warped prizes of a depraved mind. They marked the plunders of Mrs. Turney's kills or assisted suicides or whatever outlandish euphemism would be used in her defense as she was clearly insane and would be judged as that. Beatrix willed her knees not to buckle, and for the vomit threatening her throat to stay there.

"How long has she been killing people? How did this start? How could she be so vicious?" Those answers were not as obvious, but the truth could not be denied. Bunny Turney was deranged and ruthless and sick. Had been for decades.

Never in her worst nightmares had Beatrix imagined anyone so unbalanced. "At least maybe the families can now be told and have some kind of closure," she whispered, touching the tiny gold cross and reading the name in lovely, old fashion cursive. It said Marlene McCall on the attached card.

From somewhere close, a noise aroused her. Then came a whimper. The sound of an injured animal, but all the windows were closed. Then there was a tiny sound, a muffled, "Mama? Daddy? Help me."

It came from a small curio cabinet, hidden, stuffed in the back of an ornate tapestry sofa. It wasn't locked, but the door was jammed closed with a large silver serving spoon. As she pried it open, there was little Sammy Conrad curled in the fetal position. He was crying and the front of his red, white, and blue striped t-shirt was wet with tears. The child was shaking with fear and when he saw Beatrix's face, he reached out for her neck and the crying stopped. The jitters did not.

She bent low, soothing him with reassurance. She lifted the child to his feet. She hugged him so close it felt as if they'd melted together and then she stood, arms tight around his compact body. "You're okay, honey. It's going to be okay now,

Sammy. You are safe. Aunt Bea has you, and nobody will hurt you. I promise you and I always keep my promises.

"Let's get you back to your mama and daddy. They're waiting for you at my house. Don't be scared," she crooned. "We're going to walk out of here and find your mama and daddy and no one will hurt you again. I promise," she kept repeating as the child's shivers slowly ebbed.

Walking to the porch, Beatrix stopped, yet still kept Sammy tight to her body. Bunny Turney was slumped over in the rocker, her head lolling to the side, eyes glazed over and open. She twitched and sighed, then her eyes shut.

Beatrix didn't need to feel her pulse., She knew the woman was dead. Whatever she'd had in that teacup, in addition to the highly toxic foxglove, the woman had ended her own life.

CHAPTER 33

ONCE MORE THE GROUP SAT in a circle, this time touching and holding one another. The patio now was shady, and in another hour, it would be dark. Police swarmed the neighborhood, asking others about Mrs. Turney and what they knew. Would they ever know all the answers or why a woman like Bunny would become a serial killer? *Probably not*, thought Beatrix, cupping a steaming mug of coffee in her hands, feeling the moistness of the fog which crept in to encapsulate the city.

"Why do people do things like this?" Louisa asked out loud and to no one in particular.

"They feel they must. It is a chemical imbalance in the brain, most of the time," Beatrix responded. "That is no justification, by any means."

Jo hugged her little guy harder, one more time. Then he whispered something before she agreed. He dashed off to once more ride his trike in circles on the expansive patio. "What a mess. You think in a small town like this, horrible things shouldn't happen."

"They happen everywhere, ma'am," Henry added. "I lived in lots of places, and it doesn't seem to matter. We just have to be as good of a person as we can and all we can hope for is that others do the same."

Louisa looked at him, and smiled after a moment of making a decision. Beatrix looked at both of them, at the same time

Jo did. The two women nodded. It was just a twitch, and they shared a smile.

Suddenly, banging all the way from the front could be heard even in the back garden. "Now who is that?" Beatrix said but didn't get up. She felt so tired.

The group sat where they'd been, absorbed in the horror of that afternoon. It was Henry who stood. "No, ma'am. With the folks clamoring for all the gory details of the murders, and old lady Turney's suicide, and Sammy's short, but frightening kidnapping, you don't need to answer that. I'll get their story and shoo them off."

The banging stopped and Henry returned. "There's a man at the door. He won't listen to me and says he'll only talk to you, Beatrix. He looks daft and I wouldn't trust him. Seen that kind before."

"Okay, I'll deal with him." The weight of the afternoon's discoveries, including the trophy room kept by Bunny, the confessions, and then Sammy missing, had taken their toll on Beatrix.

"Shouldn't we protect her?" Louisa whispered.

Henry patted her arm. "She's got this."

Beatrix straightened the bouquet of flowers on the kitchen table, and walked through the big empty house, once more eyeing all the work left to be done. She felt like closing it up, turning her back on the mess, and taking a long vacation to someplace in the world where no one would ever talk to her.

Her shoulders sagged with sadness for the girls who had died, and with sadness for Bunny, so deranged and misguided. Sadness for Frankie and Morty Ramsey, who even faced with the fact that his son had killed someone, was sticking by him. Sadness for former Major Davies, who would shortly be lost to the confusing world of dementia, dragging his family down with him. Most of all, the sadness enveloped her heart with the reality that she might never see Thomas again. If she did, and that was up for discussion, she decided to bash him right in the nose.

The banging started once more. "Just be patient," she called out and opened the door.

Thomas stood there. His black felt fedora in his hands. He blinked back tears. "I didn't think you'd answer. Didn't know what I'd do if you did not."

"Thomas Ling, you are an idiot," she shouted.

"I've told that to myself for the last two days, only I was much cruder with the choice of words."

"Are you aware of why you had that dream?"

"Mrs. Turney's tea?"

They stood two feet apart, neither reaching out, although Beatrix had to will her arms not to do so.

"Peyote. I don't know if she grew it in her succulent garden or bought it somehow, but she used it with the intention of taking advantage of you, Thomas. Somehow you stumbled home and so your virtue has been preserved."

"I don't want to be virtuous. I want you, Beatrix. I know I can't make it up to you, ever, except I plan to take a lifetime to try."

"Wait. What about clean energy, saving the planet, and the calculations on the chalkboard in your university office? What of that, Thomas? Even if Mrs. Turney drugged you, perhaps there is a chance that your premonition is correct. Unless you realized that was a nutty notion."

"What if there was truth to it, after all? I telegraphed another scientist. He's going to take photos of my blackboard and then have the photos and the board shipped here. I can solve the conundrum of our future energy tribulations from Santa Barbara as well as I could from foggy England. However, I want to make a change in our wedding plans." He took her hands and felt Beatrix flinch, although she didn't try to wiggle free. Her eyes never left his. "Let's get married at the courthouse, here in Santa Barbara, as soon as we can. Then we'll party with the family when we return to England."

"Now that's the brightest idea you've had. And it's time for you to make a move. You'd better start by walking across this threshold. We have visitors in the garden, so testing the strength of your virtue against my alluring charms is going to have to wait until later."

"Am I exonerated?" he asked, shyly cocking his head, and producing a hint of a smile that appeared to tease one side of his mouth. "Say yes," he managed only after a welcome back kiss that lasted almost as long as he'd been gone.

"No, I will not, not yet. I will, however, think about it. Besides, that kiss was a good start," she whispered.

ABOUT THE AUTHOR

EVA SHAW is one of the country's premier ghostwriters and the author of more than 100 award-winning books including *Doubts of the Heart, Games of the Heart, Ghostwriting: The Complete Guide, Writeriffic 2: Creativity Training for Writers, Write Your Book in 20 Minutes, Garden Therapy: Nature's Health Plan,* and *What to Do*

When a Loved One Dies. She teaches university-level writing courses available online at 4000 colleges and universities.

A breast cancer survivor, Eva is an active volunteer with causes affecting women and children and with her church. She loves to travel, read, shop, garden, play the banjolele and paint, focusing on folk art and California landscapes.

When not at her desk, you can find Eva walking around the village of Carlsbad, California with Coco Rose, a rambunctious Welsh terrier.

Connect with Eva at:
evashaw.com
facebook.com/eva.shaw.96
instagram.com/shaw.eva

YOU MIGHT ALSO ENJOY

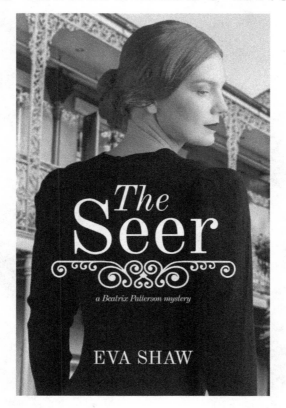

It's February 1942. War grips the world. Beatrix Patterson is a good liar with an excellent memory, which in truth is her only gift—well, that and conning the well-heeled out of their money and secrets.

Hired by the US Army to use her connections to expose Nazi saboteurs and sympathizers, Beatrix pits her skills against a government conspiracy, terrorist cells, kidnappings, and murderous plots. Exposing the Nazi war machine about to invade the country could cost Beatrix everything she's worked so hard to build but could also change the outcome of the war.

The question remains: will anyone believe a liar and a suspected traitor?

CPSIA information can be obtained
at www.ICGtesting.com
Printed in the USA
BVHW050823071022
648585BV00012B/13